Burning Bright

Also by E.J. Stevens

IVY GRANGER PSYCHIC DETECTIVE

Burning Bright

E.J. STEVENS

Published by Sacred Oaks Press
Sacred Oaks, 221 Sacred Oaks Lane, Wells, Maine 04090

First Printing (trade paperback edition), June 2014

Stevens, E.J.
Burning Bright / E.J. Stevens

ISBN 978-0-9842475-5-4 (trade pbk.)

Printed in the United States of America

PRONUNCIATION GUIDE

Pronunciations are given phonetically for names and races found in the Ivy Granger series. Alternate names and nicknames have been provided in parentheses. In some cases, the original folklore has been changed to suit the city of Harborsmouth and its environs.

Ailinn: ah-lynn
Aleya: uh-LEE-yuh
Arachne: uh-RAK-nee
Athame: ah-thaw-may
Banshee: ban-shee (Bean Sidhe, Bean Sìth)
Barguest: BAR-guyst (Bargheist, Black Dog)
Bean Tighe: ban tig
Béchuille: beh-huh-IL (Bé Chuille)
Bema: BEE-muh
Bheur: ver (like air)
Blaosc: BLEE-usk
Bogey: BOH-gee
Boggart: BOG-ert
Boitata: boy-TAH-ta
Brollachan: broll-ach-HAWN
Brownie: BROW-nee (Bwca, Urisk, Hearth Faerie, Domestic Hobgoblin)
Bugbear: BUG-bayr (Bug-a-boo, Boggle-bo)
Bwca: BOO-kuh (see Brownie)
The Cailleach: kall-ahk (The Blue Hag, Cailleach Bheur, Queen of Winter, Crone, Veiled One, Winter Hag)
Cat Sidhe: KAT shee or kayth shee (Faerie Cat, Cait Shith, Cait Sith)
Ceffyl Dŵr: keff-EEL dore (Kelpie King, Ceff)
Chir batti: CHEER bhut-TEA
Clurichaun: kloor-ih-kon (clobhair)
Cu Sith: KOO shee
Daeva: DAY-va
Demon: DEE-mun
Djinn: JIN
Draugr: DROW-ger
Duergar: doER-gar

Each Uisge: erk OOSH-kuh (Water Horse)
Elphame: EL-faym
Emain Ablach: EH-van ah-BLAH
Faerie: FAIR-ee (Fairy, Sidhe, Fane, Wee Folk, The Gentry, People of Peace, Themselves, Sidhe, Fae, Fay, Good Folk)
Fear Dearg: far DAR-rig (The Red Man)
Fionn mac Cumhaill: FIN mac COO-will
Forneus: FOR-nee-us (Demon, Great Marquis of Hell)
Fragarach: FRAG ah roch
Fuath: FOO-ah
Gaius Aurelius: GUY-us aw-REE-lee-us
Galliel: GAL-ee-el (Unicorn)
Ghoul: GOOL (Revenant)
Glaistig: GLASS-tig (The Green Lady)
Gnome: NOHM
Goblin: GOB-lin
Griffin: GRIF-fin (Gryphon, Griffon)
Grindylow: GRIN-dee-loh
Gwarwyn-a-throt: GWAR-win-uh-THROT
Hamadryad: ha-ma-DRY-ad (Tree Nymph)
Harborsmouth: HAR-bers-MOUTH
Henkie: HEN-kee
Hippocampus: hip-po-CAM-pus
Hob-o-Waggle HOB-oh-WAG-gul (Brownie, son of Wag-at-the-Wa)
Hy Brasil: HY bra-ZIL
Ignus fatuus: IG-nus FATCH-you-us
Inari: i-NAH-ree
Jenny Greenteeth: JEN-nee GREEN-teeth (Water Hag)
Kelpie: KEL-pee (Water Horse, Nyaggle)
Lamia: LAY-me-uh
Leanansídhe: lan-awn-shee (Lhiannan Sidhe, Leanhaun Shee, Leannan Sìth, Fairy Mistress)
Leprechaun: le-pre-khan (leipreachán)
Loup garou: LOOP guh-ROO
Mab: MAB (Unseelie Queen)
Manannán mac Lir: MAH-nah-nahn mac leer
Mauthe doog: MOW-thee DOO
Melusine: MEL-oo-seen
Mermaid: MER-mayd (male Merman)
Merry Dancer: MER-ree DAN-ser (Fir Chlis)

Murúch: mer-ook (Merrow, Moruadh, Murúghach)
Nixie: NIX-ee
Nuckelavees: NOOK-uh-LAY-veez
Oberon: OH-ber-on (Seelie King)
Peg Powler: PEG POW-ler (Peg Powler of the Trees, Water Hag)
Peri: PER-ec
Pixie: PIK-see (Pisgie)
Pooka: POO-kuh (Phooka, Pouka, Púca, Pwca)
Redcap: RED-kap (red cap)
Roca Barraidh: ROH-ka BAR-rah
Saytr: SAY-ter
Selkie: SEL-kee
Shellycoat: SHEL-lee-cote
Sidhe: SHEE (see Faerie)
Succubus: SUK-you-bus (male Incubus)
Tech Duinn: tek DOON
Tezcatlipocan: tehs-cah-tlee-poh-cahn
Tir na nOg: TEER na NOHG
Tir Tairngire: TEER TEARN-geer
Titania: ti-TAY-nee-uh (Seelie Queen)
Troll: TROHL
Tuatha Dé Danann: tootha DAY da-NAN
Tylwyth Teg: TILL-with TEEG (Seelie Court)
Unicorn: YOU-ni-korn
Unseelie: un-SEE-lee
Vampire: VAM-pyr (Undead)
Will-o'-the-Wisp: WIL-oh-tha-wisp (Gyl Burnt Tayle, Jack o' Lantern, Wisp, Ghost Light, Friar's Lantern, Corpse Candle, Hobbledy, Aleya, Hobby Lantern, Chir Batti, Faerie Fire, Spunkies, Min Min Light, Luz Mala, Pinket, Ellylldan, Spook Light, Ignus Gatuus, Orbs, Boitatá, and Hinkypunk)
Ynis Afallon: un-NIS AH-fuhl-on
Yue Fei: yweh-fay

Tyger! Tyger! burning bright
In the forests of the night,
What immortal hand or eye
Could frame thy fearful symmetry?

In what distant deeps or skies
Burnt the fire of thine eyes?
On what wings dare he aspire?
What the hand dare seize the fire?
-William Blake, *The Tyger*

Pluck the keen teeth from the fierce tiger's jaws,
And burn the long-lived phoenix in her blood;
-Shakespeare, *Sonnet XIX*

INTRODUCTION

Welcome to Harborsmouth, where monsters walk the streets unseen by humans...except those with second sight.

Whether visiting our modern business district or exploring the cobblestone lanes of the Old Port quarter, please enjoy your stay. When you return home, do tell your friends about our wonderful city—just leave out any supernatural details.

Don't worry—most of our guests never experience anything unusual. Otherworlders, such as faeries, vampires, and ghouls, are quite adept at hiding within the shadows. Many are also skilled at erasing memories. You may wake in the night screaming, but you won't recall why. Be glad that you don't remember—you are one of the fortunate ones.

If you do encounter something unnatural, we recommend the services of Ivy Granger, Psychic Detective. Co-founder of Private Eye detective agency, Ivy Granger is a relatively new member of our small business community. Her offices can be found on Water Street, in the heart of the Old Port.

Miss Granger has a remarkable ability to receive visions by the act of touching an object. This skill is useful in her detective work, especially when locating lost items. Whether you are looking for a lost brooch or missing persons, no job is too small for Ivy Granger—and she could certainly use the business.

We can also provide, upon request, a list of highly skilled undertakers. If you are in need of their services, then we also kindly direct you to Harborsmouth Cemetery Realty. It's never too early to contact them, since we have a booming "housing" market. Demand is quite high for a local plot—there are always people *dying* for a place to stay.

CHAPTER 1

Ever play whack-a-mole with a jincan? No? Well, then aren't you the fortunate one. Not only do jincan look like overgrown caterpillars with pointy teeth, but they also breed like bunnies and have a knack for undermining integral weight-bearing structures, leaving piles of rubble in their wake. Oh, and they smell like rotten eggs when squished—just my luck.

I scanned the cratered parking lot and sighed. Ever since Jenna was shipped off to Europe on some top-secret Hunters' Guild mission, Harborsmouth's supernatural pest problem had grown out of control. Jenna was one of the youngest members in the Harborsmouth Guild office and, as such, was responsible for the less desirable hunting jobs—like taking care of a nest of jincan. Now that she was gone, that job fell to the private sector.

I tightened my grip on the iron hammer and scowled. With Jenna gone, and the Guild in no hurry to find a replacement, jobs had come rolling in. I guess I should have been happy for the work, but no amount of money would make this feel like a real case. These jobs were just trumped up pest control. I'd much rather be working a case that required more than whacking some creature over the head. Better yet, I wanted more time to focus on the search for my father.

I'd recently learned that I was half-fae and that my deadbeat dad was Will-o'-the-Wisp, or Willem as my human mom knew him, King of the Wisps. Most of my life I'd spent feeling abandoned by the guy, which pissed me off. My psychic abilities had labeled me as a freak and an outcast, relegating me to the sidelines where I watched other people live their safe, happy, normal lives. Even my mother and step-father had distanced themselves from their freak daughter. To say I had abandonment issues was an understatement.

Imagine my surprise when I discovered, in a search for answers about my awakening wisp abilities, that my dad had been a victim too. He'd been tricked by a demon, possibly

Lucifer himself, to carry a cursed lantern that brought disasters wherever he walked the earth. In an attempt to keep me and my mom safe, Will-o'-the-Wisp had left Harborsmouth. Now I not only needed to find my father, I desperately wanted to.

But time was running out. As if my psychic gift and second sight weren't bad enough, I was growing into a whole new set of wisp abilities that I had no idea how to control. And fae who can't keep their supernatural side hidden from humans don't have a long lifespan—even for immortals. If I don't find my father soon, I'll be facing a fae firing squad. In fact, I could already feel the chill of fae assassins breathing down my neck.

Yeah, sorting out my family issues and finding a way to control my wisp powers should have been my one and only task, but information doesn't come cheap. It takes money to grease those kinds of gears, hence my jumping at the chance to fill the void that Jenna had left in her wake. Jobs like these paid in cash and favors, both of which were in short supply since beginning my search for answers.

As it was, I was accruing debt with the wrong people. Take, for example, my debt to the vampire master of Harborsmouth. I'd promised to work one case of that pompous, old dust bag's choosing. Yeah, that was bound to go well. As if that wasn't bad enough, I'd made not one, but two faerie bargains with The Green Lady. I just knew the glaistig would be calling in her favors soon. I'd caught her guards watching me more than once. I knew she was keeping tabs on her investment and that scared me worse than the threat of faerie assassins.

Unfortunately, the vamp and the glaistig weren't the only ones I'd made bargains with over the past few months. Their bargains were just the most likely to result in death or insanity. By comparison, my alliance with Sir Torn and the local *cat sidhe* was a walk in the park. And that was saying a whole lot about just how potentially deadly my bargains with The Green Lady and the vampire master of the city really were. Torn was a shadowy, feline, pain in my ass who obviously thought my roommate and business partner was catnip—like I didn't have enough to worry about.

One of the caterpillar creatures burst up through a pile of rubble to my left and, with a blur of writhing golden fur, ducked inside the ruins of a video store. Damn, these things were fast. I ran toward the alley at the back of the store, hoping to corner the jincan before it escaped back into the ground or into the multi-level parking garage. Chasing the jincan around in that warren of concrete and steel was something I'd like to avoid. There were fae who liked to inhabit those shadows and I'd rather not come toe to toe with any of them.

I gulped air as I came around the back of the building, scanning the area around the dumpster and metal exit door for signs of the jincan. No eight-foot caterpillar here. Maybe I'd been wrong to think it would come this way. Heck, it could be tunneling through the shop floor this very moment. In fact, I could hear a rhythmic thud coming from inside. Crap, I wouldn't collect my fee if I let this critter slip away.

I spun on my heel, ready to sprint back down the alley when a furry steam-train came barreling through the cinderblock wall. The owner of the strip-mall wasn't going to be happy. There was hardly anything left of the place. Too bad I had more to worry about than pissing off my clients.

I needed to stay alive.

A chunk of concrete whizzed past my head and I ducked into a crouch. I blinked away the dust and debris that filled the air and honed in on the creature's location. There, it was halfway through the wall, its head already dipping into the parking garage.

"Oh no, you don't," I said. "Hey, Goldy, over here!"

The jincan raised its head and gnashed its large, brown teeth. Oh yeah, that's attractive. These critters could use some serious dental care.

With a bellowing cry it lunged toward me. I jinked to the right, avoiding those nasty teeth with a few feet to spare. As the creature's momentum carried it forward, I lifted the hammer, bringing it down at the base of its skull. Do caterpillars even have skulls? Whatever, the blow stopped the deafening chomp of its teeth—too bad it also squished the thing's head like a water balloon.

Smelly jincan goo hit me square in the face, on bare skin. I froze, hammer locked in unmoving gloved fingers, as a vision held me rigid in its icy grip. I tried to calm my breathing and ride it out. It wouldn't do me any good to fight it, and I needed to get this over with. If another jincan came along while I was imprisoned by the goo-induced vision, I'd be getting an up close and personal look at those rotting, pointy teeth.

I'd be caterpillar food for sure.

In fact, it looked like I'd be fed to this guy's queen if he had any say in the matter. Oh, goody.

Psychometry is a funny thing. If a strong psychic imprint is made on an object, then someone with my rare gift can read the information that's left behind. In this case, the caterpillar goo was giving me a vision whammy that made my stomach churn. This jincan had three images playing on a compulsive loop and the message of what drove the beast was clear. He wanted to kill, eat, and mate—not necessarily in that order.

And, oh boy, the gal he wanted to impress was a golden-skinned, furless grub the size of a semi truck. *Protect the Queen, feed the Queen, and mate with the Queen.* Oberon's eyes, I needed brain bleach.

Oh yeah, this vision was no joyride—they never were—but visions of jincan males lining up to hump their gelatinous queen? That was sure to give me nightmares. Damn that shit was nasty.

I gagged and shook off the last of the vision. Psychometry is a bitch of a psychic gift, but the thing is, sometimes it comes in handy. Now I knew how to stop these creatures from destroying another city block, even if it was out here in the suburbs. I just needed to squash their hive leader, and I knew right where to find her.

Aware of the gathering gloom, I sprinted into the parking garage. For the second time today, I wished that Jenna hadn't pissed off the Guild and got herself shipped off to Europe. This was one job where I could use some backup. The obese hive leader didn't seem like much of a threat—heck, she looked like a pulsating marshmallow—but I was pretty sure the masses of horny jincan males I'd seen in my vision weren't about to welcome me with open arms, even if they did have about twenty extra sets of the damn things.

I sighed and ducked into the parking garage as the first stars appeared in the darkening sky above the alley. It was going to be a long night.

CHAPTER 2

"Ivy!" Jinx yelled.

I startled awake, heart pounding, wondering briefly if the scream had truly originated from my loft apartment or if it had followed me from the depths of a nightmare. I reached for my blades and stumbled out of my bedroom, hoping that I wasn't about to give anyone a show. I couldn't complain too much if Jinx brought a guy home with her, especially after the bedroom acrobatics Ceff and I had been up to lately, but I sure didn't want to run naked into some stranger. After being inside a jincan's head, I wasn't ready for another vision. Plus, I didn't think that meeting someone while brandishing blades and wearing only panties and leather gloves would make a good first impression.

Then again, I wasn't about to hesitate if Jinx needed me. She was my best friend and, until recently, the closest thing I had to family.

"Jinx?" I asked, calling out while scanning the apartment for threats.

I squinted against the bright light that rose from my skin. Turning into a freaking light bulb was one of the side effects of my fae blood. I took a deep breath, trying to calm my nerves and dampen the glow. For once, I sent up a silent prayer that Jinx hadn't brought any human guys home with her. If a human witnessed my fae abilities and told his friends, I'd be as good as dead.

"In here!" she shouted.

I turned toward the bathroom, making it to the door in two quick strides. Our loft apartment was small, a fact I was now thankful of. I shifted my blades and reached out with one gloved hand, but hesitated, hand hovering over the doorknob.

"Are you okay?" I asked.

"I don't know," she said, from behind the closed bathroom door. "Is your wispness contagious?"

"Are you serious?" I asked.

What the heck was Jinx going on about? I set my blades on the kitchen counter at my back, adrenaline washing from my system. She'd gotten me out of bed for some fae trivia? I slid a gloved hand over my face and yawned. Mab's bones, I was tired. I wanted nothing more than a nice, warm bed. My side ached and my head throbbed. Clearing out jincan nests was exhausting work.

"Please say yes," she said, her voice going small and weak.

My hair stood on end. Jinx never sounded weak. My tattooed, rockabilly best friend may be human, but she was tougher than an ogre's hide. I had a very bad feeling about this.

"No, my being fae isn't a virus," I said. "It's more like a congenital disease or birth defect. Why? What's going on in there?"

I heard a rustle of fabric behind the closed door, but Jinx didn't come out.

"N-n-nothing..." Jinx stuttered.

"Nothing, my shiny wisp butt," I said. "Come out and we can fix whatever it is."

I crossed my fingers, toes too. Jinx was the most unlucky person that I knew. I didn't even dare venture a guess at what was going on in that bathroom.

"You promise you won't laugh?" she asked.

"Pinky promise," I said. I wasn't about to link pinkies with my best friend, and she knew it, but the sentiment was there all the same.

"Okay," she said.

The knob turned and Jinx let the bathroom door swing open. I bit my lip, stifling the urge to laugh. I'd promised, after all, and breaking a promise doesn't come easy to the fae, even a half-breed like me. Fortunately, my weak blood left me wiggle room for telling lies. Thank Oberon for small favors.

Jinx stood awkwardly in a t-shirt and fuzzy slippers, her hair a mess, dark circles under her eyes, and arms crossed with her hands shielding her neck. I gave her an encouraging nod. She let her hands drop from her neck to reveal a trail of glowing, lip-shaped marks that began behind her ear and traced along the line of her pulse, a pulse that now jumped like a grasshopper on Red Bull.

"It's not so bad," I said, shrugging my shoulders.

But it was bad. Very bad, indeed. In fact, if I didn't know better, I'd say she'd even lost some weight. Her face looked haggard beneath the harsh bathroom lights.

I no longer felt like laughing, that was for damn sure. This wasn't about a bad hair day, something was seriously wrong with my friend.

"Really?" she asked, tugging down the oversized t-shirt she'd slept in to expose more of the luminous kisses. "I look like I spent the night at a rave."

Actually, she looked like a throwback from an eighties music video, but I kept that thought to myself. The offending marks followed her collarbone to the curve of her shoulder, down her arm, along her rose tattoo, and across the rise and swell of her chest. I brought my eyes up to Jinx's face and blinked.

"I have to ask," I said. "Where the hell did those come from?"

"That's just it," she said, tears welling up in puffy, red-rimmed eyes. "I went out to Club Nexus last night. J-j-just for a drink. I thought I'd bump into Torn, but he wasn't there..."

"I thought we'd agreed, no entering Nexus without an escort," I said, narrowing my eyes.

"But you were busy on a case," she said. "And I thought Torn would be there! I didn't think I'd be alone."

"Okay, so what happened next?" I asked. I crossed my arms to keep from strangling my friend, visions or not, and settled against the breakfast bar. I had a feeling I wasn't going to like what she had to say. "I take it from the luminous hickies that you didn't turn around and come straight home."

"Well, no," she said. "I had a drink or two. No faerie wine! I made sure they knew I was your vassal, or whatever. So, I had a few drinks and I think I was dancing, but..."

"But you don't remember the rest," I said.

"Not really," she said, shuffling her feet.

Crap. Jinx had probably partied too hard and left with some sleezeball guy from the club. Someone paranormal who could leave a trail of glowing kisses behind like a magical brand. Had the marks been intentional? If so, who would want to claim ownership over Jinx?

There was one scoundrel who immediately came to mind. When I'd asked what the hell had happened, I hadn't realized how right on the money I'd been. Those marks may very well have come from the fiery depths of Hell itself. And if I found out that a certain demon attorney had laid a finger on my roommate, avenging angels could learn a thing or two from the revenge I'd rain down on Forneus' well-coiffed head.

"Stay here in the apartment and rest," I said, quickly formulating a plan.

I retrieved my knives from the counter and ran to my room. I pulled on jeans and a t-shirt and grabbed my knife sheaths. The sheaths were a custom job, clurichaun craftsmanship, so the straps held my blades securely and comfortably along my forearms without giving me any unwanted visions. I shrugged on my leather jacket to hide the blades and protect my arms and stomped into a pair of leather boots. I checked that the throwing knives slid easily from their sheaths and shoved a dagger into each boot.

That would have been more than enough for me to handle a human adversary, but I had bigger creeps to fry. Opening the bedside table drawer, I withdrew a large utility belt already laden down with wooden stakes and charms. Slinging the belt across my hips, I added a clip of tiny water balloons. The industrious pooka wore these things as hats, but I'd found another use for the condoms they hand out at the free clinic. I'd filled these babies with holy water, blessed by my pal Father Michael. I slid a crucifix pendant over my head, wound my hair into a tight bun at the nape of my neck, and rushed for the door.

I was ready for anything, but most importantly, I was armed for demon. If Forneus thought he could take advantage of Jinx, he was in for a nasty surprise. No one was going to give my best friend a supernatural STD and get away with it.

CHAPTER 3

I stomped along Congress Street, heading away from the cobbled streets of the Old Port quarter and up into the more modern financial district. Plan A was to find Forneus, a no-good demon attorney, and use my blades to nail the bastard to the wall and make him talk.

I just had to find him first.

My gloved fingertips skirted the catch on my wrist sheaths as I made my way toward the tallest buildings in Harborsmouth. Good thing I knew where the creep liked to drum up business. Forneus may moonlight as an attorney, but he was still a demon with a quota to fill—and there were plenty of souls for sale in these glass and steel towers of commerce.

Knives hit my palms as my brain registered the scent of sulfur, but by then I was already shoulder to shoulder with the demon. Damn, Forneus was fast when he wanted to be. I'd seen the guy in action more than once.

My chest tightened as a memory of Forneus saving Jinx's life pushed its way to the surface. Thankfully, it was followed by the image of the man in his full demonic splendor, horns, cloven feet and all. That made it easier to tamp down the rising guilt and hold onto my anger.

I still wasn't sure of the guy's motivations toward my friend, but catching him with his tongue down her throat was a clue. The dogged way he followed her around was another hint. Did the glowing marks on her skin mean he'd already laid claim to her? If he thought Jinx would become his demon bride without a fight, he had another thing coming.

Hell was not getting a new rockabilly soul to add to their collection. Nope, nada, not gonna happen.

"Ah, Miss Granger, fancy meeting you in this part of town," he said. "You don't often venture beyond the squalor. What brings you here? Decide to sell your soul for the location of your accursed father?"

I have to admit, for a moment I was tempted. Oberon's eyes, I was tempted, but I held onto the rage that had fueled

my every move since seeing those marks on Jinx's body.
Nostrils flaring, I stepped toward Forneus and with absolute
precision held a knife blade to the bulge in his Armani suit
pants.

"You will never get my soul, Forneus, but we will
discuss my father later...if I let you live," I said.

He raised an eyebrow, and tilted his head to the side,
careful not to make any quick movements.

"Touché," he said. "So then, *princess*, to what do I owe
this honor?"

Yeah, I wasn't acting like a good little princess.
Whatever. I was pretty sure that I wasn't the only faerie
princess to get her hands dirty. In fact, Queen Mab had left a
trail of corpses on the way to her throne. Now that was a
cheery thought.

"Jinx," I said. I paused, watching his face for clues.
"Jinx is in trouble, but I imagine you already knew something
about that."

His reaction wasn't what I'd expected. Instead of a
smug grin, he looked like he'd been poleaxed.

"What do you need?" he asked. "I am at your service."

Crispy hellspawn on a stick, the guy was just full of
surprises. Either that or he was a damn good actor, which was
likely considering he was an attorney...and a demon who
tricked people into selling their souls.

"What I need is for you to tell me what you did to her
last night, and how to reverse it," I said.

"As you made it so very clear at our last encounter, you
wished that I stay away from your friend," he said. "I have
respected that wish." I twitched the blade in my hand and he
rolled his eyes. "Okay, fine, I have respected that wish...most
of the time. But I can assure you that I have not seen Jinx in
nearly a week. Though you should know that if I had been
following her last night, nothing ill would have befallen her.
Whatever assumptions you have made about my intentions
couldn't be further from the truth."

My body stiffened and my breath hitched in my throat
as his words sunk in. Unless Forneus was lying, he had no
idea what happened to Jinx last night. And the implication
was there that if I'd let him into my friend's life, she'd have
been safe.

"How can I trust you?" I asked.

Forneus snorted, letting out a puff of stomach churning brimstone. How the hell could Jinx kiss this guy? Whether he was telling the truth or not, I was glad for her sake that she didn't remember that kiss. Locking lips with a demon was bound to give a girl nightmares.

"You will never trust me, but if you care about your friend, then you will let me help you," he said. "Tell me what has happened to Jinx and I will scour all of Hell and earth to make this right."

The guy made a good speech. I just hoped he wasn't pulling a fast one. But with Jinx at home covered in glowing marks and looking like death warmed over, I didn't have much of a choice. I could kill him or ask for his help. So help me, I opted for the latter.

"It's a long story," I said with a sigh.

"Then perhaps you could remove your blade from one of my most impressive assets," he said. "I am rather fond of this body."

Right, wouldn't want to diminish the guy's sex appeal, *geesh*.

I took a step back and lowered my knife, returning the blade to the sheath beneath my leather jacket. I tried to cover my relief by muttering something about his sulfuric breath, but the shaking in my hands gave away my discomfort. Getting inside Forneus' defenses had been a necessity—who expects someone with a touch phobia to move toward you?—but now that the adrenaline was wearing off, the reality that I'd come within inches of a million mind scrambling visions hit me like an ogre's fist.

"At least you're in your human body," I said. "It's one of your better looks. Can't say I'm a fan of the whole cloven hoof thing."

I should really learn to keep my mouth shut. Forneus narrowed his eyes where a firestorm was brewing, and flame danced along his fingertips. Great, next he'd be sprouting horns and leathery wings. Note to self; don't unnecessarily piss off the demon. I'd seen Forneus transform into his demonic form and it wasn't pretty. Like I said, I'm not a fan.

"You should learn to hold your tongue, Miss Granger," he said. "My feelings for your friend do not extend to your company. I prefer not to upset Jinx by killing you, but there are other ways to silence that unpleasant mouth of yours."

"Fine, I'll play nice, yada yada yada," I said. "You want to know what's wrong with Jinx, or not?" Forneus nodded stiffly. "She woke up this morning covered in glowing marks that look like...well, lips."

The demon's eyes bulged, but I continued on. Yeah, didn't think he'd like that part.

"Anything else unusual?" he asked, his voice tight.

"She also looks like she hasn't slept in a week," I said. "It might be that she just has a really bad hangover, she may have had something weird to drink, but I'm not sure. Her last memory is of walking into Club Nexus. Everything after that's a blank."

"There are many concoctions that cause amnesia and fatigue when imbibed by a human," he said, pacing the sidewalk while he talked. "We require more information."

"Fine, I'll take Jinx over to The Emporium," I said with a heavy sigh.

I'd have to go home and convince Jinx to leave the apartment, which she wasn't going to like, but it was the best I could do. Part of me had been hoping that Forneus was the culprit, which just shows how much I didn't want to resort to asking the rest of the supernatural community for assistance. I'd exhausted my resources searching for my father, and there weren't many people I could still turn to for answers.

"I too will establish contact with my informants," he said. "Someone must have seen whom she left the club with."

The air around the demon blurred and, just like that, Forneus was gone.

Oh well, Plan A was a bust. Why couldn't it have been Forneus who'd left the marks? I swallowed hard, staring at the spot where the demon had stood. You know your life is complicated when you'd rather fight a demon than ask your friends for help. I groaned and turned back toward the Old Port. I needed to collect Jinx and try to get some answers.

Crap, plan B it was then.

CHAPTER 4

If there was one person who could identify Jinx's malady and help me find the perp who did this (assuming it wasn't Forneus), it was Kaye. I trudged up Water Street, Jinx close on my heels. She'd abandoned her usual low-cut dress for a turtleneck sweater and skin-tight jeans. The glowing marks on her skin were hidden, but she couldn't seem to keep her hand from tugging at the neck of her sweater.

"Do they itch?" I asked, breaking the silence.

It was still early for a Monday morning, and the city around us was quiet. Jinx flashed me a sheepish look and let her hands drop to her sides.

"No, sorry," she said, staring at her platform shoes. "Guess I keep wishing that I could rub the marks off or something. I can't believe this is happening to me."

I shook my head, lips pulling into a wry grin.

"I just hope that whoever this guy was, he wasn't too ugly," I said. "You wouldn't be the first chick to drink too much at Nexus and end up in bed with a snot goblin."

Jinx pulled up short, nostrils flaring, hands going to her hips. Now that was the girl who stared down demons without batting an eyelash.

"You think I'd bed some nasty faerie just 'cause I had too much to drink?" she asked. "I have standards!"

"It could happen," I said with a shrug.

"That, that's...god, Ivy," she said. "You're joking aren't you?"

I let out an affirmative snort and continued up Water Street, no longer so worried about Jinx. We needed to figure out what the marks on her body meant, sure, but it was a relief to see Jinx acting like her old self. She tossed her hair back and quickened her stride to catch up.

"Snot funny?" I asked.

"Is there even such a thing as a snot goblin?" she asked, eyes narrowing.

"I hope the hell not," I said. "I've seen enough monster goo for this lifetime."

We turned onto Wharf Street and I crossed to the opposite sidewalk, avoiding a vodyanoy. Slime and muck oozed from his froglike skin and dripped onto the cobbled street.

"Make that two lifetimes," I muttered.

"What?" Jinx asked.

"Nothing," I said with a shrug.

One of my fae talents is second sight. I can see through the glamour that most supernatural creatures cloak themselves with in order to hide amongst humans. With Kaye's help, we'd come up with a recipe for faerie ointment, a concoction that allowed Jinx to see through fae glamour, but the ingredients weren't cheap and it didn't allow to her see vamps and other supernatural beasties—only faeries. Due to the price and its limitations, Jinx saved the ointment for night jobs and trips to Club Nexus. Which meant all she saw was a sweaty guy with a long, tangled beard and a skin condition. Too bad I couldn't be so lucky.

I flicked my eyes to Jinx as we passed the drippy vodyanoy. She was biting her lip and fidgeting with the neck of her sweater. In other words, she was totally freaking out.

"Do you really think Kaye can help?" she asked.

We'd come to a stop in front of a wood and brick façade decorated in blue, purple, and gold. Madam Kaye's Magic Emporium may look like a total tourist trap where suckers spend their hard earned money on useless charms and gaudy kitsch, but it was also the home of Harborsmouth's most powerful witch.

Kaye O'Shay is a tough old bird with a gift for magic and a penchant for mischief. She also used to run with the local Hunters' Guild, which gave her ties to the secret society and access to their arcane records. If there was one person in town likely to have the knowledge we needed, it was Kaye.

Too bad she considered Jinx to be a flaky liability. Jinx was a human with a knack for racking up injuries and Kaye, grudgingly, was good at patching people up. It didn't take long for the two to get on each other's nerves. But in our own way, Kaye and I had become wary friends over the years and where I went Jinx followed. If the old witch had a problem with it, that was just too bad.

I winced inwardly and shook my head. I had a reputation for being stubborn, and where Jinx was concerned I could be as bull-headed as a minotaur, but I knew I'd back down if push came to shove. Thing is, not only was Kaye one of the most powerful witches on the eastern seaboard, but I also owed her big time. When the *each uisge* invaded Harborsmouth, Kaye had helped to turn the tide against the bloodthirsty creatures and she'd been saving my butt, one way or another, ever since.

Instead of voicing my concerns, I nodded and flashed Jinx what I hoped was an encouraging smile.

"Sure thing," I said.

I reached for the door, but paused in mid-motion at the *snick, snick* of claws on the bricks above my head. My fingers itched to draw my blades, but I stifled the urge and turned a smile to the massive stone face peering down at me.

"Hey, Humphrey," I said. "How's it hangin'?"

The gargoyle chuckled, making his dog-like ears twitch.

"Dude, I will never get used to that," Jinx said, shaking her head.

"Get used to what?" I asked. "Laughing statues or my poor attempt at gargoyle humor?"

"Humphrey's laugh is definitely way creepy, but I was actually referring to the way he seems to teleport around," she said. "Without faerie ointment, I can't see him move. So one minute he's up on that rainspout and then, poof, he's hanging over the door. It gives me the heebie freakin' jeebies."

Jinx's comments made Humphrey chuckle all the more. It sounded like someone tossed rocks into a coffee grinder.

"Is Kaye inside?" I asked, hooking a thumb toward the door. Humphrey nodded, spread his bat wings, and flew back up to his perch. "I'll take that as a yes. Ready?"

"I was born ready," Jinx said.

She tossed her hair and strode confidently forward. Too bad the effect was ruined by her tripping and falling headfirst into the shop. No one ever accused her of being graceful. I just hoped she wasn't hurt. I was pretty sure that asking Kaye to patch Jinx up wouldn't put the witch in the best of moods, and take it from me—it's never a good idea to ask the favor of a pissed off witch.

A black cat was the only one to witness our ridiculous entrance, though I didn't kid myself for a second that Kaye

couldn't see through the eyes of her familiar. Heck, for all I
knew the thing could be one of Sir Torn's spies. But I turned
my back on the cat and crouched down beside Jinx.

"You okay?" I asked.

Jinx fell all the time, no big deal. Thing was, she didn't
look okay. If I didn't know better, I'd have thought she'd been
without sleep for a week. The dark circles that ringed her eyes
were joining together, making her look like a bugbear bandit.

"Yeah, yeah," she said, pulling herself up and dusting
off her hands and knees. "I'm fine."

"Good, let's get this over with," I said.

I picked my way through the winding maze of the occult
shop, stopping only when Jinx tripped or knocked something
over. If I didn't know better, I'd say Kaye was using her magic
to make this difficult, but I didn't think she'd waste her powers
on Jinx. Then again, the witch was known for her love of
pranks and practical jokes. I shook my head, unlocked the
hatch in the oddments counter, and continued down a hallway
to an unmarked door at the back of the building, Jinx close at
my heels.

I didn't have time for practical jokes. We needed to get
to the bottom of Jinx's marks before one of us started glowing
in public. Mab's bloody bones, when did my life become so
complicated?

CHAPTER 5

I walked into Kaye's spell kitchen and Jinx nearly toppled over as I stopped dead in my tracks. Arachne was inside Kaye's spell circle working a casting. Since when did Kaye allow Arachne to practice real magic?

Don't get me wrong. The kid was from a long line of Wiccans and she was well versed in herb lore, but Kaye never trained her would-be apprentices. What had changed?

"I'm getting old, Ivy," Kaye said, as if reading my mind. She waved a tattooed hand toward the spell circle. "It's time I had an apprentice."

It had taken Kaye over 300 years to utter those words. There was nothing I could say in response, so I continued to watch Arachne in silence. Purple-streaked hair floated around the kid's face, and a ball of energy spun in the middle of the circle, as she chanted something under her breath. I had to admit. The girl was impressive.

But the longer I watched, the more Arachne showed signs of fatigue. Sweat rolled down the girl's face and her hands were starting to shake. I frowned, but resisted the urge to rush forward. I had to remind myself that this was what Arachne wanted.

"Do you have her parents' consent?" I asked.

Kaye snorted.

"Don't be daft," she said. "Of course I have their consent. That family has been forcing its progeny on me for decades. They're so happy, they threw a party."

I was glad I'd missed that party. Wiccan gatherings tended to have a strange dress code; clothing optional. Not to mention the orgies. Start pouring the mead and brandy wine and the local coven was nearly as bad as the clan of pooka who lived in my old tree house.

"Things are changing in the world," Kaye said. "I can feel it like a storm brewing on the horizon."

"What kind of storm?" I asked. "Something magical?"

I had a feeling I didn't want to know, but I had to ask.

"War," she said. "There are signs, if you know where to look for them. Even Jenna being sent to Europe demonstrates just how desperate the Hunters are. They feel it too."

"Wait, what do you mean?" I asked. "Is Jenna in trouble?"

I'd thought that Jenna had been sent away as a punishment, but maybe there was more to the story.

"The balance of power is shifting and there are those who would use that change for their own benefit," she said. "The Guild is mobilizing for war. They are rushing the training of young Hunters like Jenna and calling up old retired souls like myself who have aided them in the past."

"So this trip to Europe is part of her training?" I asked.

My head spun trying to keep up with Kaye's unusual outpouring of information. The witch was normally tight-lipped about her Hunter friends—unless she herself was deep into the brandy wine.

"Yes, the final step in a young Hunter's training is a solo assignment to the Old Country," she said. "But Jenna was years away from her testing. The fools at Guild headquarters are advancing journeyman Hunters into the ranks of masters with little or no preparation."

"Is it really that dangerous?" I asked.

"The supernaturals who haunt the Old World cities are ancient and deeply entrenched," she said. "Locals often worship them, which only adds to their power. I do not know to which city Jenna has been assigned, but I hope for her sake that she has made allies. The girl will need all the help she can get."

Icy cold spider's legs skittered up and down my spine. If the highly skilled Hunter needed help, then the Old Country was indeed a dangerous place to be. Apparently, Jinx was thinking the same thing.

"Whoa, remind me never to vacation in Europe," she said. "We've got enough supernatural nut-jobs right here in Harborsmouth. Bigger and badder doesn't sound like my idea of fun."

"Sounds like a dream vacation for Jenna," I said.

It was true, Jenna loved a good fight, but my gut twisted all the same.

"What is *she* doing here?" Kaye asked, arching an eyebrow and pointing a tattooed finger at Jinx.

"Um," Jinx said, looking down at her shoes.

"We've got a case we need help on, but if you're busy with Arachne, we can come back later," I said, waving a hand at the spell circle.

Kaye sighed, making a *tut tut* sound, and shook her head.

"Go have a seat by the hearth," she said.

We'd been dismissed. Getting the hint, we gave the casting circle a wide berth and headed toward the large stone hearth at the back of the room. The front of the kitchen was modern looking with bright, white cabinets and wide open spaces to accommodate the large spell circle, but the rear of the room was all stone, thatch, and dark beams. It was like walking into an old pub, a pub that happened to have its own hearth brownie.

"Hi Hob," I said, lowering my head to acknowledge the brownie and bowing slightly at the waist. "May we enter?"

The top of Hob's crumpled hat only came to my knee, but I sure as heck didn't want to anger the little fellow. Brownie's can be ornery, and if you piss them off, you'll be in for a world of hurt. Brownies have made an Olympic sport out of pranking, and some of those pranks are pure evil.

Hob nodded his oversized head and waved a knobby hand, allowing us to enter his domain. And don't be fooled, Kaye may own this place, but the old portion of the kitchen was Hob's territory. Even the witch respected that fact.

"Thank you, Hob," I said.

"Thanks, Hobster," Jinx wheezed.

She dropped onto a wooden bench and slumped over the old oak table. Crap, she didn't look so good. The circles around her eyes seemed darker than before and she sounded out of breath from our short walk to The Emporium, which wasn't like her at all. Jinx may be curvaceous, but she was in great shape. If she was that tired from our walk, then something was seriously wrong with her.

"Got me gift?" Hob asked.

Right, time to get down to business. Hob had allowed us entry into his domain and now it was tradition to reciprocate with a gift. Since I'd been on the receiving end of Hob's ire once or twice in the past, I came prepared.

I held out a small pendant in the shape of a gnome standing beneath a mushroom. It was made of a gold that

matched the twinkle in Hob's eye. His fingers twitched, but he
didn't reach for the trinket, yet.

"Gnomes don' look li' dat," he said.

Hob scowled at me from beneath thick, bushy eyebrows.
I smiled back and winked.

"I know," I said.

I did in fact know. I'd helped to relocate a family of
gnomes when the land their home was on was sold to
developers. The gnomes now lived in my mother and
stepfather's garden, spitting distance from the tree house
where I'd stashed a clan of pooka. If I didn't watch out, their
yard would soon be inhabited by an entire freaking fae
menagerie.

Me a soft touch? No way. I just seemed to have a knack
for picking up strays. That old lady who lived in a shoe? I
wondered if she was half-wisp.

"Hah!" he exclaimed, slapping his thigh. "Me wear dis
bit o' pretty next time me see Olga."

Olga was one of the female gnomes I'd help to relocate.
She usually stops by my office once a week with fruit pies (real
fruit pies, not goblin fruit or grasshopper pies, I checked) as her
way of saying thanks for the new digs, and I've noticed that
Hob has made a habit of visiting at the same time. I was
pretty sure the brownie was harboring a gnome sized crush.

I was happy for the guy. Olga was kind and sorta cute,
if you could get past the facial hair. It took me weeks before I
realized that female gnomes have beards, though I should have
guessed sooner with all the catcalls coming from the tree
house.

"You do that, Hob," I said. "It'll be good for a laugh."

The pendant disappeared into one of Hob's many
pockets as a shadow crept across the floor at my feet.

"So who is your client?" Kaye asked.

I turned to face the witch, and tried not to flinch. She
looked as drained as Jinx. The arcane tattoos that crept across
her body had spread down her arms and up her neck during
our battle with the *each uisge*. In recent months, the marks
had snaked across her wrists and hands, bringing with them a
frailty I'd never before witnessed in the woman, no matter how
old she really was.

"You're looking at her," I said, pointing to Jinx.

Kaye gave me the stink-eye, no surprise there, and turned her steely gaze on Jinx.

"Come with me," Kaye said.

She turned and marched toward the spell circle where Arachne was still sweeping away a pile of salt. Jinx shot me a questioning look and I shrugged. There was no point arguing with Kaye. If the witch said jump, you asked off which bridge. I just hoped that she could help my friend.

Jinx pulled herself upright and shuffled zombie-like across the room. By the time she reached the spell circle, Arachne was done with her cleaning and striding toward the hearth. Hob was nowhere to be seen. Knowing the brownie, he was probably down in his home beneath the hearthstone, counting his gold.

"Hey, Ivy," Arachne said, toweling her face and pulling her purple-tipped hair into a ponytail. "What's wrong with Jinx?"

I raised an eyebrow at the kid, wondering what she could see. She'd always been the gangly teenager who worked the register at The Emporium. Aside from being the butt of Kaye's magical jokes, and being brought up in a Wiccan family, I hadn't thought she had much real experience with magic. Maybe I was wrong.

"You tell me," I said.

"I don't know," she said, forehead wrinkling. "Maybe the flu? Her aura's all messed up, like she's been drained of energy."

"Does the flu leave behind glowing hickies?" I asked.

Arachne's eyebrows disappeared beneath purple bangs.

"Guess it could be mono," she quipped.

Mono—the kissing disease. A chill ran up my spine. Kisses that left behind glowing marks and drained the victim of energy? I really didn't like the sound of that.

"Guess we can rule out normal human ailments," I said.

"Yes, you can, dear," Kaye said.

I jumped. Not many people can sneak up on me, but Kaye wasn't most people. That was something I'd be smart to remember.

I frowned, scanning the room for Jinx. She wasn't standing behind Kaye, like I'd expected. Heart racing, my eyes came to rest on her prone form at the center of Kaye's spell circle.

"What have you done?" I asked.

I took a deep breath, trying to remain calm, but the light coming from my skin betrayed my emotions.

"Calm yourself, child," she said. "She will be safe inside my circle. I've given her something to help her sleep. She needs rest if she's to recover."

"Recover from what?" I asked.

"From being eaten, dear," she said. "Someone has been feeding off her life force."

"Someone or something?" I asked.

At some point my blades had found their way into my gloved hands, my fingers cramping around the hilt.

"A succubus or incubus," she said. "Judging by your friend's proclivity for 'bad boys' I'd say we're looking for the latter."

"Fuck," I muttered.

"That is one way they feed, though if things had gone that far, I don't think the girl would still be alive," she said.

An incubus could steal your life energy during sex? That gave a whole new meaning to getting screwed.

CHAPTER 6

I left the Emporium determined to find the perp who'd been tapping into my friend's life force like she was a freaking battery. The fact that he'd been doing it under the guise of sex just made it all the worse. My stomach twisted at the thought of some incubus violating my friend.

I gripped my knives and strode toward the waterfront. There was one place I knew harbored incubi and succubi, and there was one succubus in particular who might have some answers. Too bad Delilah and her friends were under the glaistig's protection. The Green Lady was the last person I wanted to face right now.

But this was Jinx who needed my help; my business partner, my roommate, my best friend. Jinx had always been there for me, through all the weirdness, and there was nothing I wouldn't do for her.

According to Kaye, the incubus who'd fed on Jinx wasn't finished. He'd linked himself to Jinx and was continuing to siphon off her energy, bit by bit. She was safe inside Kaye's spell circle, but if I wanted to keep her alive, Kaye speculated that I needed to break the connection.

That's where Delilah came in. I needed someone who could help me find the incubus and reason with him. It would be best for Jinx if I could sweet talk the incubus into willingly breaking his hold.

If that didn't work, we'd do things the hard way. I didn't like killing. The guilt from taking down Ceff's psycho ex-wife still gave me nightmares. But I'd learned that in the fae world, you couldn't show weakness. Most of the fae were deadly predators. I just hoped that the knowledge that this creep was feasting on my best friend would help alleviate the guilt, if it came down to using my blades.

A shriek filled the air and I tensed until I recognized the source. I was so focused on my mission that I didn't hear the fire engines until they were turning onto the narrow street. I slipped my blades back into their wrist sheaths and stepped out of the way just as a horn honked and the truck came barreling down the hill. Heart racing, I continued down the hill, taking to heart the harsh reminder that there were things bigger and more powerful than me in this city that could squash me like a bug.

The breeze shifted as I moved closer to the harbor and I caught the scent of smoke. Something was on fire that was for sure. Normally, I'd be curious, but I didn't have time to check it out. Protecting the people of Harborsmouth was a job I normally took seriously, but not today. The whole city could burn for all I cared, Jinx needed me. For now, that was all I could think about.

I hurried to the waterfront, passing the shops and cafes without really seeing them. I made a cursory sweep for potential threats and hurried on. I needed to reach the carnival and gain an audience with The Green Lady.

Kaye had looked so weak and frail when I'd left Jinx in her care. How long could the witch maintain the spell circle that kept Jinx safe? What would happen if the circle fell?

I blinked rapidly and broke into a run. I wouldn't pass for a morning jogger in my jeans and leathers, but who the hell cared? For once, attracting unwanted attention was the least of my worries.

I passed more police and fire engines as I ran, but no one stopped or questioned me. Flames leapt from a nearby building and I tamped down the guilt that rose as I passed. I couldn't save them all, but I could try to save my friend.

A trashcan a few yards ahead of me burst into flames and I sighed. Shit, this was getting out of hand. What the hell was going on? It was like this part of the city had turned into a warzone.

"The Guild is mobilizing for war." Kaye's words niggled at the back of mind. Was this part of the war she was talking about? Here, so soon?

I hadn't given it much thought at the time, but I realized Kaye had also mentioned the Hunters requesting her help in the war ahead. Did that mean she'd be going away too? I had hoped that my friends would be here to help during the upcoming Summer Solstice, but now I wasn't so sure. It was starting to look more and more like this was something I'd have to face alone.

Could I survive breaking into a death god's domain on my own? I'd been training with Jenna these past few months, but I was no Hunter and I was still healing from a nasty wound in my side. Kaye had nullified the lamia poison, but Melusine had left me with scars to remind me that her fangs had punctured my left flank. The wound slowed me down so that even the pesky jincan had given me trouble. If I could barely take care of supernatural lawn pests, how could I possibly hope to successfully sneak through the Otherworld and into Faerie?

I glanced at the fire from the corner of my eye and caught a flicker of movement within the dancing flames. There, grinning from ear to pointy ear was a tiny fire imp. With a flick of my wrist, my blades reached my gloved palms, but the fiend was already gone. I scowled at the mocking flames.

Damn it all to Hell. The city was being plagued by demons.

CHAPTER 7

I massaged my temples with gloved hands and waited at the railing. I didn't want to get sidetracked, not with Jinx's life on the line, but as much as I tried, I couldn't let my city go to Hell in a hand basket. I just hoped that didn't make me the worst friend on the planet.

"Tell Ceffyl Dŵr that I require his presence," I said.

My voice was drowned out by the crash of waves and the ever present echo of sirens, but I needn't have worried about being heard. Within seconds an equine head emerged from the water. The kelpie whinnied and ducked back below the surface. The creature had heard my summons, now I just had to wait.

"Come on Ceff," I muttered. "I don't have all day."

Ceffyl Dŵr, king of the kelpies, was my lover and official suitor. When we'd fallen for each other, I'd assumed there was no way to make things work between us. I was a half-breed wisp who couldn't be touched without triggering unwanted visions and he was a kelpie whose people had a reputation for eating humans. But somehow, against all odds, he'd managed to nuzzle past my defenses.

But dating each other didn't change our personalities or our duties. I continued to live on land and run my private investigation business and Ceff returned to the sea where he ruled over his people. Of course, we managed to find time for each other in our busy schedules and sending him a message via one of the kelpie or selkie sentinels who patrolled the harbor was the best way to get in touch.

Unfortunately, this time I wasn't looking for a rendezvous with the sexy water fae. I needed his help as the local kelpie king. I just hoped he was within swimming distance. It wasn't unusual for Ceff to be called off on official business, trade negotiations and border wars with the local water fae were common, but I prayed he'd be nearby.

I fidgeted with my knives as my eyes obsessively watched the water. I'd give it five minutes and then I'd have to book it out of here. Thankfully, I didn't have to wait that long.

A handsome face pushed its way up through the water, followed by a well-muscled chest. Blushing, I looked away as Ceff pulled himself up over the railing and onto the sidewalk. I gave him a moment to shake off, and put on some clothes, before turning around.

My belly tightened with need as I took in the rippling muscles and his wet, tousled hair, but I swallowed my desire. This was no booty call. I pulled my gaze from his low-slung jeans and met the dark, green pools of his eyes.

The raw desire I saw there didn't make this any easier. I took a step back and shook my head.

"I gather this is not a date," Ceff said, gesturing to my knives.

I sheathed my weapons, but nodded.

"Jinx is in trouble," I said. "I have to find a way to get her butt out of hot water, but..."

I lifted my arms, indicating the smoke and flames that engulfed much of the waterfront.

"What can I do to assist?" he asked.

Just like that, Ceff had agreed to help. Whoever said chivalry was dead had never met the kelpie king.

"Something, or someone, is setting the city on fire," I said. "I don't know how far it's spread, it may only be here on the waterfront, but I'm pretty sure that fire imps have something to do with it. I saw one of the gleeful little fiends over there."

Imps were lesser demons and as such weren't entirely malicious. The tiny creatures were the pixie equivalent of demonic society—irritating, but not too destructive. The problem arose when you encountered fire imps, which were thankfully somewhat rare here in the human world. The little fellas tended to prefer the fiery pits of Hell—to each his own.

Mix the mischievous nature of a brownie with a fire imp's proclivity toward setting fires and things could quickly get out of hand. Like now.

"And you need someone with the ability to control water to help you put out the flames," he said.

"Yeah, can you do it?" I asked.

"Of course," he said.

I owed Ceff, big time, but I didn't say that. If those of us
with fae blood skate too close to a faerie bargain, we'll be held
to the deal. I'd show him my gratitude later, but I wanted it to
be on my terms, not part of some supernatural compulsion.

I took a step closer, not quite touching, and whispered
in his ear.

"I love you," I said.

"I know," he said, eyes twinkling. "And I love you more
than the air and sea, Ivy Granger."

I ducked my head and smiled. Damn, Ceff always knew
the right thing to say.

"Now go to your friend. My entourage and I will take
care of these flames. I will do my best to hold the demons at
bay."

With one last glance, I spun on my heel and sped toward
the carnival grounds. The sound of hooves hitting cobblestones
filled the air at my back. Ceff's "entourage" was a battalion of
his elite royal guards. With their water magic, they'd make
short work of the fires along the harbor. The close proximity to
the sea lent power to their kelpie magic. Any fires burning
deeper within the city would be more difficult to fight, but I
knew that the kelpies would do their best to extinguish the
flames...and keep Ceff safe.

After Ceff's kidnapping last autumn, his elite guard
weren't letting their king out of their sight. Sometimes it
meant a lack of privacy, which was a total pain in the ass, but
right now, I was more than happy to have them at Ceff's back.
I already had Jinx to worry about. I couldn't be afraid for his
safety as well. I suppose my growing circle of friends were my
weak spot, but I wouldn't trade them for the world.

I just hoped that Jinx hadn't been targeted in an
attempt to get to me. I'd been struggling to come to terms with
her marks and psychic assault, and the thing I kept coming
back to was motivation. Was she attacked because she was a
weak human or because she was my vassal? Vassals were
supposed to be protected, and to the fae world I was royalty.

As Will-o'-the-Wisp's daughter, I was a princess, but as I
was quickly learning, being a faerie princess wasn't all it was
cracked up to be. For every handful of fae who respected my
role as leader of the wisps, there were at least ten more who'd
gladly slit my throat. The fae had a long history of

backstabbing and political infighting that made the Byzantine Empire look like bumbling preschoolers.

If I found out that someone had gone after Jinx as an indirect attack on me or my theoretical throne, I'd bring their ass to Mag Mell—a land where death resulted in immediate resurrection—so I could kill them over, and over, and over again.

A grin tugged at the corners of my mouth. I may even invite Torn along for the ride. The *cat sidhe* lord would appreciate that particular trip to the Otherworld. Cats do enjoy toying with their prey, after all.

CHAPTER 8

With a supernatural fire brigade fighting the flames at my back, I approached the main carnival gates at a dead run. The carnival, the domain of The Green Lady, was on the old amusement park grounds that straddled a pier that thrust the gaudy vaudeville acts, circus sideshows, and rusting rides out into the harbor.

I shoved my twenty bucks at a pimple-faced kid with an overbite, yelled for him to keep the change, and vaulted over the turnstile. The carnival was a maze of tents, gaming booths, food vendors, and amusement rides. It would be easy to get lost, but I'd been here before, during the *each uisge* attack on the city—and that night wasn't one I was apt to forget.

I hurried past the carousel where I'd faced down a very different kind of horse, and hurried to the heart of the carnival.

Of course, the heart of the carnival was where I'd find the glaistig, her pavilion nestled in a ring of smaller tents advertising peculiar physiology and feats of strength. Fae with no other place to go had found a home in the carnival's freak shows. The Green Lady provided a haven for faeries who could not glamour their true form, an affliction that struck close to home.

The carnival may be a safe haven, but it felt like a prison. I'd spent more than one sleepless night picturing myself on a stage where humans came to gawk at the strange, glowing girl. Unfortunately, that nightmare would become a reality if I couldn't find my father and learn how to control my wisp abilities.

Surprised, I blinked away traitorous tears as I ran. This path had been strewn with the torn and bloodied bodies of human parents and their children, as well as brave carnival fae, the last time I was here. I shook my head, dispelling the ghosts my subconscious had conjured. I was already walking a fine line with my emotions. I was anxious about Jinx and, as much as I hated to admit weakness, thinking about the night of the *each uisge* attack could push me over the edge. I needed to focus or I wouldn't be doing anyone any good.

I took a deep breath and slowed my pace to match the families milling about me. If I started glowing in front of humans, the faerie council would have my head on a platter and if The Green Lady discovered my particular malady she'd try to keep me here for my own "protection." A blade or a leash, I wasn't sure which was worse.

I checked my warped reflection in a funhouse mirror and felt my muscles tighten. I wasn't glowing, thank Mab, but I did have a tail. Make that two.

I pretended to fix my hair as I surveyed the area at my back. Apparently, my hasty entrance had gained the attention of the carnival fae. That was fine by me. This wasn't a stealth mission.

I needed an audience with The Green Lady and I needed it yesterday. The fae liked to stand on ceremony, but this was no time for red tape and lengthy traditions. Jinx was counting on me. And honestly? I sucked at diplomacy anyway.

Of course, that didn't mean I was stupid. I kept my blades out of sight and held my hands at my sides as I turned to face my escort.

"Hey, Delilah, who's the new guy?" I asked, tilting my head toward a scruffy *nagual* with amber eyes and, judging by the pelt worn across his shoulders, a bad case of mange. "He doesn't seem like your type."

The succubus dropped from her perch and sashayed across the sawdust strewn path. The *nagual* frowned, keeping his weapon trained on me, but he wasn't the one I was worried about. When I'd visited the carnival in the past, there'd been a faerie bard who'd stuck to Delilah like snot on a boggle's finger.

Despite the succubus' feeding methods, the bard seemed to have genuine feelings for her. I figured if Delilah was here, the trigger-happy bard wasn't far behind. And that guy? He had incredible skills with a bow. Even Jenna would have been impressed.

As it turned out I didn't have long to wait. The bard stepped out from behind the funhouse mirror, a haughty look of amusement on his breathtakingly handsome face. Like I said, the faerie had skills. I'd been within inches of him and hadn't known he was there. I was impressed, not that I was about to advertise that fact.

I scowled and lifted my gloved hands to the air.

"About time you guys showed up," I said. "I need an audience with The Green Lady, stat."

"Our Ladyship does not take orders from you, wisp princess," he said.

So, the carnival fae knew about my new royal status. Apparently, word gets around. Good to know.

"No, but you take orders from her and I'm sure she'd like to see me," I said. I took a deep breath and met his gaze. "I owe her a bargain."

"Last I heard, you owed her more than the fulfillment of one bargain, princess," he said, a twitch of his lips letting me know he thought this was amusing.

"Whatever," I muttered. "Just take me to The Green Lady and let her decide if she wants to see me or not."

The bard gestured and the *nagual* took the lead, heading toward The Green Lady's pavilion. I took my place behind the shifter on this crazy, freak show train and tried to ignore Delilah's purr of pleasure at my side and the bard's arrows at my back.

I focused on the *nagual*, startled when I noticed the furry tail sticking out of his deerskin pants. That might explain why he had joined the carnival fae. Shapeshifters who can't fully hold their human or animal form are a risk to the secrecy that fae society holds so dear. I guess he wouldn't have had much choice coming here, but it had to be hard for someone who's half wild animal to be penned up in an amusement park. Judging by his mangy pelt, I didn't think the carnival life was agreeing with him.

I pulled my eyes from the pendulous tail and winced. Delilah matched my stomping footsteps with her rolling gait, doing her utmost to sway her hips right up to her elbows. The succubus caught my eye with a wink, tongue darting out to suggestively lick her lips.

Mab's bloody bones, I didn't want to encourage the succubus, but this might be my only chance to pick her brain. I smiled, trying not to reach for my blades. Jinx was going to owe me, big time.

"So, um, Delilah," I said, clearing my throat. "I hope this doesn't sound rude, but could you describe your, um, feeding process? I'm...curious."

"Ah, come find out for yoursssself, wisssp princesss," she said, hands moving up and down her body to show me what was on offer.

I took one step to the side, putting more space between us, but kept the smile plastered on my face. It was all I could do not to run.

"No thanks," I said. "I don't need a demonstration. A description will do me just fine."

Delilah pouted artfully, but I just shook my head.

"I take away energy and in return I give pleasssure," she said.

The way she put it, a succubus feeding sounded like an equal exchange, but I was pretty sure that wasn't the case.

"What happens to the other person when you're done feeding?" I asked.

"They die," she said.

Her eyes dilated and I wished I hadn't asked.

"That is enough," the bard said, placing his bow between me and the succubus. "Save your questions for Our Lady. Now move."

I took a hurried step before he could nudge me forward. I didn't want to risk that bow touching my skin. If that happened, I'd probably end up a gibbering mess on the sawdust strewn pavement.

I flicked my eyes to Delilah and tried to smile. She mouthed "later" with her pouty, bee-stung lips and I nodded. If I found out that The Green Lady was harboring the incubus who'd fed on Jinx, I may need Delilah's help. As a succubus and a carnival fae herself, Delilah might be able to convince the guy to release his hold on Jinx, maybe.

It was a long shot. Being nice to Delilah wasn't without its own risks. I didn't need a hungry succubus on my hands. Encouraging a succubus was playing with fire and, like the city outside, I didn't want to go down in flames.

CHAPTER 9

The whir of rusting metal punctuated by loud carnival music and human shrieks grated on my nerves as we skirted a rickety, old tilt-a-whirl ride. I shook my head and followed the carnival fae toward a large, forest green pavilion. I didn't need to fork over my hard earned money to feel the world spinning beneath my feet. I could get that gut in the throat feeling all on my own.

The *nagual* lifted the flap and Delilah sauntered inside. The bard waved his bow, gesturing for me to follow.

I stepped inside, the sounds from the amusement park cut off as the shapeshifter dropped the heavy cloth to the ground. The pavilion was large, but it felt cramped with the hundred or so guards crowded inside. They each had at least one weapon trained on me and I froze.

I'd received the royal audience that I'd wanted, but apparently, The Green Lady had taken measures to make sure I stayed in line. I took a deep breath, wondering how to begin without pissing off the faerie queen. I sucked at diplomacy. I was going to have to dig deep for the tiny bit of manners that I had.

"Um, nice dress," I said.

Okay, that was lame, but I couldn't think of anything else nice to say. And the long, green, formal gown did cover up the glaistig's goat legs, making it an improvement over the dress she'd worn on my last visit.

"Whilst I appreciate your attempt at civility, I am guessing that you did not come all the way here to compliment my dress," she said.

Oh well, so much for playing nice. Might as well say what I came to say and try not to get killed in the process.

"I am here to fulfill our bargain, but on the condition that you provide information that I seek," I said. I held my breath, waiting for one of the guards to run me through with one of their pointy spears for my insolence. I counted to ten and, when no one tried to turn me into a pin cushion, I continued on. "Once I have the information, I'll need a day and a night to act on it, and then I'm all yours."

"I see you have learned something of faerie bargains since our last meeting," she said. Her lips curved, but the smile didn't reach her eyes. At any moment, with the slightest twitch of her hand, she could signal her guards to kill me. It was a sobering thought. "You offer me what is already my due. Why should I agree to your terms?"

"Because if you do this for me, I will fulfill my side of the bargain—without fighting it," I said.

More than one of the stoic guards let out a gasp and The Green Lady shot me an incredulous glare.

"You would think to defy me?" she asked. The faerie queen rose in stature, gathering her power.

"It's nothing personal," I said with a shrug. If she was going to order her guards to kill me, there was nothing I could do to stop them and if she twitched her nose, she could smack me into the ground with her magic like an episode of Bewitched, just much, much bloodier. I figured if she was preparing to kill me, I might as well go down being a wiseass. "It's who I am. I just can't help myself."

To my surprise, she laughed. The sound danced along my nerves like shards of razor-sharp glass, but I held my relaxed pose. Let her think I faced down faerie queens every day.

"Yes," she said, eyeing me up and down, scrutinizing me from head to toe. I tried not to cringe as her eyes glinted like the sun on a guillotine's blade, apparently liking what she saw. "It is what you are—half fae and half human. It is in your very nature to fight the shackles of our bargain, and shirk our traditions. That might make you a useful tool yet."

Mab's bloody bones, I didn't like the sound of that.

"So, um, do we have a deal?" I asked.

"Ah, I see you have also inherited impatience from your human mother," she said.

"What can I say, I'm a busy woman," I said. "People to see, monsters to kill."

Her eyes narrowed and I swallowed hard. Okay, maybe I shouldn't have mentioned that last part. The Green Lady may act like a cold-hearted bitch at times, but the faerie queen cared deeply for her loyal subjects. Many of the carnival fae could pass for monsters. Heck, for all I knew she was

harboring the incubus who'd fed on Jinx. I snapped my mouth
shut and waited.

"Listen carefully, wisp child, for I will not say this
again," she said. "If you ever harm one of my people, I shall
torture you for eternity—no matter who your father is."

Oh shit. She was serious. I nodded and tried to look
sheepish, which wasn't all that hard. I should really learn to
keep my mouth shut.

"Good," she said. "Now that we have that matter out of
the way, let us discuss our terms." I blinked and nodded.
Apparently, we were back to bargaining. "As it happens, I do
have a situation that requires someone of your particular
talents."

"That is...fortuitous," I said. Look at me with the big
words. Hanging out with Ceff must be rubbing off on me.

She grinned like a *cat sidhe* eyeing a mouse.

"Yes, perhaps," she said. "As for this question of yours,
how do I know it is not worth a bargain of its own?"

"You don't," I said. Her eyes narrowed, and I held up a
gloved hand. "But I can assure you that I will do my best to
fulfill my end of the deal. You can ask any fae who've come to
me for help in the past. I bring results."

"Fine," she said. The skin around her eyes looked
pinched and I wondered what kind of job she needed my help
for. If it was big enough to have the glaistig worried, I
probably wasn't going to like the answer.

"And it's information on one topic of my choice, not just
the answer to a single question," I said hurriedly.

"Yes, alright," she said, waving her hand. "It is not like
this is the last of my hold on you. You will still have a
remaining bargain to fulfill."

Ugh, I was hoping she'd forget about that. No such
luck.

"So you give me the information I need and, after a day
and a night, I will come to you to fulfill one task of your
choosing," I said.

"I will agree to providing the information you seek, but
not to the delay," she said. "Do what you will with the answers
to your questions, but you must fulfill your side of the bargain
immediately."

I'd rather have a day to focus on saving Jinx, but this was better than nothing. I needed answers that the glaistig may have. I nodded.

"Fine, do we have a deal?" I asked.

"Yes," she said, a cold grin on her lips.

There was something hinky about the glaistig that I just couldn't put my finger on. I had a bad feeling that she was somehow getting the better end of our bargain. Too bad I didn't have the luxury of time to come up with a better idea.

"Okay," I said. "I accept the terms of our agreement."

I let out a yelp and staggered back a step as the changing nature of our bargain settled across my shoulders like a yoke.

"It is done," she said. "What information do you seek?"

I took a deep breath, in through my nose and out through my mouth, and met the glaistig's eyes.

"Tell me about succubi and incubi," I said.

The Green Lady raised an eyebrow at my question, but steepled her fingers and continued on.

"Succubi and incubi are the result of the coupling of a demon with a highborn fae," she said.

"Sounds cozy," I said.

"I can assure you, it is not," she said, perfect little nose wrinkling. "To become impregnated with a succubi or incubi is a death sentence to the mother, whether she be fae or demon. From the time of conception, the child relies on the mother for nourishment and therefore feeds on her life essence. To my knowledge, no mother, fae or demon, has ever survived the birth of their succubi or incubi offspring."

I swallowed the bitter tang that rose in my mouth and flicked my eyes toward Delilah. Succubi and incubi came into this world with blood on their hands. I knew they couldn't help it, but it didn't endear me to the life-sucking temptress.

Which made me wonder, how had Jinx become seduced by an incubus? I'd made sure we'd been well stocked in crucifixes and holy water and Jinx never went anywhere these days without a weapon. I mean, she was only human, and attracted to bad boys, but after all that we'd been up against in the past year, I had my doubts that she'd just willingly throw herself at an incubus. Had he invited her back to his place? How far had things gone?

Oh, Oberon's eyes, if succubi and incubi were the product of a demon and fae union, then—if a human survived the experience—what was the result of incubi and human sex? God, Jinx, what have you gotten yourself into?

Another slimy thought wormed its way into my brain, making my stomach churn. What would happen if a demon and a human did the horizontal mambo? When I'd caught Jinx and Forneus in the basement of Club Nexus, they were just a few pieces of clothing away from sex.

Remembering Forneus' appearance when he transformed into his demonic form still gave me nightmares— the fact that he'd done so to save Jinx was beside the point. I was sure that if the two ever got together for real, there'd be consequences. And bouncy, little, essence-sucking demon babies sounded like a possible deal stopper.

If Jinx ever remembered that kiss, she'd need to know the risks of taking things further. But I didn't think The Green Lady would be willing to toss that tidbit of knowledge in for free. And I sure as hell wasn't going to make another bargain for it. I'd have to get that information elsewhere. In the meantime, I'd have to pick her brain for information on incubi.

"So what happens if a human and an incubus get...intimate?" I asked.

"If the two had sex, the human would die," she said.

"And how fast would that happen?" I asked, trying to ignore the quiver in my voice. "The dying part."

I silently prayed that Jinx hadn't already signed her own death certificate. If she'd had sex with an incubus, could that be why she was losing energy? Was she just dying a slow death? If so, I wasn't sure if Kaye's magic would be strong enough to keep her alive. My chest tightened. If Jinx was dying, there may be nothing I could do except stand by and watch it happen.

I held my breath, and tried to calm down. If I started glowing, I wouldn't be doing anybody any good. I'd either be recognized as too weak to control my powers or viewed as a potential threat.

"Death would be instantaneous upon completion," she said, gaze flicking upward as if exasperated by my line of questioning.

Relief hit me and I let out a nervous laugh that earned a look of pure scorn. God, this entire line of questioning was

awkward. When I imagined my next conversation with the
faerie queen, it sure as hell hadn't involved discussing incubus
sex. I felt like a kid sitting in Incubus Sex 101 class. The urge
to shoot spitballs at The Green Lady almost made me laugh
again. Yeah, that would be a sure way to get on her bad side.
If I spit anything at the glaistig, I'm pretty sure I'd be facing
far worse than detention.

"And if an incubus and human only got as far as
kissing?" I asked.

The faerie gave me a knowing smile and I wondered
again what game she was playing at. She was answering my
questions, but I could swear that she was holding something
back.

"There would be an energy exchange, of course, which
would immediately begin to weaken the human," she said. "A
link is formed that ensures continued feeding until the human
dies or the link is broken. Though it is rare that an incubus
does not proceed to sex and complete the consumption of the
vessel's energy."

That sounded a lot like what Kaye suspected had
happened. But why had the incubus stopped? I mean, I was
glad he had, or my friend would already be dead. But if the
guy was facing an all-you-can-eat buffet, why settle for an
appetizer?

"You said it's rare for an incubus to stop feeding, once
he's started," I said. "So, what would keep an incubus from
continuing on with sex. It would be against his nature to stop,
right?"

"There are reasons," she said slyly. "He could already
be well sated...or his queen may have asked him to stop."

It took a second for her words to sink in, but when they
did my skin began to glow. Let them think I was doing it
intentionally. I didn't care.

I was pissed.

"You're the one behind the attack on Jinx?" I asked.

I held the glaistig's gaze, but I could feel her guards
closing in. I didn't have enough blades to fight them all—there
were too damn many—but the bitch would pay. She might
survive this moment, but someday soon she would pay.

The Green Lady's tinkling laughter filled the pavilion
and I held myself rigid. It was all I could do to restrain myself

from lunging forward and shoving a blade down her throat. But first, I wanted answers.

"I sent my messenger to your vassal to ensure your timely arrival," she said.

Leather creaked as my hands tightened into fists.

"Jinx is human," I said through clenched teeth. "She never stood a chance against your incubus."

"It was a necessary means to an end," she said with a shrug. "You are here and our deal has been made. So far you have done everything I expected of you."

I felt like I'd been punched in the gut. I'd become predictable. The faerie bitch had found my weakness and used it against me. Jinx was in this mess because of deals I'd made.

She was dying because of me.

I'd known there were risks involved when I'd made those bargains, but I'd been foolish and naïve enough to think the danger was only to me. Now Jinx was paying the price for my stupidity.

"I may be bound by our bargain, but next time you deal directly with me," I said.

"You are in no position to give me orders, little wisp," she said. "My incubus continues to feed from your human friend. If you do not do as I say, and pay your debt to me, then she will die."

The Green Lady had me exactly where she wanted me. I seethed with anger at how easily I'd become ensnared by her web of manipulation. Getting me here to help her with this job had been the glaistig's plan all along. I'd been played, plain and simple.

"So what's the job?" I asked.

Maybe it wouldn't be so bad. I was good at finding lost items and missing people, and I wasn't half bad at the odd extermination gig. Perhaps the carnival had a rodent problem. The harbor was infested with the things.

"I want you to kill the witch Kaye O'Shay," she said.

Oh, shit.

CHAPTER 10

Kaye had been right about one thing, there was certainly a shit-storm on the horizon. But I didn't think this was the war she'd been talking about.

The Green Lady's guards escorted me to the carnival gates, never giving me a chance to rendezvous with Delilah. The succubus made my skin crawl, but I'd been holding out hope that she could somehow help me make contact with the incubus who was feeding off Jinx.

I pulled out my phone and texted Forneus, updating him regarding The Green Lady's involvement. That done, I stared back at the carnival gates and ground my teeth in frustration. Unbeknownst to the frolicking humans, dozens of heavily armed fae watched my retreat. I wouldn't be making it back inside the carnival until I'd fulfilled my end of the bargain—and killed the most powerful witch in the city, an ally and a good friend.

It was weird thinking of Kaye as my friend. She'd filled the role of informant and mentor, helping me out of more than one jam, but at the end of the day that's what she was, a friend. How could I possibly kill one friend to save another?

The fact was, I couldn't. I'd rather cast myself into one of the buildings burning by the harbor than harm the old witch. I'd just have to find another way to save Jinx. When that was done, I wasn't sure what I could do. I was bound to the deal I'd made with The Green Lady. That was the danger of a faerie bargain.

I turned my back on the carnival and hunched my shoulders against the itchy feeling between my shoulder blades. Shoving my gloved hands in my pockets, I trudged past the smoking wreckage left from this morning's fires and made my way back toward The Emporium.

My gut churned as I pushed forward, pumping my legs to carry me up the hill. I was headed toward two of my friends. Too bad one was my potential victim.

CHAPTER 11

It was still light out when I reached The Emporium, but a "sorry, we're closed" sign hung in the front window. I tried the door, but it was locked. Weird, Kaye didn't usually close the store this early in the day.

I sighed and tilted my head back, trying to catch a glimpse of Humphrey. I hoped that Kaye and Arachne had closed up shop early in order to focus on curing Jinx. I didn't think I could handle another problem on my hands.

I caught sight of the gargoyle on his rainspout perch and waved. I heard the snick of stone claws against the brick wall and knew I'd caught his attention, but he was taking his time, eyes intent on a pigeon flying nearby. While I waited for Humphrey, the pungent smell of burnt garbage tickled the back of my throat and I scanned the street. There, beside a wrought iron lamppost, smoke drifted from a city trash bin.

The fire had been extinguished, fire retardant foam spilling over onto the sidewalk, but my heart raced as if the entire street was in flames. I prayed the fire had been set by bored teenagers, but something told me this wasn't the result of human pranksters. Not with those fires at the harbor being set on the same day. That was too much of a coincidence, and I didn't put much faith in coincidences—they tended to be Fate's way of smacking you upside the head with a wake-up call.

"Hello, Wisp Princess," Humphrey said, gravelly voice grinding out the words.

"Hey Humphrey," I said. "Mind letting me in?"

The gargoyle stared at me so long that I thought he'd fallen asleep. Just when I was ready to try to rouse him, he lifted a clawed hand and the door clicked open.

"Um, thanks," I said. "Rock on, Humphrey."

Okay, my attempts at gargoyle humor were lame, but I'd cling to anything that resembled normalcy in my chaotic life. Plus, Humphrey seemed to get a kick out of it. He chuckled and waved before turning and climbing back up to his perch.

I walked inside, locking the door behind me. No one was at the counter, but with the shop closed for the day that was no surprise. Heck, half the time Kaye just used her magic to mind the store. It's not like a person could steal anything. The place was warded against theft and Kaye had more than one nasty spell in place to keep her customers in line—and keep herself amused. If someone ever came in with the intent to rob the place, they'd be in for a world of hurt.

Not that I really wanted to think about how powerful and temperamental the witch was. I was, after all, the sucker who'd been sent to take her life. Mab's bones, how had I ended up a faerie's freakin' hitman? My life was seriously screwed up.

"Kaye?" I called out. "You in here?"

I made my way to the back of the occult shop. I gave the witch's black cat a two fingered salute as I unlocked the hinge on the rear display case, but still no sign of Kaye. Heart in my throat, I reached the hallway marked "employees only" and took a deep breath.

"First things first," I muttered to myself.

I'd check on how Jinx was doing and then face the reality of my misguided faerie bargain. I gave a quick rap on the door and gingerly pushed it open.

Someone was inside the spell circle, hovering over Jinx's prone form, but it wasn't Kaye. Judging from the purple hair, Arachne was the one with Jinx. Had Kaye retreated to her office to consult one of the many books in her arcane library?

I hesitated, wavering between the urge to see Jinx and the need to consult with Kaye. My ties to the sleeping rockabilly beauty won out. I walked toward the spell circle, careful not to touch the ring of silver that was set deep into the floor.

Disrupting a witch's circle while she worked was never a good idea. Circles were built as a means of protection for when a witch was at their most vulnerable. It made sense. It also meant that if my boot scraped the ring of silver from this side of the circle, I'd probably end up the way I liked my vampires—extra crispy.

This spell circle kept both bad things out and the nasty effects of miscast spells in. If Kaye or Arachne blew something up, it would only destroy the area of the kitchen within the spell circle. Watching my friend lying there defenseless didn't make that particular piece of knowledge all that comforting.

"Arachne?" I whispered. "It's me, Ivy. Got a minute?"

I kept my voice low. If the young witch-in-training was deep in a casting, I didn't want to disturb her. I also didn't want to startle her into thinking I was a threat. It was a bit like talking to a bugbear cub—"hey, kiddo, please don't eat my face off"—except with a witch I could end up like that guy from the Indiana Jones movie who opened the Ark. I really didn't want to be turned into a pair of eyeballs in a pile of melted skin.

Arachne's eyes flew open, gaze unfocused. I waited, giving her a moment to ground herself. She blinked rapidly and turned toward me, an embarrassed flush to her cheeks.

"Hey, Ivy," she said. "Sorry, I didn't hear you come in."

"That's okay," I said. "Where's Kaye?"

"I don't know, she just said it was important and took off," she said, frowning. "She's been going out a lot lately, but she never tells me why or for how long."

Sneaking off to consult her Hunters' Guild friends perhaps? Kaye was embroiled in some kind of battle preparations while I still had no idea what kind of war was coming. Did it have anything to do with the glaistig's request for me to kill the witch? I didn't like that line of thought, not one bit.

"Don't worry, Ivy, I can do this," Arachne said, misreading my expression.

My attention returned to the teenager standing there, hovering over Jinx. Arachne chewed on a piece of purple hair while she shifted side to side in her matching Chuck Taylors.

"Wait," I said, the reality of the situation making tingles of anxiety dance along my skin. "You're in charge of watching Jinx?"

No offense to the kid, but her cauldron still had training wheels.

"I've learned a lot and, unlike Kaye, I actually like Jinx," she said, pushing her hair behind her ear. "I want to see her get better."

I suppose, put like that, she had a point.

I turned my attention to Jinx, though still careful not to disturb the spell circle.

"How's she doing?" I asked.

"The same," she said, frowning.

"And that means...?" I asked.

"She's, like, stuck, you know?" she asked, lifting her hands in frustration.

"If I understood any of this, I wouldn't be asking," I said.

I tried to soften my expression, but my voice was hard. The kid was trying, I'd give her that.

"Okay, it's like this incubus, or whatever, cast a spell on Jinx," she said. "Except, it's not like witch magic, so we can't just create some counter spell to fix her. Faerie magic is complicated, like algebra complicated, so the best we can do right now is keep her stable."

"Hence the circle?" I asked.

"Yeah," she said. "Think of it like a force field. It's like Jinx is superman and the connection to the incubus is kryptonite. The spell circle keeps her from getting any weaker, but she's already been drained of a lot of energy."

"And the second she steps outside that circle, she dies, right?" I said, swallowing hard. "Kaye didn't just put her under a sleeping spell to get better, did she? It's to keep her from doing something stupid—like trying to leave the circle."

Arachne nodded, still chewing her hair.

"So is there any benefit to her sleeping?" I asked.

Oberon's eyes, I'd hoped she was getting better. Please say she was regaining her strength.

"Um, it helps a little," she said. "And I'm trying every healing spell I can think of, just in case."

"Okay," I said, rubbing a gloved hand down my face. I wanted to talk to my friend and shake her in equal parts, but I'd have to settle for leaving her under Arachne's care. I sure hoped the kid knew what she was doing. "You keep watch and continue your efforts to heal Sleeping Beauty over there. I'll deal with the creep who's got his hooks into her."

The kid stood up straight and gave a curt nod. I knew I could trust her to do her best. I just hoped that her best was enough. I returned her nod and turned to leave.

"Ivy?" she asked. "I'm glad you're okay. There've been sirens wailing past the shop all day. I was starting to think you might have gotten yourself into real trouble this time."

"Nope," I said, holding up my hands to show my wrists. "No cuffs or IVs. The sirens were due to all the fires that broke out along the harbor."

I felt a pang of worry for Ceff, but tamped it down. He could take care of himself and when he tried to be a hero his elite guard would keep him safe.

"Fires?" she squeaked.

"Yeah," I said. "It's okay. Don't worry about it. You focus on Jinx."

"B-b-but..." she stuttered.

"No buts," I said. "Do what you can for Jinx, and if you hear from Kaye, let me know. She and I need to have a chat."

I wasn't looking forward to that conversation. *Oh, hey, by the way, I just signed up to take your life.* Yeah, that was going to go over well.

I'd rather play grab ass with an eight-armed goblin spider, but if I couldn't find another way to take down the glaistig's pet incubus, then Jinx would be trapped inside that spell circle forever. One way or another, Kaye and I were going to have to have that chat.

Some girls just have all the luck.

CHAPTER 12

Thick, black smoke stung my eyes and left an acrid taste in the back of my throat. The flames may have been extinguished, but Harborsmouth hadn't escaped the morning's fires unscathed. I clenched my fists. Someone was going to pay for the damage to my city.

I remembered the fleeting glimpse I'd caught this morning of a fire imp dancing in the flames by the waterfront. If it hadn't been for the current situation with Jinx, and the added matter of my bargain with The Green Lady, I'd be out hunting the little bastards right now.

Too bad my hunting partner had been exiled halfway around the planet, my best friend was stuck inside a magic hamster ball to keep from dying, and my mentor in all things paranormal had gone missing. Oh yeah, and when she returned, we'd have to address the small matter of me being pledged to kill her.

I blinked hard against the smoke-filled air and stomped toward Private Eye, the detective agency I ran with Jinx, and the adjacent loft apartment we both shared. The loft was situated on the floor above our office, but I hesitated before reaching out for the door that led to a flight of stairs and the promise of a shower. Someone, or something, was hunched in our office doorway.

I hadn't been into the office today, but I'd heard Jinx clearing our schedule before walking to Kaye's earlier today. Had that really only been this morning? She'd sent out calls, emails, and text messages to our clients, so who was lurking on our doorstep?

With the philosophy that it was better to be prepared than dead, I flicked my wrist to release one of my throwing knives from its sheath and with the other hand slid a holy water dipped stake to rest along my thigh. I really wasn't in the mood for vamp games or fae politics and there was no way I'd take on a new case right now. Whoever it was needed to leave…or face the consequences of a very grumpy wisp princess.

I stalked forward, careful to keep my weight balanced, ready to strike or dodge as need be. Thankfully, I wouldn't need my blades, this time.

Ceff sat there waiting on my doorstep, a smudge of soot on his face. His eyes fluttered open and he waved me off.

"What…?" I gasped. "Are you okay?"

Wincing, he pulled himself upright. He wobbled, unsteady on his feet, and I hurried forward. I reached out to steady him, but he took a step away.

"I am uninjured, just…tired," he said. "No need to risk a vision. Unless, of course, you would like to join me in a shower? I seem to have acquired an inordinate amount of filth while fulfilling your wish to extinguish fires throughout the city."

His dark eyes gleamed and warmth spread through me and tightened my belly. God, Ceff was gorgeous when he smiled. The smudge of soot did nothing to mar the chiseled features of his face. In fact, it made me want to touch him all the more. Sharing a shower? Yeah, that sounded like a grand idea. Too bad this was neither the place or the time.

I shook my head and took a step back, putting more distance between us, struggling to keep my hands to myself. If I touched Ceff now, it would be awhile before I could stop, and I didn't just mean sex.

Coming into contact meant experiencing visions of every significant, emotionally charged moment in the immortal kelpie king's life. We'd shared those visions before. It was a necessary part of our relationship, one that had brought us surprisingly close, but it did have a downside. There was no such thing as a quickie where Ceff and I were concerned, and right now I didn't have time to play in the shower. We could go horizontal when everything else in my life stopped going sideways.

"Come on, we can talk upstairs," I said. "And I do mean talk. It's been one hell of a day."

"Of course," he said.

Ceff waited patiently for me to lower the wards and unlock the door before crossing our threshold and mounting the stairs to the loft. My human blood, as well as the door ward's custom design, allowed me to enter, but Ceff was a pureblooded faerie. He could only enter if Jinx or I let him in. Which was…awkward.

The fact that my supernatural security system kept the good guys out left a sour taste in my mouth, not unlike the acrid tang of soot that currently coated the back of my throat. Just a few months ago, I'd have been happy that my home was protected against the fae—every damn one of them.

Until last summer, the only faerie I'd considered a friend was a churlish brownie who would just as soon pix you as sweep his own hearth. It's funny how a battle to protect the city could change so much in such a short span of time. Since then, I'd learned that being fae didn't necessarily make you an enemy. Hell, we'd even allied with vamps—dusty old bloodsuckers. War makes strange metaphorical bedfellows and if Kaye was right, there was another war brewing, which was just freaking ducky.

In the past few months, I'd gained some amazing fae friends and was literally sharing my bed with a kelpie king whose ancestors ate humans for breakfast. I'd also learned the secret of my own fae lineage—something I was obviously still struggling with. After years of thinking of the glamoured beings who walked the city streets as monsters, it was hard to resist the urge to stab first and ask questions later.

And don't get me started on demons. My city was being vandalized by pyromaniacal hellspawn and I was wondering when Forneus would call with an update on Jinx. Since when had my hopes hung on a demon?

Everything I'd thought I'd known was turned on its head in such a way that even setting my door wards made me feel guilty. Mab's bones, this was messed up. It also didn't go over my head that the very wards and charms protecting my home were created by the witch that the glaistig had ordered me to kill.

I brushed salt and herbs from my gloves and followed Ceff up the stairs. Oh well, if I was having a crisis of conscience, I might as well enjoy the view. Yeah, I was going to Hell, but at least I'd go happy.

CHAPTER 13

Ceff went to the kitchen where he started opening cupboards, pulling down packages of food, and setting a pan on the stove. It wasn't the first time he'd cooked for me, but today the sight of Ceff wearing Jinx's apron felt wrong. My roommate usually cooked my meals. She'd made it her mission to make sure I didn't forget to eat, something I had a bad habit of doing, especially when I was wrapped up in a case. I swallowed hard and dropped onto a tall stool, watching Ceff as he found his way around the small kitchen.

"How is Jinx?" he asked.

He kept his attention on the food, which was now simmering on the stove, giving me a chance to regain my composure. I took a deep breath, waiting until I could speak without breaking out into big, ugly sobs. My skin began to glow and I bit the inside of my cheek. When it came to Jinx, I could be such a wuss.

"For the moment, she's being kept inside a spell circle at The Emporium," I said. "An incubus fed on her. He's one of the carnival fae, and if I want to save Jinx, I have to either kill the bastard or convince him to relinquish his hold on her."

Ceff's hand paused as he reached for a kitchen knife. I could read his emotions by the tension in his shoulders and the way he worked his jaw, but when he spoke, his voice was calm, controlled, the voice of a king.

"When you called for my help with the fires, you were going to speak with The Green Lady?" he asked.

"Yes," I said.

He slowly turned off the stove, and carefully set the pan aside.

"And did she punish her subject, this incubus who attacked your vassal?" he asked.

"Punish him?" I snorted. "Nope, she's the one who ordered him to make contact with Jinx in some freaking Machiavellian attempt to get my ass down to the carnival and pay up on one of my bargains. A ploy which worked, by the way."

Ceff spun around so fast that my half human eyes couldn't follow the movement. One second he was staring at the cooling food on the stove and the next he was facing me across the counter. His dark green eyes bled to black and I stifled a chill. Ceff was pissed and giving off his king of the sea vibe. Or maybe it was his, "I'm going to drown your ass and pick your bones" vibe. Sometimes I just can't tell the difference.

Thankfully, his anger wasn't directed at me.

"What does The Green Lady want of you?" he asked.

He started to pace and I suddenly wished we'd splurged on a larger apartment. Ceff may have been in his human form, but the energy coming off him was that of a wild stallion—and yeah, he was still giving off that drag you down and feast on your bones kind of feeling.

"Look, you sure you want to know any of this?" I asked. "Cause I understand if you don't want to get involved. She's a faerie queen and you're a faerie king. I'm guessing that means that things could get messy if you join team Ivy on this one."

I wanted him by my side so bad it set my teeth on edge, but I didn't want anyone else I cared about getting hurt. My human mother still couldn't write her own name after she'd tried to help give me answers about my real father. Jinx was on her deathbed because of me, spell circle or no spell circle, and if the glaistig got her way, Kaye would be next. If I could save my friends, I would. The least I could do was give Ceff the choice, no strings attached.

"As you would say, I am all in," he said. "Now what does she want?"

"She wants me to kill Kaye," I said.

Just saying the words was like taking a punch to the gut. Judging from the way Ceff's face paled, he felt the same.

"The Green Lady, queen of the carnival fae, has asked you to take the life of the most powerful witch on the entire eastern seaboard?" he asked. "The same witch who came to your aid on more than one occasion, who has fought to save this very city...the witch you call your friend?"

"Yes, the one and only," I said.

"You agreed to such a thing?" he asked, incredulous.

"Yes, but, in my defense, I didn't know what I was agreeing to at the time," I said. "And she was holding Jinx's life as bait."

"You owe The Green Lady a boon," he said with a sigh. "In all likelihood, there was not much that you could have done." Ceff shook his head and returned to his cooking, lighting the flame and placing the frying pan back on the burner. "So what are the terms of this agreement, be as precise as you can."

I chewed on my lip, thinking back to my conversation with the glaistig. Yeah, she'd dangled Jinx's welfare like the carrot that it was, and I was not a happy bunny. I'd have to be more careful when it came time to fulfill my second bargain with The Green Lady. Fool me once, shame on you—fool me twice, shame on me. I'd learn from this and move on. Too bad learning experiences with the fae tended to be so costly.

"She says I have to kill the witch Kaye O'Shay to fulfill our bargain," I said. "And just to make it worse, she said that I had to do it or else she'll let her incubus continue feeding and kill Jinx. I suppose that's her little insurance policy, in case I find a way around the bargain." I pounded the counter with a gloved fist. "Mab's bloody bones, there's got to be some way to win this thing!" I muttered.

I felt like a *cat sidhe* chasing its own tail. No matter how many times I thought the problem over, I kept coming up with the same thing. I needed The Green Lady to order her incubus to break his connection with Jinx, but the only way to do that was to fulfill our bargain by killing Kaye. I couldn't bring myself to kill Kaye, which meant that my best friend was going to die.

Ceff turned and raised an eyebrow at me as he slid a pile of seasoned eggs and buttered toast onto a plate.

"What?" I asked, suddenly ravenous.

"You are stubborn," he marveled.

"Well, yeah, that's a given," I said. "Of course I'd try to find a way out of the bargain if it was nasty enough. I just never thought she'd ask me to kill someone, least of all Kaye."

"And if you move against her directly, she has the incubus as leverage," he said.

I nodded, shoveling a forkful of food into my mouth.

"Oh yeah, and she said that if I ever harmed one of her people, she'd torture me for eternity."

The memory of The Green Lady's words rang in my ears as if the glaistig were still in the room. The threat had been clear—mess with the incubus and die a long, painful death.

"Hmmm..." Ceff mumbled.

Other than the mumbling, Ceff remained silent, but a small grin tugged at his lips.

"Talk to me, Ceff," I said. "Give me something to go on, anything."

He leaned back against the far counter, muscular arms across his chest, legs wide apart.

"I do have a suggestion, but you are not going to like it," he said.

"Go ahead, shoot," I said. "I'm fresh out of ideas. At this point, I'll take all the advice I can get."

"I was thinking that the first thing you need to do is find a way to kill the witch, hence freeing you of the bargain," he said.

I coughed, choking on a piece of toast.

"Are you nuts?" I asked.

He couldn't be serious. Could he? Fae morals were different than the human ones I'd grown up with, but I'd bet my life that Ceff wasn't like that. He'd never put my life before my friend's lives, would he?

"Wait," he said. "Hear me out. If you disagree, you can stab me later."

Was that a knife in the palm of my hand? Why yes, yes it was. I pushed the knife back into my sleeve and went back to eating my eggs. Me, embarrassed of wanting to stab my boyfriend? Nope, not one bit. I was hungry and there is nothing worse than cold eggs.

"I'm listening," I said around a mouthful of food.

"You must fulfill the terms of your bargain with The Green Lady," he said. He lifted his hands, but let them drop. "The longer you resist, the weaker you will become. The laws of the fae run within your blood. You may have more time than most purebloods, but eventually, you must obey or die."

"Wait, you mean The Green Lady will siphon off my energy just like her incubus leach is doing to Jinx?" I asked.

I blinked at Ceff and pushed my plate away, suddenly not so hungry. Going against faerie law was something I hadn't thought about. I'd known there were consequences to fighting against the chains of a faerie bargain, but I hadn't bothered to ask what those consequences might be.

"It is our way," he said, looking down at his hands.

"So I have to fulfill my side of the faerie bargain, or I'll be no use to anyone," I said.

"Yes," he said.

"I have to kill Kaye," I said. "Mab's bones, I'd rather die first."

"Yes, you have to kill Kaye," he said. He moved across the kitchen and leaned across the counter, bringing his lips close to my ear to whisper. "It is a good thing that all death is not permanent."

I jerked my head back and marveled at the gleam in his eye.

"Are you suggesting what I think you're suggesting?" I asked.

"You have read Romeo and Juliet, have you not?" he asked.

If the circumstances had been different, I'd have rolled my eyes. The fae have an unhealthy fascination with The Bard. My mother, while dating my wisp father, had become a Shakespearephile herself. I'd grown up on all the classics.

"Yeah," I said. "So you're suggesting I convince Kaye to brew up a sleeping potion that mimics death? Would that even work?"

"Not exactly," he said. "In this case, the potion would need to, at least temporarily, kill the witch. She must die in order to fulfill the terms of your bargain. But there is no rule saying that you are not allowed to revive her."

I lifted my hands and pushed away from the counter.

"No way," I said. "The only necromancers I know are vamps, and those old dustballs aren't about to help a witch, especially not one who used to be chummy with the entire Hunters' Guild. Plus, I've seen what happens to people who come back from the dead." I swallowed hard, remembering the way Stinky's guts had exploded all over me on a recent trip to vamp headquarters. There was no way I'd do that to Kaye. "It's not pretty."

"No, not necromancy," he said with a grimace. "I was thinking of having an antidote prepared, or perhaps one of those lifesaving machines that restarts the human heart."

"A cardiac defibrillator?" I asked.

Now that was one crazy plan, but it might just work—if I could find Kaye and get her to agree to letting me kill her and zap her with electricity.

"Kill the witch, fulfill your debt to The Green Lady, and then bring your friend back to life," he said.

I licked my lips and fidgeted with my gloves. Kaye forgive me, but I was considering Ceff's plan.

"You make it sound so simple," I said.

"No, not simple," he said. "Elegant."

"Damn, you sound like Forneus," I snorted. "You guys and your elegant plans. I'd rather go in there blades flashing."

Which reminded me, I needed to check in with the demon. I should have heard from him by now.

"If you meet The Green Lady head on, you will die," Ceff said.

"Yeah, there is that," I said. "But I'm still not sure how this helps us save Jinx. I mean, being free of the bargain is great and all, but if The Green Lady discovers that I've found a way around it, then what's to keep her from trying to worm her way out of fulfilling her side of things? If her incubus doesn't willingly release control of Jinx, our only option will be to kill him. And if The Green Lady finds a way to weasel out of our deal, I'm sure she'll have her incubus' ass protected night and day."

"Do not let the glaistig know that she is being bamboozled," he said. "Keep Kaye's resurrection a secret long enough to find a way to break the incubus' hold on Jinx."

"You really think that's possible?" I asked.

He nodded, eyes beginning to glow green.

"You encompass the best qualities of both fae and human," he said. "You are clever, strong, stubborn, and unpredictable."

It was a strange compliment, especially coming from one's boyfriend, but his words gave me the kick in the pants that I needed. I lifted my chin and let out a throaty laugh.

"The Green Lady will never know what hit her," I said.

Ceff grinned.

"Indeed."

CHAPTER 14

Our plan had sounded good in theory, but it would only work if I could convince Kaye to let me kill her. That was kind of difficult considering the fact that at the moment, I had no idea where she was. I stared at my reflection in the bathroom mirror and frowned.

"This is a shitty plan," I muttered.

I shook my head and splashed water on my face, careful not to disturb any of Jinx's things. Cherry red lipstick and a box of tissues sat precariously on the edge of the sink. Like Jinx herself, her things were poised to fall—and if I failed The Green Lady, I wasn't sure who'd be here to pick up the pieces.

I toweled off my face and sighed, but it came out like a strangled hiccup. Maybe coming back to the apartment had been a mistake. Seeing Jinx's things made me miss her all the more. But I hadn't expected to find so many traces of her here in the bathroom. My eyes blurred as I looked at the cherry red lipstick. My roommate was usually so careful not to leave her things lying around, just in case they gave me an unwanted vision. But this morning had been different—way different, and not in a good way.

Just this morning, Jinx had looked at her reflection in this very mirror, struggling to see the glowing marks on her skin through unshed tears. She'd tried to put on her lipstick, like it was a normal day, like nothing was wrong. And when the realization hit that she was in deep shit, she'd reached for the box of tissues—and cried out for help.

She'd called my name, believing that I could fix this. I couldn't let her down.

I pulled my hair back into a ponytail, securing it with an elastic band, and twisted it into a tight bun. I slid four wooden stakes and four silver pins into the bun, helping to secure it. Keeping my hair out of an opponent's grasp was prudent, and if someone did try to grab it, they'd get a nasty surprise.

I continued to weapon up, sliding blades, stakes, crosses, and small charms into sheaths, boots, and pockets. What was it that Jenna liked to say? Oh yeah, "keep your enemies close and your weapons closer." It was good advice. I just wished she was here to join in the fight.

And it would be a fight, in the end. There was something on the wind, a promise of blood that lingered in the smoky air. In order for our plan to work, I'd have to find a way to get to The Green Lady's incubus and break his connection to Jinx. Double-crossing a faerie queen and messing with one her loyal subjects? That promised a fight.

But first I needed to find Kaye.

"You look beautiful, and deadly," Ceff said.

He was leaning in the open doorway, looking me up and down.

"Um, thanks," I said. "That's the idea. The deadly part, that is. Think the glaistig will be shakin' in her boots?"

He nodded. Right, it's hard for the pureblood fae to tell an outright lie. Ceff was trying to make me feel better, but telling me The Green Lady would tremble in fear at the sight of a half-breed with a few trinkets was probably asking too much of the guy.

I pushed away from the sink and he moved out of my way, smart man. Grabbing the last of my things, I took one final look around the apartment. The handwoven tapestry on one wall, the ticking Felix-the-Cat clock over the kitchen sink, and the old comfy couch suddenly looked drab and worn like someone had sucked the life out of the entire loft and its furnishings. This place would never be the same without Jinx. If I couldn't save her, I might as well not come back.

"You will save her," he said.

He came to stand beside me. Not close enough to trigger a vision, but within reach if I desired it. Ceff was a steadying presence and I nodded curtly. When we cleared the front door, I said a silent prayer as I reset the protection wards that only allowed Jinx or me to enter. I just hoped that one of us would be coming back.

CHAPTER 15

"Miss Granger?"

Crap. That was the problem with living over your business. It made it way too easy to be found. Just wait long enough and I'd turn up. I'd have to remember that the next time I needed to dodge potential clients and deadly enemies. This one, thankfully, looked like the former.

I turned to see a short, heavyset man standing in front of my office. I focused on him with my second sight, but he looked much the same either way; a stout man in a pinstripe suit, watch fob and all. He could have been a vertically challenged human, but I was guessing dwarf.

Though what a dwarf would want with me was anyone's guess. There weren't many in the area. Dwarves were miners and we were at sea level without a mountain in sight. A few had excavated The Hill centuries ago, but word on the street was that they'd all cleared out when the vamps moved to town and took over the underground chambers for their own headquarters.

I studied the dwarf, wondering what could have brought him to the city and onto my doorstep. He held an old, bowler hat to his chest, exposing the top of his head—which appeared to be the one spot on his body not covered in shaggy hair. His beard, which covered most of his face, was split down the middle and braided into two plaits that brushed the top of his large boots.

He turned the hat in a circle with his stubby fingers and looked pleadingly up at me. I hated it when they did that. I was no good at this sort of thing, which is why Jinx dealt with our clients. But she wasn't here to run interference, not today, maybe not ever again.

I bit my cheek and gave myself a mental kick in the pants. Being depressed about Jinx wouldn't do my friend any good. I had to think positive, and if Jinx were here, she'd want me to be nice to the potential client. Whoever, or whatever, he was.

"Yeah, um, that's me," I said with a shrug. I hoped that owning up to my name hadn't just painted a big target on my chest, but then again, this guy would be hard put to reach that high to stab me. Of course, he could have a gun in that fancy hat...or rabid ferrets or something. With the fae, you never know. "But the office is closed today—family emergency."

It wasn't a lie exactly. For the longest time, Jinx had been the closest thing I had to family. My wisp blood didn't react—it was close enough to the truth.

"M'lady, I am Benmore, leader of the dwarves of Harborsmouth," he said. "I bear a missive from the vampire master of the city."

He lowered his hat in one hand, the other hand reaching inside his pinstripe vest. With a flick of my wrist, a throwing knife hit my palm, ready to throw if necessary. Better to be paranoid than dead. Apparently, Ceff was thinking the same thing. He held his telescoping trident in both hands, ready for a fight.

The dwarf's eyes widened—at least I think they widened, since they became much more visible in his hairy face—and he froze.

"Would you prefer to retrieve the missive yourself, M'lady Wisp?" he asked.

"I'd rather not," I said. No way was I touching some strange dude's vest, no matter how impressive his beard. "No offense. Ceff?"

Ceff stepped forward and reached two fingers into the man's vest pocket, retrieving a dusty scroll tied with a ribbon. He carried it toward me and I groaned. The thing reeked of vamps. It had the stink of dust and decay all over it.

"You're working as a messenger for the vampire master of the city?" I asked.

The dwarf shrugged and placed his hat on his head.

"We have an arrangement, m'lady," he said. "They rule the city above from below, while I rule the city below from above."

"So when the vamps took over your halls, you did what? Went topside while your people dug deeper?" I asked.

Benmore nodded, beard wagging, and held out his hands in a "what can you do?" gesture. I could think of a lot of things, like staking all the vamps, but I kept those thoughts to myself.

"Shall we open it?" Ceff asked, eyeing the scroll in his hand like a viper that may strike at any moment. Knowing vamps, it just might. Vampires love theatrics.

"Okay, fine," I said. The dwarf mayor or whatever seemed to be waiting for us to read the letter and we needed to get a move on if we were going to find Kaye. "Let's get this over with."

Ceff tugged at the red ribbon, which was the color of blood, of course, and broke the wax seal that held the scroll together. As he unrolled the scroll, the parchment—please god, tell me that's not human skin—made a dry, whispering sound that scraped along my nerves like claws on a chalkboard. Leave it to the vamps to use a means of sending a message that was both dramatic and annoying. God forbid the Luddites pick up a telephone.

"What does it say?" I asked.

I leaned toward Ceff, careful not to get too close to the scroll. I sure as hell didn't want to touch something that came from vamp headquarters, even if it wasn't human skin—and the jury was still out on that one.

Ceff tilted the scroll toward me with a grimace. The spidery handwriting danced along the page with dark blotches where the nib of the pen had caught the paper. The ink looked dark brown, but I knew by Ceff's look of disgust that it had run red when it was fresh.

The scroll was written in blood.

I swallowed hard, choking down my revulsion and focused on the flowery words. Too bad the message found within wasn't any better than the vile manner in which it was written. The vamps meant to collect on my debt.

When it rains it pours. It seemed like everyone was out to collect a piece of me. Too bad for them, I was busy.

"What shall I inform the vampire master of the city?" Benmore asked.

"Like I said, we're closed, family emergency," I said.

"Oh, but the master will be very displeased," he said, beard twitching.

"A moment," Ceff said.

He gestured and I followed to where he stopped a few feet away from the dwarf. It wasn't private, but we didn't have time to go back inside and have a long chat. Plus, as far as I was concerned, the vamps could wait.

"We don't have time for this," I said, speaking through my teeth.

"Would you agree that there is nothing more to be done until you hear back from Forneus or Arachne?" he asked. "We do not know Kaye's whereabouts and we are no closer to breaking the incubus' hold on Jinx."

"But you're the one who said I had to complete the bargain before it started to sap my strength," I said, sotto voce.

"All I am suggesting is that we hear the vampire out," he said. "Breaking a bargain with the master of the city while trying to do the same with the queen of the carnival fae may be too much, even for you."

I scrubbed a gloved hand over my face and groaned.

"Fine," I said. I turned to Benmore who was not-so-subtly checking the time on his pocket watch. "Tell the vampire master of the city that I've accepted his invitation."

I ground out the words and stormed up the street. I didn't have time for games, but Ceff was right. It would be foolish to piss off the vamps. The last thing I needed was the council of dusty leeches on my ass. *Ewww.* That would suck, pun intended.

CHAPTER 16

I punched in Forneus' number and scowled when I was sent to voicemail. The demon wasn't answering his phone, the bastard. Strains of violin music played in the background as his smooth voice informed me that it would be his pleasure to return my call if I would be so kind as to leave a message after the beep.

"Where the hell are you?" I asked. "Get your ass back from wherever you've slithered off to and call me."

Okay, it wasn't the nicest of messages, but Forneus was on my last nerve. He claimed that he wanted to help Jinx, and then he off and disappeared. That was typical of a demon, so I shouldn't have been so worked up over it. I guess I'd started to let the guy weasel inside my defenses with his apparent worry over Jinx. Ceff raised an eyebrow and I snorted.

"The bastard said he was going to help," I said. "I'm not holding my breath."

But I had been. I'd been waiting for Forneus to dramatically appear in a puff of sulfurous smoke and bring me a way to save Jinx. I could be Grade-A stupid sometimes.

Next, I speed dialed Arachne, hoping that she wasn't in the middle of casting something. Or if she was, that she'd had the foresight to turn off her screeching ringtone.

"Ivy?" she answered. "Is that you?"

"Yeah, it's me," I said. "How's Jinx?"

"Okay, the same," she said. "Sorry."

I'd been hoping for more, but if wishes could be dollars, and all that.

"You're doing your best," I said. I knew the kid would do anything to help Jinx get better. For now, that was enough. "Any word from Kaye?"

"Nothing yet," she said. "But as my mom always says, a watched cauldron never boils."

"And that's supposed to mean what exactly?" I asked.

"It means I'm focusing on Jinx and trying not to hover by the phone waiting for you and Kaye to call," she said.

She yawned and I realized the kid probably hadn't slept since yesterday. She'd been busy with her training when I'd interrupted this morning. Knowing Kaye, they'd been at it all night, which would explain why she was sounding grumpy.

"When was the last time you ate?" I asked.

If you have to go without sleep, food is a good substitute. So was caffeine, but I'd never seen the kid drink coffee.

"I dunno, yesterday I guess," she said.

"Is Hob there handy?" I asked.

"Think so," she said. "Yeah, he's polishing his hearth. Why?"

"Ask him to make you something to eat, something that is safe for humans to eat," I said.

"Anything else, mom?" she asked.

"Yeah, ask nicely," I said.

"Okay, okay, fine, I'll make sure to eat, but I'd rather order out for pizza," she said. "No offense to Hob."

Huh, why hadn't I thought of that? Pizza was sure to be safer than negotiating a meal with a hearth brownie. Of course, we couldn't let the spell circle fall that was protecting Jinx and with Kaye AWOL that left Arachne to maintain the circle.

"Your spell circle will hold if you go out front to pay the delivery guy?" I asked.

I was pretty sure that proximity mattered, at least with less experienced witches like Arachne.

"Yeah, I'm not a total loser," she said.

"I didn't mean to imply that you were," I said. "Look, you watch out for Jinx and you can eat all the pizza you want, my treat."

I gave the kid my credit card info, thankful Jinx made sure to pay the bills each month, even if I was spending too much of our profits on the search for my father.

"Cool, thanks, Ivy," Arachne said.

Well, that put the kid in a better mood. Nothing like free pizza to raise the spirits.

"No problem," I said. "Call me if anything changes."

"I will," she said over the sound of shuffling paper and hung up.

I put the phone in my pocket and turned to Ceff who was on high alert. He'd been keeping pace with me as I strode across the cobbled streets of the Old Port quarter, heading toward Joysen Hill and his eyes were searching the shadows of every door and alleyway as we approached. We were heading into a nasty part of town and it was nice to know he had my back.

"Jinx is stable," I said. He continued to watch for potential threats, the tightening around his eyes the only sign he'd heard me. "We can do this, there's still time."

He nodded, but the words fell flat, even to my ears. For the first time since this morning, I questioned whether or not I was kidding myself. Doubt gnawed at me like a ravenous ghoul.

Speaking of ghouls, I wondered how the vamp's doorman—who I'd nicknamed Stinky for the foul putrescence that leaked from every open wound and orifice—was doing. Last time I'd visited vamp headquarters, Stinky's abdomen had done a water balloon impersonation—and exploded all over me. I grimaced at the memory. Visiting the council of dusty leaches and their grand poobah, Sir Gaius Aurelius the vamp master of the city and chairman of the northeastern vampire council, was bad enough without exploding ghoul grenades.

"Come, we should not keep the vampires waiting," he said.

I grunted my reply and fell into step beside Ceff. We stomped our way through the Old Port quarter and up The Hill—well, I stomped while Ceff managed to glide along silently in that otherworldly way that only a pureblooded sidhe can—which gave me plenty of time to mull over my upcoming visit with the most powerful vampire in the city.

Sir Gaius, who'd I'd aptly named The Boss on my first visit, was an ancient vamp. Through centuries of machinations and cunning, he'd achieved his current position as leader of the local vamps. It wasn't healthy being on The Boss's radar and I'd given him his very own open invitation to call me in. God, I was stupid.

I'd come to the vamps for answers, and in my rush to save a group of missing fae children, I'd made a deal with The Boss. I'd agreed to work one case of his choosing, pro bono. Working a free case may not sound like a bad exchange for information that could save numerous lives, but this was the vampire master of the city we were talking about. Bargains with vamps never ended well.

CHAPTER 17

I hesitated halfway up the steps to vamp headquarters, wondering idly if the ghoul Stinky would be the one to open the door. Could a ghoul survive losing all of its internal organs? Do ghouls even need organs? I mean, ghouls do eat, when their masters allow it. Ghouls are the scavengers at a vamp's table, eating dead things (ie, humans) that the dust bags cast aside. But I'd had an up close and personal look at Stinky's insides and his organs had been long liquefied. So how does a ghoul gain sustenance without any digestive system?

Contemplating the eating habits of ghouls? That was a surefire way to lose my appetite and add a few more nightmares to my repertoire. I was definitely procrastinating. With a heavy sigh, I took the last two steps in one long stride, placing myself beside Ceff. It was time to face the drama queens of the paranormal community, find a way to appease whatever ridiculous demands they made, and get back to work.

I gave Ceff a curt nod and he reached for the doorbell. I may be wearing heavy duty, leather gloves, but I wasn't crazy. If I could avoid touching anything in this place I would. Thankfully, Ceff understood my aversion and rang the bell without me even having to ask.

I'd expected Stinky, or maybe even the recently demoted vampire Gerald, but the vamp holding the door was a stranger to me. I stepped over the threshold, glad to avoid Stinky's malodorous stench and happy not to have Gerry at my back—that vamp hated me with a passion—but my relief was short-lived.

Stinky's replacement was a vamp armed to the fangs with weapons. The handles and blades of two sai, a three-pronged weapon similar to Ceff's trident, fanned out from the small of the guard's back, a third sai was slung at his hip, and he held a spear sporting a large, red, horsehair tassel in one hand.

That was new. The bloodsuckers had never bothered with armed guards to escort their visitors in the past. An overt

show of force by a race that preferred stealth and subterfuge?—
that could not be good. The scales must really be tipping
toward war if the vampires were so uncharacteristically edgy.
I filed it away for something to think about later.

Ever since Kaye mentioned trouble brewing, there
seemed to be signs of war everywhere I looked. The
paranormal community was on edge and, until now, I hadn't
even noticed. The ability to observe and put the puzzle pieces
together was integral to my job. It is part of what makes me a
good detective—that, my second sight, and a stubborn streak a
mile long.

So why hadn't I recognized the signs sooner? Because
I'd been a selfish fool, that's why. I was so focused on finding
my father that I couldn't see the obvious signs of trouble in my
city. Now that I could see the truth, I vowed to do what I could
to protect Harborsmouth, and my friends. I just hoped that it
wasn't too late.

But for now, I had more immediate things to worry
about—like the pair of sai now inches from touching me. The
vamp had moved so fast, I hadn't even followed the movement.
One second he was standing in the flickering, artificial
torchlight and the next he had me penned in with his spear
blocking the tunnel and his body blocking the door at my back.
And, of course, we couldn't forget the blades.

I froze, eyes wide, taking in the sai—one aimed at my
jugular, the other at my solar plexus. I was one quick jab away
from death or incapacitation. Not to mention the potential for
skull crushing visions from contact with some old-school
samurai vamp's weapons.

Yeah, this visit was going well.

"Ceff?" I whispered, careful not to move.

"On it," he said. From the sound, he'd removed his
trident from its ankle sheath, flicking the telescoping handle
bringing the weapon to its full length. "It seems that we are at
an impasse."

Straining my eyeballs until they hurt, I could just make
out where Ceff stood holding his weapon. The vamp had his sai
aimed at me and Ceff had his trident aimed at him. We were
deadlocked.

"As much as I'd like to continue this little testosterone
tea party, I have an appointment with Sir Gaius," I said.

Sweat trickled down my back, but my voice came out normal. No quivering, go me.

"Prove it, human," he said, the disdain clear in his voice.

"Oh, dude, you have this all wrong," I said.

Someone had obviously given the order to stop any humans from entering vamp HQ and this guy had mistaken me for the enemy. Looks like I'd have to set him straight.

I grabbed hold of the anger and fear churning deep inside of me and set it free. My lips parted in a sigh of relief as my wisp magic flowed through my body. Letting my powers loose was much easier than keeping them chained. My hair began to float around my head, though there wasn't a single draft in the underground tunnel. A blinding light erupted from my skin and I knew that if I'd had a mirror, I'd see my eyes glowing like two miniature suns.

"I'm not human."

Funny how that was getting easier and easier to say.

"My mistake, mistress fae," the vamp said.

He reached behind his back and slid both sai into the wide belt at his waist in one smooth movement. He bowed his head briefly and stood with his empty fists at his side.

Even without the weapons, the vamp looked like a badass. He was wearing armor made up of hundreds of small, red, lacquered scales that appeared to be threaded together with gold wire. His greaves matched the armor with the exception of a hexagonal pattern at the knee. All of this was worn over heavy, black and red, padded clothing that I would have mistakenly assumed would impair a man's movements—if I hadn't already seen the vamp in action.

But most striking was the helmet that covered most of his face in the visage of some kind of demon. The vampire's fangs protruded from the grimacing demon's open mouth—a sight I'm sure had set terror into the hearts of many a mortal man. Seeing that thing charging into battle would surely make most men want to turn tail and run.

Ceff slowly returned his own weapon to its sheath and carefully pulled my "invitation" from his back pocket. With a rustle of parchment, he held it out to the vamp. After a cursory glance, the guard nodded.

"I will take you to Aurelius-Daitoryo."

The guard turned in a series of birdlike, vamp-fast movements and the red lacquer of his armor shone like wet blood in the dampening wisp glow. I stifled a shiver and forced myself to follow.

I'd never liked the dark descent to the vampire's council chambers. The torch-lit tunnel always gave me the sensation of being swallowed whole. Too bad becoming vamp food was always a possibility. I just hoped that Sir Gaius and I could reach an agreement that we could both live with. Otherwise, I'd become tonight's entertainment...and dinner.

CHAPTER 18

My skin tingled as we made our way down the tunnel. As we grew closer to the inner chambers, and the master of the city, every alcove was filled with a suit of armor. The culture and time periods represented varied, but each piece of armor was old—and if the hairs along my neck were to be believed, so were the vamps wearing them. Yeah, I was pretty sure there were vamp guards lurking in that old armor. Just because the armor wasn't moving, didn't mean it was empty. Vampires could stand immobile for eons if not for the occasional need to feed.

Doing my best to ignore the vamps lurking in the shadows, I examined the fast approaching double doors. The ornate doors were warded with heavy magics, and could only to be opened safely with the consent of the master of the city. Crossing that threshold without Sir Gaius' permission meant sudden death, which I suppose was a better way to go than becoming some vamp's chew toy. I just hoped that tonight there was a third option.

According to his summons, The Boss wanted me to follow the terms of our prior agreement and work one case for him, free of charge. If he was sending dwarf messengers and escorting me with armed guards, I'd take a wild guess and say the vampire master of the city was desperate. If I was reading things right, that meant he needed me, for now. Maybe death by immolation was off the menu, I just hoped that held true for both me and Ceff.

The demon-faced guard stopped at the doors and tilted his head as if listening to a conversation I couldn't hear. Which, I suppose, he was. One of The Boss's talents was telepathy, and he never missed a chance to show off. After a brief, albeit silent, conversation, the guard moved aside. My ears popped and the wavering of the air, like the heat above an open fire, dissipated.

The guard waved an arm toward the doors and they opened with an ominous creaking of the hinges.

"You may enter," he said.

I rolled my eyes and strode into the vamp council chambers—and stopped short. No, I hadn't been struck down by the door wards, but my heart had stopped beating all the same.

I'd been ready for the vulgar artwork and stained glass images depicting scenes that would make the Marquis de Sade blush. Maybe even a public and bloody settling of a dispute between rival vamps. After being tricked into interrupting a council meeting on my last visit, I even half expected a fully assembled council of dusty leeches. What I hadn't expected was a fully disrobed master of the city stepping into a raised tub filled with red liquid.

Fucking hell. When I'd pictured a bloodbath in the council chambers, this was not what I had in mind.

I tried to pretend that the master of the city was bathing in tomato juice. Who knows, maybe he'd been sprayed by a skunk. The image of a cartoon skunk nailing Sir Gaius with a stink bomb nearly set off a fit of giggles. I coughed into my gloved hand and cleared my throat.

Ceff raised an eyebrow at me, but I waved him off. Now wasn't the time for sharing vamp jokes. *Le sigh.* I cleared my throat again and Gaius caught my gaze as he submerged deeper into the crimson liquid.

For a moment, I was ensnared by the pale Adonis who was lowering his body into the bath. I nearly wept with the need to join him, to feel his embrace. I struggled to take a step forward, but something held me back.

I twisted in Ceff's grip on my leather jacket, breaking eye contact with Gaius and severing his hold on me. Shivering, with equal parts rage and fear, I took a step backward. Ceff released my sleeve, though he stayed within easy reach—just in case I decided to be a total dumbass and fall under The Boss' spell again.

Mab's bones, that was stupid. I knew better than to let a bloodsucker hold my gaze, but I'd been trying to avoid staring at other more *shriveled* parts of the ancient vampire's anatomy. My second sight allowed me to see through vamp glamour, which in this case wasn't necessarily a good thing. There were some things that should remain a mystery.

Though if Jinx ever woke up, I'm sure she'd want to know. Ever since I told her vamps didn't sparkle, she'd been wondering why so many people throughout history thought they were so hot. I tried to explain vamp glamour, and their ability to enthrall, but I think my friend had her own theory. Too bad I was going to have to burst her bubble—there was nothing sexy about a dusty, old vamp. Nothing.

Thinking about Jinx helped me shake off the last remnants of the vamp spell.

"Cut it out, Gaius," I said, my teeth grinding together as I spit out the words. "I'm here to fulfill our bargain, not play games."

A dry chuckle, like the scrape of dead leaves on a coffin lid, rose from the tub.

"You could not handle me, little *corpse candle*," he said. "And for now, I require your services."

Yeah, he had a point. Sex with the vampire master of the city—if such a thing was even possible with that equipment—would be the death of me. One touch of his ancient skin and I'd be flooded with a raging sea of visions. I'd be dead before our first kiss, though I'm not sure if that's entirely what he meant. Probably better not to think too long and hard about it.

I snorted and rolled my hand in a "let's get on with it" gesture. The sooner Ceff and I could get out of here the better. I really didn't want to be around when Gaius was done with his bath. Ogling him naked once was bad enough, but seeing his desiccated body dripping blood was something I sure as hell didn't want to experience again in this lifetime.

"What is it you want, Gaius?" I asked. "Other than the usual sex and blood."

The vampire master held out his arm, turning it to examine his slender hand, a sigh passing between his fangs. I wasn't sure if it was my imagination, but the vamp's matchstick thin fingers seemed to be plumping up, like a raisin set in a glass of water. *Ewww.*

"I am in need of your services...your professional services," he said.

Yeah, whatever. We all need something. I thought the words, but didn't say them out loud. Contrary to popular belief, I didn't have a death wish. And as much as I hated to admit it, I owed the vampire master of the city. We'd made a deal. He gave me information leading to the missing fae children and I agreed to work one case of his choice, free of charge. I could try and be civil, for now.

"Um, okay," I said. I swallowed hard, pulling my attention from the vamp's spongy appendages and stared at a drop of blood in stark contrast to the rim of the ivory tub. I was done looking at Gaius. "What's the case?"

"As you may know, there are forces at work in the supernatural community," he said. "The scent of war is in the air; the weak skitter into hiding while the powerful amass their troops, preparing for battle."

So it was true then. There was a war coming. I just didn't understand why, not yet. Suddenly the rash of monster infestations and local territorial disputes made sense. Fae, vamps, hunters, and witches were on the move, maneuvering their assets like pawns on a chessboard, and those with enough power were drawing the proverbial line in the sand.

I flicked my eyes to Ceff. My boyfriend was a kelpie king. Had he known about this? Judging by the flush of color that rose in his cheeks, I'd say that was a yes. Damn it, why hadn't he told me any of this? I studied the way he stood, hands flexing and body at an angle to the bathing vamp.

I sighed, the answer obvious. Ceff would do anything to protect me, even if that meant sheltering me from the truth. He knew how important the search for my father was to me and how fragile my control was over my wisp powers. Worrying about a possible war would be a distraction and a stressor, a potentially deadly one if I started glowing on the city streets. Ceff had been trying to shield me from the truth. He may have had all the right reasons, but that didn't mean we weren't going to have a serious talk later—as soon as I was done dealing with Gaius.

"You want my help in this war?" I asked, brows rising as the vamp's words sunk in.

He had to be kidding. I might have gained some skill at squashing the occasional fae pest, but fighting as a soldier in a vamp war was way outside my job description.

Gaius chuckled, making the hairs along my neck stand at attention.

"No, corpse candle, I do not need a soldier," he said. I heard the sloshing of liquid and kept my eyes glued to the edge of the tub. "I need you to put an end to the fires plaguing our city. I only speak of the approaching war to let you know why I do not take care of this minor trouble myself."

Ah, yes. No matter what The Boss would like to have me think, fire was never a "minor trouble" to a nest of vamps. He could bathe in blood all he wanted, like that freaky ass Countess Bathory chick from history class, but the truth of the matter is that vamp bodies are tinder dry. No amount of feeding or bathing could change that fact.

Vampires are basically kindling with fangs. That was the reason the torches in here were lit by LED bulbs, not open flame. Suddenly, I saw the fire imp infestation through the eyes of the vampire master and I understood just how much he needed me.

If the city burned, the vamps would die.

"Let me get this straight," I said. "You want me to help stop the fires raging across the city, right?"

It would be a lot to handle, what with needing to find and kill Kaye and rescue Jinx, but with Ceff's help, we might pull it off.

"Yes," he said.

Blood splashed and dripped onto the marble floor tiles as the master of the city rose and stepped out of the tub. Ugh, time to go.

"Sure, I'll do it," I said. "But this makes us even."

"It is done," he said. I staggered a bit under the weight of his words, but kept my eyes focused just to the right of where Gaius was standing. "Yue Fei will see you out."

The Boss gestured toward the door with his newly plump hand and I turned to see the samurai vamp waiting for us. As I made my way into the adjoining tunnel, with Ceff at my side, Gaius' voice floated up from the cavernous council chamber.

"Be careful facing your demons, little *corpse candle*," he said. "I would not want you to get burned. Mwhahahahahahahaha!"

His sinister laughter was cut short by the doors slamming shut on our heels, just as the tunnel lights were extinguished.

Yeah, that wasn't creepy or anything. Damn vamps.

CHAPTER 19

Suddenly grateful for the night vision gifted to me by my wisp blood, I followed the guard up the steady slope of the tunnel. I ignored the burning in my calves as I walked, chewing on the new pieces of information I'd learned. I knew better than to think the vampire master of the city had let anything slip unintentionally, but I had to wonder what his motivations had been for bringing up the coming war.

Had he been trying to warn me about a potential threat to Harborsmouth, or was he just trying to emphasize how busy he was in an effort to downplay my role in ridding the city of the fire imp menace? Either way, I now knew that a war truly was brewing and I'd been the last to know.

"We are going to have words later," I muttered out of the corner of my mouth at Ceff.

He gave the barest nod, acknowledging that he'd heard me, and continued on. An annoying part of my subconscious pushed an image to the forefront of my brain and I shook my head. Ceff had kept the truth from me in an attempt to keep me safe. How different was that from me keeping the truth of Jinx and Forneus' kiss from my best friend? Yes, I was a hypocrite. Point taken, but I still didn't trust Forneus.

Maybe if the demon contacted me soon with a lead on how to solve our incubus problem, I might start to trust him. I checked my phone for missed calls, but there was no signal this far underground. I sighed and shoved the phone back in my pocket and trudged up the tunnel.

"So, um, Yue Fei," I said. "You new in town?"

I'd been distracted over the past few months sure, but I figured I'd have noticed a vamp dressed as a samurai warrior. Even in a dark tunnel lined with suits of armor from all over the world, the man tended to stick out.

"Yes," he said.

Right, man of little words that Yue Fei.

"You don't happen to know a kitsune named Inari, do you?" I asked.

Inari was a Japanese faerie who, according to Torn, was queen of the kitsune. But no matter how much I badgered Torn, he wouldn't tell me anything else about the kitsune woman, even though she was one of the few leads I had on my father. I was pretty sure that Yue Fei was Chinese, not Japanese like Inari, but it couldn't hurt to ask, right?

"The red fox lady, patron of swordsmiths, is known to me," he said.

We'd reached the outer door and Yue Fei stood to the side, gesturing for us to leave. I opened my mouth to ask what he might know about the woman, but Ceff took a step forward, facing me, and shook his head.

I growled in frustration and stormed out into the night.

CHAPTER 20

"What the hell was that about?" I asked.

I kicked the door behind me, slamming it shut, and threw my hands up into the air. To say that I was pissed was an understatement.

"Not here," he said.

I flashed Ceff a glare as I stomped toward Sacred Heart Church. If we were already this far up The Hill, might as well check in with Father Michael. The ex-Vatican scholar had a thing for demon lore. Maybe the priest could give me some pointers on how to deal with fire imps. Hell, he might even know where I could find Kaye.

I spun on Ceff as we turned onto an empty side street. If we were going to have an argument, this was as good a place as any.

"What. The. Hell?" I asked, biting off the words. "That guy might have known something about my dad!"

With the help of my *cat sidhe* allies, I'd been searching for my father, but the trail ran cold a few years ago in Fukushima, Japan. The fact that the one name my mom had managed to give me, before a magical geis nearly killed her, was that of Inari a Japanese faerie queen, couldn't be a coincidence. With Torn being frustratingly close-lipped about his former relationship with Inari, I was low on options. For a moment, I'd hung my hopes on Yue Fei, only to have Ceff step in and act like a jealous boyfriend. He better have a damn good reason for interfering, and I wanted to hear it, now.

"The walls of vampire headquarters have ears," Ceff said, keeping his voice low.

Shit, he was right. I remembered the creepy suits of armor filling every dark alcove along the tunnel. Yeah, I'd suspected those suits of armor weren't empty, but I wasn't sure why a bunch of vamps would care about my search for my father.

"So?" I asked. "What could Gaius possibly do with information about Inari?"

"Have you considered why your father does not wish to be found?" he asked.

Ceff's soft voice was like a lonely stream burbling over smooth pebbles, but his words hit me like a slap in the face. That and the look he gave me when I turned on him was one of utter sadness. He knew how much finding my father meant to me, and how badly I needed to find a way to control my wisp powers. He hadn't overstepped in my dealings with Yue Fei in some macho attempt to flex his muscles and take control of the little lady. He was trying to help, and he'd obviously given this a lot of thought.

I'd hear him out, though I suspected that I wouldn't like what he had to say.

"He left to protect me and my mom," I said. "I'm guessing he still thinks he's protecting us by staying away, by remaining hidden."

"And why does he need to protect you from his very presence?" he asked. "Why would your father believe that he could not be a part of your lives?"

I grew up thinking that I'd been abandoned by my real father, but that wasn't entirely true. My father, who turned out to be not only fae but king of the wisps, had left me and my mother after being tricked by a demon. I still didn't know all the details, but the end result was that my father was cursed to carry an unholy lantern, taking on the title Jack-o'-Lantern.

"Because he's cursed to carry the demon lantern," I said.

"A lantern that carries an ember from the deepest pits of Hell," he said. He paused, letting the words sink in. "...a lantern that brings chaos, destruction, and tragedy in its wake."

I thought of the plagues and natural disasters attributed to the lantern. The Tohoku earthquake and tsunami which caused the Fukushima Daiichi nuclear disaster was one of the more recent disasters, but there'd been many more over the years. The history of the lantern went back centuries, maybe longer. The lantern was a conduit to Hell, bringing pain and suffering wherever it was carried.

It was the reason why my father kept running, kept hiding from us.

To make matters worse, the one cursed to carry the lantern could not be rid of it, not without someone else being tricked or convinced into willingly taking it up. My father may have been suckered into a deal with a demon, but he was an otherwise honorable man. There was no way he'd trick another poor soul into carrying his burden.

"I fear that they would use him as a weapon," he said. "Whoever gains control over Will-o'-the-Wisp would wield a powerful weapon in the coming war."

Oberon's eyes on a stick, I was a fool. I'd been so focused on finding my father and somehow making things right, that I'd never considered what others may attempt if they found him first.

"I do not wish to see your father mistreated this way, and such a weapon in the hands of the undead could bring doom to us all," he said.

Shit, I could see it now, the dust bags dragging my dad into some warzone so that the lantern could wreak havoc on its fae or human inhabitants. Thousands could be killed and injured, but what did the vamps care? They could send in their ghouls to clean up the piles of corpses. Ghouls would feast on the dead while the vamps themselves rounded up those who lived. Humans and fae would become like cattle and the world would be ruled over by a bunch of night loving bloodsuckers.

And that was just the undead. Who was to say what the Seelie or Unseelie faerie courts would do if they got their scheming hands on my father.

"The vamps aren't the only ones, are they?" I asked. "If war really is coming, every side will want the ultimate weapon."

"It is a very real possibility," he said.

I let out a shaky sigh and wrapped my arms around my middle. It wasn't the answer I wanted to hear, but it was the truth. Ceff may have tried to protect me from his suspicions, but now that the *cat sidhe* was out of the bag, he'd give it to me straight. All I had to do was ask.

"If that's true, then who can I trust?" I asked.

"You can begin with trusting me," he said.

Yeah, he was right. It was a good place to start.

CHAPTER 21

We continued walking to Sacred Heart Church. I was hoping that Father Michael's obsession with demon lore would come in handy with the fire imp problem, and as a friend of Kaye's, he may know where I could find her. I might be able to kill two pixies with one visit, so to speak.

During the short walk to the top of The Hill, Ceff and I discussed the search for my father and the need for allies. Aside from Japan, my only lead was a box that my father had left me containing a key to Faerie. That key would open a gateway through the Otherworld and into the wisp court. I was sure that I'd find answers there, but the roads to Faerie had been sealed when Mab, Oberon, and Titania disappeared centuries ago.

The only way for me to gain entry to the wisp court was to follow a hidden pathway that only became accessible on the summer solstice. Unfortunately for me, that pathway led through Tech Duinn, the house of Donn—the Celtic god of the dead.

The door you seek is one that hides. You must await midsummer tides. Upon the summer solstice when the moon doth wane, the wisp princess shall sit upon her throne again. Muster your allies and gather your power. You must reach Tech Duinn's steps by the witching hour. Brandish the key and do not lose heart. On solstice night the ocean shall part. Go to Martin's Point at final light of day, and the stones of Donner Isle will lead the way. Not by sea, but by land. You all will take your stand. To the house of Donn you must carry, king Will-o'-the-Wisp's key to Faerie. Inside Donn's hearth bend your knee, close your eyes and turn the key.

If Béchuille was any indication, the Tuatha Dé Danann were more cryptic than demon attorneys. Or maybe it was the fact that she was a druid. Either way, I'd puzzled out the meaning behind her words and knew what I had to do. It just wouldn't be easy, hence the need for allies.

As we walked, Ceff and I hashed out a list of associates who we figured we could trust with information about my father. Sadly, the list was pretty damn short.

In fact, there was one person on the list who we both decided wouldn't have been made a confidant under different circumstances. Neither one of us fully trusted Sir Torn, but the *cat sidhe* lord was already in this up to his whiskers.

Torn had manipulated me into revealing that the key was in my possession when he brought me to Mag Mell to see the druid Béchuille. Yes, being tricked by the *cat sidhe* lord was one reason why I didn't trust him. But since he already knew about the search for my father and the key in my possession, there was nothing to do now except hope Torn honored our alliance, and watch our backs.

"There are less than two months until the summer solstice," Ceff said.

I sighed at the reminder. How did I end up with these solstice the-end-is-nigh deadlines? Oh, right, because I was knee deep in faerie drama.

"I'm sick of being on a solstice deadline," I said, thinking back to my troubles with Leanansídhe on the winter solstice. "Been there, done that, got the t-shirt to prove it."

He raised his eyebrow, mouthing "t-shirt," and gave me a questioning look, but I just shook my head. Poor Ceff, sometimes I forget he's an immortal faerie king who, unlike Jinx, only has a stunted arsenal of pop culture references with which to make sense of my snarky comments.

"I'm just tired," I said, forcing a grin. "With Jenna gone, Jinx's situation, and my possibly being on the outs with Kaye with the whole needing to kill her thing, I'm down to me, my boyfriend, a grumpy brownie, a teenage bridge troll, and a pain in the ass *cat sidhe* who neither of us trust. Oh, and the entire paranormal community is itching for a fight and may try to use my father as a weapon in their war. It's a lot to take in."

I yawned and dragged myself up the stone steps. My hand shook as I reached for the door, not a good sign. Ceff said that the longer I delayed in fulfilling The Green Lady's bargain, the worse I'd feel. My human blood might give me a little extra time, but apparently, it wasn't enough to completely block the energy drain.

I steadied my hand and said a silent prayer that Father Michael knew where I could find Kaye. I needed to find the witch, sooner rather than later. Otherwise, Jinx wouldn't be the only one doing a Sleeping Beauty impersonation, and then who'd save the city when the vamps and fae turned Harborsmouth into their very own sandbox?

The Hunters' Guild claims to be the protectors of humans against rogue paranormals, but what will the Hunters do if the entire paranormal community goes rogue? Would the Hunters' Guild stick around and fight if the vampires and fae went savage? I swallowed hard, thinking about the family and friends who called Harborsmouth their home.

I ignored the fatigue that had been slowly chipping away at me and headed into the church, suddenly determined to keep this city, and everyone in it, safe. I had to find a way to survive in order to protect them all. I couldn't count on anyone else to do that for me. I wasn't willing to take that risk.

CHAPTER 22

"So there's nothing in there that can help Jinx and we're no closer to finding Kaye," I said, scowling at the priest.

"We've only done a cursory search," Father Michael said. He blinked, giving me an owlish look from behind his reading glasses, and waved his long, thin hands over the books and scrolls stacked on his desk. "With time, I'm sure I can learn of a way to break the connection between this incubus and your friend Jinx."

We were seated in his cramped office in the back of the church. At the priest's suggestion, we'd called The Emporium, but there was still no word from Kaye. That little tidbit set my teeth on edge, but I tried not to grump at Arachne over speakerphone. It's not like it was the kid's fault that Kaye had gone missing.

With no leads on Kaye, we'd moved on to Jinx's incubus problem. Father Michael had been eager to pull out a pile of dusty tomes relating to incubi behavior, but none of the books gave any hint as to how to break the incubus' hold on my friend. The priest wanted more time to pour over the books in his extensive library, but I shook my head.

"Sorry, padre, time isn't a luxury we have," I said, holding up my phone.

Jinx had forced me to upgrade to a new smartphone a few months ago. I was still getting used to all the new features, but one thing I knew how to do was check the news. While Father Michael had clucked over ancient manuscripts, I'd scanned the local headlines—and it wasn't pretty.

According to the news, fires were springing up all over Harborsmouth. There must be dozens of the demons at large to cause this much chaos. It was obvious that the fire imps were no longer content with a little public vandalism, and they were moving into residential neighborhoods where damage could equate to lives lost.

So far most of the fires were small, but the damage was escalating and at this rate, things could get out of hand fast.

Something as trivial as a sea breeze coming off the harbor could turn a contained fire into an uncontrollable blaze, destroying homes, taking lives, and giving the vampire master of the city a reason to bleed me dry.

The priest read the headline, let out a chirp of surprise, and crossed himself.

"We must save the city," he said.

I ground my teeth and let out a frustrated growl. The fire imps had to be stopped, but first, we needed a plan. Otherwise, we'd be chasing our tails.

I tilted my head back to stare at the ceiling. I knew from past visits that the wooden beams that arched above me were carved with a pattern of flowers and vines, but today my eyes stared up unseeing. My attention turned inward as I mulled over the problem of how to control the fire imps who were setting fire to the city. Each time I felt close to a solution, it slipped just out of my reach.

"There's two damned many of them," I said. "No offense, Father."

"No offense taken," he said benevolently.

Apparently, the priest was feeling gracious. Last time I swore inside his church, he threatened to have Galliel dunk me in the baptismal font.

I stroked Galliel's head in my lap, struggling to come up with a workable plan to take down the fire imps. Usually, the unicorn's presence brought me a great sense of peace and happiness, but I was too keyed up with worry. I bit the inside of my cheek, stifling a scream of frustration. It had been bad enough when the imps were targeting businesses down on the waterfront, but now they were burning down people's homes.

"If only we could get them all in one place," I said.

I jumped as Arachne's voice came through the desk phone's speakers. I'd forgotten she was still there. Thankfully, the unicorn in my lap kept me from toppling over backward.

"Um, I might know a way to get the fire imps to gather together," Arachne said.

"How?" Father Michael and I asked in unison.

Ceff leaned forward and Galliel lifted his head. I gently bit my lip and held my breath. Mab's bones, we needed a break in this case. *Please, please, please* be something we could use.

Arachne spoke rapidly, reminding me that we were hanging our hopes on a teenage kid.

"There's this artifact and it holds demons, or at least it did, and I think it could again..." she said.

"How do we acquire this artifact?" Ceff asked.

Yeah, that was a damn good question. I'd already sucked down an entire carafe of coffee that I'd nabbed from the church's kitchen, but the caffeine wasn't working its usual magic. The more time that went by without fulfilling my end of the faerie bargain, the worse it would get. A long journey to retrieve a lost artifact, no matter how useful, was definitely off the menu.

"It's, um, here," she said.

"Are you saying that you actually have it, there at the shop?" I asked.

"Well, yeah, duh," she said. I could almost hear the kid rolling her eyes. "That's why I brought it up in the first place."

I exchanged a look with Ceff and Father Michael. The priest sat on the edge of his chair, licking his lips. Ceff just scratched his jaw and shrugged.

"And Kaye just left this thing out for the taking?" I asked.

Because that didn't sound like the witch I knew. The Emporium may look like the holy smorgasbord of occult objects, but most of the stuff for sale in the shop was harmless trinkets. The real arcane items were locked up in the cupboards of Kaye's spell kitchen or secreted away behind her office door. Last I knew, that office was off limits to Arachne, and for good reason—there was some powerful shit in there.

"It's a l-l-long story," she said.

"Yeah, I'll bet," I said.

I wanted to tell the kid to spill the beans—she was obviously hiding something—but I didn't want to risk an argument over the phone. Like it or not, Arachne was the one maintaining the spell circle around Jinx—the circle that was keeping my friend alive. I'd get my answers from the young witch, that was for damn sure, but it would just have to wait until we were face to face. I couldn't risk her storming out of The Emporium and leaving Jinx on her own.

I wished, not for the first time today, that Kaye would return from who knows where. I'd come to rely on the crafty, old witch.

"I would like to see this artifact," Father Michael said, fingers twitching greedily.

Yeah, of course he would. The guy was obsessed with arcane lore and anything related to demons was like porn to the priest.

"I can send a pic to Ivy's phone," Arachne said.

"A pick?" he asked, tilting his head to the side.

"A picture," I said.

"Ah, I will never live long enough to understand the lingo these days," he said.

"Neither will I," Ceff muttered.

I grinned, that last comment striking me as funny, seeing as it came from the lips of an immortal.

"Here," I said, holding out my phone so the priest could see the screen. I narrowed my eyes at his fingers darting toward my phone. "Just don't touch it."

The priest held his hands to his chest and nodded, eyes already glued to the picture that Arachne had sent. The artifact was small, about the size of a teacup—a proper teacup, not the head-sized troughs I drank my coffee out of—and resembled a gold censer, the kind of incense burner used in church services.

"But even with the ability to lure the foul creatures to one location, where could we possibly send them?" Ceff asked. "It is not as though we can set the creatures loose on one neighborhood. An entire city block could burn to the ground if the imps were brought together."

"Do not plan evil against your neighbor, who dwells trustingly beside you," Father Michael said, quoting the bible.

"Yes, not even the grindylow deserve such a plague of pests," Ceff said, nodding. "I would not wish those imps on any of my neighbors, would you?"

A grin tugged at my lips, the beginnings of a plan forming. Warmth radiated through my body and I let out an evil laugh.

"Oh yeah, I would," I said.

In fact, I could think of more than one neighbor I'd like to sick the nasty, little pyromaniacal demons on. Let the fire fiends burn up a nest of dusty vamps? Yeah, that was tempting. But there was the problem of getting past my bargain with Gaius. Thankfully, I didn't even have to worry about circumventing my agreement with the master of the city. The vamps wouldn't be the target, not this time.

I had an even better idea.

If my ruse of only temporarily killing Kaye worked (and, granted, that was a big IF), then I'd be back in The Green Lady's favor—and able to enter her territory. But I had a bad feeling that the glaistig would find a way to retain control over Jinx, and thus me. I needed a backup plan, and figured that a horde of fire imps would come in handy when she double-crossed me.

If I wanted to be sure of Jinx's safety, I'd have to find a way to convince the incubus to break his hold on my friend, one way or another. But I wasn't naïve enough to think that I could just waltz onto the carnival grounds and strike up a chat with the incubus. We needed a distraction capable of keeping The Green Lady busy long enough to make contact with her incubus.

That's where the fire imps come in. I'd enter The Green Lady's territory, bringing Arachne's magic artifact with me. If the artifact worked the way it should, the fire imps would follow, giving the incubus and I time for a little chat.

Of course, it wasn't a perfect plan. I'd be relying on a lot of shit to go my way, but just knowing there was a possibility of success sent a jolt of energy through my body.

"You would send those fire fiends to one of your neighbors?" Father Michael asked, recoiling.

"Yes, I would," I said. "They'll be a gift to The Green Lady, a reminder not to mess with my friends."

"You publicly claimed Jinx as your vassal," Ceff said, nodding. "You are within your rights to fight for her safety, and to seek recompense."

"Cool, kick that faerie queen's ass!" Arachne piped in.

Galliel chuffed into my hand. I guess we were all in agreement, all except for the priest. Father Michael's fingers danced over the documents on his desk, his head bobbing nervously.

I stayed quiet, waiting for the priest to work it out. It couldn't be easy for the man. He may have a loose interpretation of some church doctrine, or he never would have stolen all those artifacts and documents from the Vatican archives, but that didn't mean he was morally bankrupt. He believed in turning the other cheek and loving your enemies. Thankfully, he loved his parishioners more.

"I will not watch my flock burn," he said. "I will do what I can to help, but on one condition."

I nodded.

"You will not lead the demon spawn onto carnival grounds during opening hours," he said.

"Agreed," I said.

I felt the bargain settle onto my shoulders, but that was one promise I wouldn't have to worry about trying to break. There was no way I'd pick a fight with The Green Lady when the amusement park was open for business. I may act like a cold hearted bitch, but I wasn't okay with collateral damage.

A battle when the carnival grounds were filled with innocent human families was just asking for casualties. I'd wait until after hours to strike. In fact, I hoped that I could keep most of the carnival fae themselves from getting hurt. If we led the fire imps to The Green Lady's pavilion, and away from the worker's sleeping quarters, then maybe we could pull this off in a way that I could live with. Saving the day without accumulating a shit ton of guilt would be nice for a change.

"Ceff, do you think some of your people would be willing to help keep the fires from spreading to the tents where the carnival fae live?" I asked.

"My people cannot cross into The Green Lady's territory," he said, rubbing his chin. "But yes, we could help. Direct magic would be blocked, I'm certain of that, but we could remain outside her territory and send water in the direction of the tents."

"Good, then that's settled," I said.

I turned back to Father Michael. I knew he preferred a world of black and white, but he'd spent enough time in our world to know that nothing involving the fae was that simple. It was all shades of grey. Those of us good guys had to try to keep shit from getting too dark—it was the best we could do. I just hoped the priest saw it that way. I bit my lip and held my breath.

"I will continue my research," he said grudgingly. He looked longingly at the artifact on my cell phone's screen until I picked up the phone and put it away. Research was the priest's strong suit, but I knew he'd rather be chasing demons and getting his grubby mitts on that artifact. Yeah, it was all about shades of grey—even the priest's soul wasn't lily white. "I will let you know if I discover anything that will help you save your friend."

"Thank you, Father," I said.

Reluctantly, I pushed Galliel's head from my lap and stood.

"I'll see you later," I said, ruffling the unicorn's mane. "You too, Arachne."

A squeak escaped the phone on Father Michael's desk. Yeah, I hadn't forgotten about paying the kid a visit.

"Bye!" Arachne said, and hung up.

Father Michael replaced the phone on the cradle and sighed. His gaunt face looked pale, paler than usual, all hard lines and angles in the low light of his desk lamp. He remained stooped over his desk, but his eyes came up to meet my gaze, and I didn't like what I saw there. Not one bit.

"What is it now, padre?" I asked. "I'm kinda in a hurry."

I didn't have time for any more problems. In fact, I was already sorting my mental to-do list and it was giving me a headache. I'd need to retrieve the artifact from Arachne soon, but first I had to find Kaye.

He rubbed a hand down his rumpled pants, fidgeting with his white clerical collar with the other.

"There is still the matter of how the fire imps entered the city," he said. "I know that dealing with the ones that are here now is the priority." He raised his hands as if to hold back an argument. "But we must consider the possibility that we are dealing with a gate."

"A gate?" I asked.

"A portal to Hell," he said. "It is likely the portal links to one of the outer rings, if the type of demons that we're seeing are any indication."

"Wait, you're saying there could be an open gate to Hell, here, in Harborsmouth?" I asked.

"As I said, it is a possibility," he said, head bobbing. "And if you encounter one, you must promise to contact me immediately. You will need my help to hold back the demons and close the gate."

Mab's bloody freaking bones, Hell gates? As if the day wasn't bad enough.

"What other demons reside in this ring of Hell?" Ceff asked.

Good question. Fire imps were a nuisance, but one that we had more than a snowball's chance in Hell of defeating. But a horde of badass demons? Not so much.

Father Michael paced excitedly in front of his bookshelves until he found the book he was looking for. With a flourish, he set a heavy, leather-bound tome on the desk and opened it to an illustration that would give Hieronymus Bosch nightmares.

"You have got to be kidding me," I said.

I swallowed hard, rooted to the spot. Most of the demons in the illustration were tiny imps, yeah sure, but the master demons who apparently ruled over them all were huge. Like brick shithouse huge. If those dudes—and yes they were male, the illustration made that painfully clear—ended up in Harborsmouth, we could kiss the city and its human inhabitants goodbye.

"If those demons come through the portal, if such a portal exists, then we are all well and truly FUBARed," Ceff said.

I snorted, but it came out more like the cry of a strangled cat. Normally I'd celebrate the fact that Ceff had used modern slang correctly—and he was correct, we'd be well and truly fucked up beyond all recognition—but I was too busy trying not to piss my pants.

CHAPTER 23

I promised to contact Father Michael if we encountered anything that resembled a portal to Hell—not that I was sure what one would look like. The priest had tossed a few books onto the desk, but the illustrations for Hell gates weren't exactly helpful. Apparently, these portals could be anything from a shimmering rift in the air, like a tear in the fabric of reality, to an ornate hand mirror. Since I couldn't go confiscating every damn mirror in the city, I focused on what I did know.

I knew where I wanted to direct the horde of fire imps, and more or less how to go about it. Now I just needed to find Kaye and get this faerie bargain off my back. Yes, I was simplifying. Yes, I was deflecting from the very real possibility of huge, nasty demons entering the city. But I had to focus on the things I had some control over, like getting rid of the faerie bargain before it drained me dry, or I'd be nuttier than a rabid squirrel.

Plus, let's face it. We'd all be better off with the witch's magic on our side. If some badass demons did come gunning for us, we'd need more firepower than a priest, a teen witch, a kelpie, and a half-breed faerie princess. It was like a bad joke, one the demons would be laughing at for centuries while they cracked the whip over their new city full of slaves.

Of course, finding Kaye was easier said than done. I still had no idea where the witch had gone. With no other leads, I decided to pay a visit to the Hunters' Guild.

On my way out of the church, I tried calling the local guild office, but no one answered and the number Jenna had given me was no longer in service. I didn't even want to contemplate what that meant. I guess I'd find out soon enough.

I scrubbed a hand over my face before beginning the descent down the stone steps leading out of Sacred Heart. The church was at the very top of Joysen Hill and I wanted a moment to catch my breath and enjoy the view. If I squint my eyes just right, I could pretend that the city below us was nothing more than party lights floating in a water garden. Well, except for the fires raging to the East.

It looked like a trip to the Hunters' Guild would have to wait.

"Oh, shit," I said. I pointed and Ceff's face darkened as he caught sight of the flames. "That's near Baker's Row. Come on!"

I started to run, but lurched to a stop when Ceff stepped into my path.

"I will attend to the fires," he said. "Confer with the Hunters' Guild. Find Madam Kaye. I will join you later."

"But how are you going to fight those fire imps without your guards?" I asked.

I hadn't seen any of Ceff's royal guard since we'd left the Old Port quarter. I assumed that they thought he was safe with me, which just showed how little his people really knew about me.

Ceff whistled and two kelpies slid out of the shadows. Damn, his elite guards were ninja stealthy. The fact that they were in their massive horse forms made their sudden appearance even more impressive.

"I will not be alone," he said. "Aminon and Dilyn will be at my side and I can call for more of my people once I am within earshot of the harbor. Once the fire is contained, and the inhabitants of the buildings to safety, I will return to you and leave the remainder of the firefighting in the capable hands of my elite guard."

I remembered the *bean-tighe* family we'd visited on Baker's Row when working the missing children case. My chest tightened at the thought of Myrtha and Glynda and their daughter Flynis trapped by the flames. I hoped that they were able to take to their brooms and flee, but not all of the inhabitants of Baker's Row had the gift of flight. Those vamp owned buildings were deathtraps.

"Okay, go, but take this," I said, reaching into my jacket pocket.

I pulled out a burner cell that Jinx had given me in case of emergencies. I had a nasty habit of losing my cell, or otherwise causing it to become a useless chunk of metal and plastic. Plus, as Jinx had pointed out, you never know when you'll need to make a call your enemies can't trace.

Having a quick, mundane way to keep in touch with Ceff was also useful.

Ceff gave the phone a nasty look, but slid it into a pocket. He may not like the technology, but at least it wouldn't give him iron poisoning. Cell phones contain copper, gold, and platinum, but no fae crippling iron—I'd checked. Thank Mab for Google.

"And don't forget the nixie who lives in the fountain on Merrion Square," I said, thinking fast. Kelpies weren't the only fae who could control water. "Maybe she can help."

"Beautiful *and* smart," he said. "I really am the luckiest man on land or sea."

I blushed, but flashed him a cocky grin.

"They don't pay me for my looks, horse man," I said.

"Ah, but they should," he said. Then he blinked and shot me a grin of his own. "Did you just call me a stud?"

I snorted and waved him away. As much as I hated to admit it, we didn't have time for flirting. When did we ever? There were always cases to solve, cities to save—you know, the usual.

I let a little heat into my gaze and made a mental promise to make it up to Ceff when all of this was over. When the city was safe and my debts were cleared, we'd take a long weekend—just the two of us. I owed it to Ceff.

I'd been a pain in the ass to be around lately, what with my obsession to find my father and my not-so-graceful entrance into fae society. I'd been especially hard on those closest to me. It was time I treated those I cared about like the precious gems that they were. I just wish it didn't take the threat of losing them all for me to realize that.

"Go on, I'll catch up with you later," I said.

Ceff's eyes glowed green in response to the rising heat between us.

"I will hold you to that promise," he said.

The guards snorted and stamped their feet, probably giving Ceff the kelpie equivalent of a chest bump. I rolled my eyes and waved them off. I thought about making some witty comment like "you boys have fun playing with water," but just the thought of Ceff manipulating his element sent a shiver of anticipation along my spine. I knew from experience that water fae could do a heck of a lot more with water than just put out fires. Hell, Ceff could set my skin aflame—literally.

I shook my head, trying to dispel naked images of Ceff. I was not going to stand here on the church steps while thinking about hot kelpie sex—that sounded like a surefire way to get struck by lightning. I gave my brain a mental cold shower, focusing on the fires raging below and the need to rescue Jinx and myself from the glaistig's clutches.

I grabbed hold of my anger and let it grow, the beating of my heart loud in my ears, nearly drowning out the sound of horse hooves as the kelpies raced toward the fire. I turned in the other direction, heading west toward the Hunters' Guild's local base of operations. I would find Kaye, retrieve the artifact from Arachne, reconnoiter with Ceff—and then we'd kick some demon ass.

CHAPTER 24

The Hunters here in Harborsmouth have used the old Herne building as their guildhall for nearly a decade. The former private school is ideal for their purposes. The school campus was easily defendable and had all of the buildings that the militant guild needed for its operations.

I knew from experience that the gymnasium and courtyard were used for weapon and hand-to-hand combat training. According to Jenna, the Hunters lived in the dormitory and the numerous classrooms were also still in use, although I'm sure the former headmaster would roll over in his grave if he discovered that the new teachers were instructing their students on such subjects as military tactics, vampire politics, fae anatomy, and demonology.

But then again, who knows. The place had been named the Herne School, and a figure similar to the pagan Green Man peered from above the door lintel, its head displaying an impressive rack of antlers. It was possible that the figure represented Herne the Hunter. Maybe the former headmaster had been fae.

At least I could see the reason why the Guild was attracted to the place.

"Come on, come on," I muttered, waiting for someone to answer the doorbell.

I shivered, pulling my jacket up around my neck and stomping my feet against the chill in the air. I stood beneath the horned face that sprouted vines from every orifice. Thank Mab the thing was inanimate stone. Humphrey was hard enough to get used to. I couldn't imagine chatting with a gargoyle that looked like it was puking a garden out through its eyeballs.

Booted footsteps drew near and I took a deep breath. *Okay, calm down Ivy.* Now would not be a good time to start glowing. Hunters might technically be the good guys, but they fought against rogue paranormals and had a tendency to strike first and ask questions later.

Of course, being run through with a sword and turned into a wisp kebab wasn't my only worry. There was a very real possibility that the guards would turn me away at the door. In the past, I'd only come to the guildhall for appointed training sessions with Jenna. Without the young Hunter here to meet me, I wasn't sure if I'd be able to get inside.

Chains slid, metal bolts were thrown, and the door swung open on well-oiled hinges. I blinked at a belt buckle the size of my fist and tilted my head back to see a behemoth of a man towering over me. Hunters only allow humans to join their ranks, with the notable exception of the occasional witch, but I wouldn't be surprised if this guy had some ogre blood somewhere in his family tree. Not only was he well over six feet tall, the guy's muscles had muscles, and strapped over those rippling masses were a staggering number of weapons.

"Um, I'm here to see Master Janus," I said.

I tried to flash the guard my best smile, which seemed to backfire when his hands tightened on the handle of an axe. Oh well, so much for polite. It wasn't really my style anyway.

"You got an appointment?" he asked.

"No, I don't, but I'm not leaving until I speak with him," I said. "Tell him Kaye's friend, Ivy Granger, is here to see him and it's urgent—as in I need to talk to him yesterday."

Muscles grunted and, with one hand still gripping the massive axe, picked up a phone that was bolted to the wall just inside the door. He angled his body away and kept his voice low, but my fae heightened hearing allowed me to make out the gist of what he was saying. Muscles was checking in with Janus' office and verifying my story.

He narrowed his eyes and shot a glance at me from beneath dark, bushy brows and I tried not to fidget. I kept my hands loose at my sides and away from any obvious weapons. Of course, I had my throwing knives literally up my sleeves, strapped to my forearms beneath my leather jacket, but he didn't necessarily know that. Not unless he'd seen me spar with Jenna.

His eye twitched and I got the impression that whatever the person was saying on the other end of the line had surprised the guy. Maybe they were going to let me in after all.

"You're cleared to enter, but stick with me," he said. "No detours, you got me?"

"Sure, whatever," I said.

Muscles looked me over, eyes hovering over my forearms, lower back, and ankle—oh yeah, this guy knew exactly where I kept my blades—his bulk blocking my path.

"Master Janus says you're not to be searched and you can keep your weapons, some kind of special dispensation due to OCD or PTSD or some shit, but I see you so much as scratch your ass and I'll cut you," he said. "Got it?"

Asshole. How does Jenna put up with these meatheads?

"I hear you," I said. "Loud and clear."

I tried to act cool, but inside I was pissing my pants. I'd never been bodily searched during my previous visits, but the new policy made sense if the Hunters' Guild was gearing up for the coming battle. Thank Mab that either Kaye or Jenna had mentioned my touch phobia to Janus or things could have got messy quick.

Of course, that also meant that the Guild knew my weaknesses. I swallowed hard and fought to keep up with Muscles.

He marched me through the parade grounds, which I was pretty sure used to be the old bus loop, and up a gravel drive. At the entrance to the administrative building, a young man in cargo pants, combat boots, and a tight fitted t-shirt came running out and saluted Muscles.

"I'll take it from here, Hendricks," he said.

Hendricks? Must be Muscles' real name, and just when I was getting used to the ring of it. Hendricks thrust out his chest and stared the new guy down. Cargo Pants was half of Hendricks' size, but he stood his ground.

"By whose orders, whelp?" Hendricks scoffed. "Yours?"

"Don't need orders, just common sense," Cargo Pants said. He nodded back toward the way we'd come. "Someone needs to watch the gate, and last time I checked the roster, that person was you."

A muscle twitched in Hendricks' cheek, but he blew out a breath and rolled his eyes.

"Whatever," he said. "You can have the bitch. She's just your type, a Grade-A pain in the ass."

With that, Hendricks turned and swaggered back toward the gate. Cargo Pants waited until the crunch of gravel beneath heavy boots faded then treated me to a brilliant, yet rueful smile. He had the most amazingly perfect, white teeth—

all except for the canines, which were impossibly long and sharp.

Werewolf? If so, then the Hunters' Guild's recruiting practices had changed as of late. Either that or the rumor that they were a solely human organization was smoke and mirrors. Hard to tell when you're dealing with a secret society with a labyrinthine hierarchical structure based on initiating its members into even greater degrees of secrecy.

I pushed away the image my brain conjured of me wearing a red cloak and holding a picnic basket—damn I was overtired—and smiled back at Cargo Pants.

"Sorry about Hendricks, he's an ass," he said. He started to reach out to shake hands, thought better of it, and rubbed the back of his neck—which meant he probably knew about my touch phobia. "You're Ivy Granger, right?"

I nodded slowly and tilted my head to the side.

"You seem to know me, but I don't recognize you," I said. "You got a name, or am I going to have to call you Cargo Pants all day—or maybe you prefer Big Bad."

His eyes flashed silver and I knew I was right. I'd be damned, the guy was a werewolf. True shapeshifters like werewolves and skinwalkers don't use a glamour to conceal their animal forms, so there's nothing for my second sight to see through. But that didn't mean there weren't ways to know what I was dealing with. Just like in poker, everybody's got a tell.

And those eyes were telling me that Cargo Pants may be a lot of things, but he sure as hell wasn't human. Skinwalkers have golden eyes, so I was leaning toward were. After Hendricks' "whelp" insult, I was thinking wolf.

"My name's Jonathan, Jonathan Baldwin," he said. "I'm a friend of Jenna's."

"Does Jenna know you're a werewolf?" I asked.

His eyes widened, mouth dropping open. *Bingo.*

"Jesus, she was right, you get straight to the point, don't you?" he asked.

"No time for bullshit," I said with a shrug. "I'm too busy saving the city from the stuff the Guild doesn't bother with, or doesn't know about. And you haven't answered the question."

"Okay, fine, but can we talk while we walk?" he asked. He looked around nervously. There were young, heavily armed men and women moving busily throughout the campus and we'd started to catch their notice. "And keep your voice down? Jenna knows what I am, but not everyone here does, and I'd like to keep it that way. In case you haven't noticed, Hunters aren't always the most tolerate when it comes to paranormals."

I snorted. That was an understatement. I couldn't imagine what some of these guys would think if they knew that a werewolf was in their midst. Though it did beg the question of how a paranormal had infiltrated such an exclusive club.

Jonathan started walking and I matched his stride.

"So how do you know Jenna?" I asked.

I kept my eyes on the corridors and galleries as we passed, careful not to look too interested in what the guy next to me was saying. If someone was watching, it probably looked like he was giving the visitor a tour.

"We're roommates, or at least we were before they sent her out of the country," he said.

I felt his body tense and knew he wasn't too thrilled with the Guild's decision to ship the young Hunter off to Europe. In that, Jonathan and I were in perfect agreement.

"Roommates, really?" I asked. "How'd that happen? I would have thought the old geezers in charge would have frowned on that."

"We're bunkmates, not lovers," he said. I caught the wistfulness in his voice and winced. Jenna and Jonathan may not have hooked up, but that didn't mean the guy wasn't interested. If I had to guess, I'd say he was nursing a crush on my Hunter friend. "Nobody else wanted to room with Jenna, not after she knocked a few heads together for idiots not respecting her personal space. So I gave up my single on the condition that Master Janus gave me permission to let Jenna in on my secret."

So the Guild did know about the fact that Jonathan was a werewolf, interesting. I filed the information away for later.

Jonathan rubbed at a scar above his right eye and I suspected that he and Jenna had come to blows too. There was probably a story there. I shook my head and paused.

"I don't get it," I said. "I know Jenna's tough as nails, but why the need to prove herself?"

"It was more than that," he said. "Girls have it harder here than guys, so she did have to prove herself more than once, but the fights in the dormitories weren't just bluster. For Jenna, it was survival."

"Are you telling me someone here was trying to hurt her?" I asked.

I had to breathe slowly and deeply to keep my rage at bay. If my skin started glowing this deep inside the guildhall, I'd be screwed.

"Not here, it was before she was initiated into the Guild," he said. He frowned. "Look I'm only telling you this because Jenna said that you're her friend and that I could trust you."

I nodded.

"She had a tough life before coming here," he said. "Her parents were murdered and she was in and out of the foster system for years."

"I didn't know," I said.

I winced. Jenna had never shared anything about her past and I'd never bothered to ask.

"It's not uncommon," he said, shrugging. "The Guild often recruits orphans when the system lets them down. But I think things were especially bad for Jenna. She was more...haunted than most, though she did a good job of hiding it during the day."

"But it's hardest to hide from your ghosts at night," I said, and Jonathan nodded.

I should know. There's nothing like sleep to tear down your defenses and let the nightmares in. I'd woken up Jinx with my screams more often than I'd like to admit.

"Yeah, which made her a bitch to room with," he said, grinning. "Though I don't imagine bunking with a werewolf was easy for her either."

"Have you heard from her since she left?" I asked.

"No," he said. "Not a word."

His face clouded over and his eyes flashed silver.

"Any idea how dangerous her mission is?" I asked.

I'd assumed that her bosses had shipped her off as punishment for attacking Hans. But Kaye's comments had been nagging at me. Maybe they had sent Jenna off on some top secret mission in order to advance her training. Odds were, it was a bit of both.

"All I know is they sent her to Belgium," he said. "That's bad."

I raised an eyebrow. When I think of warzones, I do not think of Belgium. If you're going to get shipped out of the country, it didn't sound like a bad post to me. Wasn't Belgium the land of beer and chocolate? How could that be bad?

"How so?" I asked.

"Belgium might be safe for people in the human world, but not for Hunters," he said. "Paranormals have been deeply entrenched in the European countries for centuries, and they share a bloody history with the Guild—one they're not likely to forgive or forget."

"But if that's true, why send a teenage girl there?" I asked. Jonathan bristled, but I held up a gloved hand. "I'm not saying she's weak. We both know she's a cute as hell killing machine. But she's young for that kind of solo assignment, isn't she?"

"It's unusual to be sent to the Old Country at this point in her training, especially on her own," he said, running a hand through his hair. "I should have been sent with her."

"So why do you think the Guild sent her flying solo into a viper's nest of paranormals?" I asked.

"That's what I'd like to know," he said.

He turned to stare at me and a sick feeling crept into my gut.

"Are you hiring me to find Jenna?" I asked.

If that's what Jonathan was asking, I'd have to refuse. As much as I liked and respected Jenna, there were people who needed me here in Harborsmouth. Not to mention the fact that I was running on a deadline. I was nowhere near ready for the summer solstice.

Heck, with my debts to the vamps and The Green Lady in play, I may not even survive the night.

"No," he said. I briefly closed my eyes. I wouldn't have to turn the guy down, thank Mab. "But if you learn anything, I'd like to know."

"Yeah, sure," I said.

Jonathan stopped in front of an office door and I could read the tension in his neck and shoulders.

"This is Master Janus' office," he said.

"You'll let me know if you hear from Jenna?" I whispered.

He nodded.

I rubbed my arms and looked up and down the hall. We were deep inside the administrative building, far from any exits, and the only door in this corridor was the one I now faced.

I took a deep breath and nodded for Jonathan to go ahead. There were so many questions I'd like to have had answered, but it looked like our time was up.

CHAPTER 25

At Jonathan's knock, a gruff voice barked for us to enter. I took a deep breath, squared my shoulders, and prepared to face one of the Hunters' Guild's most formidable local masters. But Jonathan didn't open the door. I shot him a questioning glance and he flicked his eyes downward.

There, held between our bodies, was an envelope folded so many times it was the size of a quarter. Jonathan held it out to me, looking furtively up and down the hall. I was loath to touch anything that came from the lovesick werewolf, but my curiosity won out.

He mouthed "from Jenna" and I gingerly grabbed the note with gloved hands and slipped it into my jacket pocket for later. With the envelope safely stashed away, Jonathan turned the knob and opened the door wide.

I walked slowly into the office, doing a quick scan for potential threats. I'd feel better having Jonathan at my back, but with a nod to his boss, the werewolf bowed and left the room, closing the door behind me. Aside from two armchairs, a heavy wooden desk, and the old books and artifacts that lined the floor to ceiling shelves, the place was empty, but my fingers still itched for my weapons. That probably had something to do with the man sitting behind the desk.

Master Janus may be the head of the Harborsmouth Hunters' Guild, but he wasn't an old geezer by my standards, far from it. The man was a powerhouse of lean muscle and sharp intellect, but the gray hair dusting his temples, sideburns, and short beard, and the creases at his eyes belied his age—and garnered respect amongst his men.

Janus was in his forties, which was ancient for a Hunter. Hunters fought hard and died young. Wrinkles were a luxury that few Hunters ever lived to receive. But living to the ripe old age of forty was only one of the man's many accomplishments.

In an organization as competitive as the Hunters' Guild, Janus had climbed his way to the rank of Master. That was no

small feat. Some said he was soon on his way to becoming
Grand Master, an honor bestowed to few Hunters. From what
Kaye and Jenna had shared, there were less than a dozen
Grand Masters worldwide.

One look at the man's sword-calloused hands, ripped
muscles, and curious hazel eyes and it was no wonder he'd
come so far in a guild that prized secrets, combat skills,
leadership, and military cunning. That didn't mean I had to
stand here shaking in my boots.

I strode forward and dropped uninvited into the chair
facing the guild master's desk. I never was one for ceremony.

Janus let out a noisy breath, posture stiffening and, for
a moment, I thought he was going to grab a sword. Instead, he
pounded his hand against the hard surface of the desk, which
made me jump. Janus let out a bark of raucous laughter.

"You're not what I expected from fae royalty, but then
again, I should have known better from a friend of Kaye's," he
said. The creases at the corners of Janus' eyes deepened with a
smile and I realized those wrinkles came from more than
squinting down the barrel of a weapon. I could see why his
men would follow him into battle. The Hunter's smile was
contagious, and I fought to keep my trademark frown intact. "I
was worried I'd lose my entire afternoon to some poncy twit
spouting Shakespeare while trying to stab me in the back with
my own blade."

"Nope, no dancing around with flowery words from me,"
I said. "I don't know which knife and fork to use at a fancy
dinner party either. I'm not your typical faerie princess. I
grew up human, same as you."

For all his reputed skill with a sword and rugged good
looks, the man was human. That was clear.

Janus smiled more widely and leaned back in his chair.

"So what can I do for you, Miss Granger?" he asked.

"I was hoping you could help me locate a mutual friend,"
I said. "Kaye took off without a word as to where she was
going, and now all hell's breaking loose."

"You talking about those bloody pyro demons?" he
asked.

Now it was my turned to gape like an idiot.

"Aye, lass, we know all about the fire imps plaguing the
city," he said. "I've got men on it, though we're short staffed

here at the moment. Timing couldn't have been worse, almost as if it happened that way on purpose."

He rubbed the back of his neck and scowled.

"You think the demons showing up now is a targeted attack on the city?" I asked.

"I don't know, but Kaye was checking things on her end," he said. "She went to walk the perimeter barrier. It may not keep things out like it used to, not enough powerful magic users left to fuel the damn thing, but the barrier still works as an early warning system for those of us who still care about protecting this city."

"So Kaye went to check the perimeter?" I asked.

"Aye, fire imps were popping up inside the city, but there was no sign of them passing through the barrier," he said. "Had our witch friend in a right tizzy."

"Yeah, I bet," I said.

I remembered how foul tempered she'd been when Forneus managed to enter Harborsmouth without triggering Kaye's magic alarm system. In fact, he never did share how he managed that trick.

I sighed. Kaye hadn't been the only one to disappear. Forneus had left with a promise to help find out how to break the incubus' hold on Jinx—and I hadn't heard from him since. I guess I should know better than to trust a demon.

"Any theories on how a bunch of rare demons are getting inside the city without setting off the barrier?" I asked.

I bit my lip, a knot forming in my belly. As far as I knew, Forneus was the only demon to pass unnoticed, until now. If I found out that the demon attorney had something to do with the fire imp plague on the city, I'd send him straight back to Hell—and I'd make damn sure he stayed there.

"Not yet, but I don't reckon we'll like the answer," he said.

No, probably not.

"Well, um, thanks for the info," I said. I thought about what Father Michael said regarding the possibility of Hell gates and winced. "Tell your men to keep an eye out for portals...mirrors, tears into the fabric of reality, that sort of thing."

God, did I just say that with a straight face?

"Already on it, lass," he said.

Master Janus rose to his feet, the universal sign for 'get the hell out of my office.' I stood slowly, every muscle in my body protesting, and went for the door.

"If you hear from Kaye, let me know," I said. "I'm in the book."

Jinx had printed up fancy Private Eye business cards, but I hadn't thought to grab any earlier. I was too busy strapping on weapons.

"Aye, will do," he said.

I nodded over my shoulder. I may not trust the man, or his guild, but I did appreciate the fact he'd seen me on short notice. I was also aware that someday, if Kaye and I were gone, the Hunters' Guild could be the one thing that came between the rogue paranormals and the human inhabitants of Harborsmouth. With Kaye's magic waning and my current situation with The Green Lady, that day may come sooner than later.

"Safe travels, Janus," I said.

"Good hunting, Granger," he said.

I just hoped that this round of hunting didn't get me dead.

CHAPTER 26

My exit from the Hunters' Guild was uneventful. Jonathan was nowhere in sight and his taciturn replacement escorted me to the front gates with no more than a series of monosyllabic grunts and mutters. I'd been ready for a fight, but Hendricks had left his post and I made it through the gate without so much as a barbed insult.

I sprinted away from the looming edifice of the Herne building, burning off unspent adrenaline while formulating a plan. Kaye's magic perimeter barrier encircled the entire city of Harborsmouth. If I started tracing it now, I could be running in circles for days looking for the woman. There was a chance I'd never encounter the witch at all.

No, I'd take my chances back at The Emporium. Kaye was bound to return eventually and Arachne had that demon vessel artifact for me. Plus, I wanted to check in with Jinx. A status report over the phone was all well and good, but I needed to see my friend for myself.

Decision made, I hastened toward the Old Port quarter which was thankfully downhill. I may run along the harbor and go through basic defense drills daily, but unfulfilling my bargain with The Green Lady was beginning to take its toll. My breathing was labored and sweat was beading on my forehead and upper lip.

Although the sweat may have had something to do with my close proximity to a dozen fire imps. Imps ran across my path, cackling and chittering as they slipped into a nearby alleyway.

Fire imps roving in packs? Now that was interesting. In fact, there was a chance they'd lead me to the Hell gate that Father Michael suspected was somewhere in the city.

I considered turning around and raising the alarm back at the guild, but shook my head and put on more speed. Why let the Hunters have all the fun? I bolted after the demons.

My limbs felt heavy with fatigue—damn The Green Lady—but I pushed forward, muscles burning. I careened around the corner and into the alley, gulping air thick with the reek of garbage, urine...and smoke. I choked on the stench, raising an arm to cover my nose and mouth.

The fire imps had definitely come this way, but they were nowhere in sight and the alley was blocked by a tall, chain-link fence. I retraced my steps, but there were no doors or windows on the first or second floors of the adjoining brick buildings. Unless there was a portal here which I couldn't see, the imps must have made their way over, under, or through the fence.

I let out an impatient growl and returned to the fence, searching for signs of the diminutive demons. A closer inspection turned up a patch of blood where one of the buggers had cut himself trying to climb up and over to the other side.

I eyed the fence, topped with barbed wire, and sighed. I'd never catch up with the imps now, not in my current bargain-plagued condition. If I wanted answers about the location of the Hell gate, I'd have to take my chances with the cooling blood.

I grimaced, not liking my options. Using my psychometry was always risky, which is why I was so selective in how I went about engaging it. Normally, I tried to play it safe, and fondling some demon blood was not my idea of safe— not by a long shot. But if there was a portal to Hell in my city, there was no way I could sit back and let demon hordes pour through unchecked.

The gate had to be closed, and the only way to do that was to find its location. I thought of the gigantic master demons that Father Michael had shown me in his books and shivered. Those demons dominated the demons of their plane. What would they do to the people of this city? Would they enslave my family, my friends?

I imagined Jinx in shackles, her spirit broken. Mab's bones, what about Marvin? Could the bridge troll take another beating? The kid still had scars from the *each uisge* attack. And I knew what Kaye and Ceff would do. They'd fight until their bodies lay broken and lifeless at the feet of the demon lords.

I tugged at the fingers of my glove, and took a long, quivering breath. *Stupid, stupid, stupid*, I admonished myself, but I forced my shoulders back. Sure, I could lose my sanity and end up a gibbering mess in an alley stinking of piss and smoke. Heck, if the convulsions were bad enough, I could break my own neck. But I continued to strip off my gloves.

There are some things that are worth the risk.

I went through my preparations slowly, all the while trying to calm my nerves. I needed to find my center, my chi, and focus my will. I slid a plastic mouthguard into my mouth and ignored the drool that immediately had me resembling a slavering barguest. The mouthguard made me claustrophobic, but my convulsions could be violent and now was not the time to bite my tongue off. I had to maintain control, at all cost.

I cleared the ground at my feet, sweeping away the refuse that littered the pavement with my boot. I thumbed off my phone's ringtone, not wanting any unnecessary distractions. This would be hard enough without the jarring sound of my ringer going off.

I was pretty sure that losing my focus while handling demon blood would be a mistake of epic proportions. Stabbing myself with one of my many weapons was also probably a bad idea. With jerky movements, I stripped off my leather jacket, forearm sheaths, and utility belt placing them all in a plastic bag I kept folded inside my jacket.

Even in the heat of the alley goosebumps dotted my skin. I felt naked, vulnerable. I tossed the bag aside and planted my feet wide.

I winced at the drool trickling down my chin, but the mouthguard was a necessary evil. Not only would it keep me from choking, or eating my own tongue, it would also muffle my screams.

I raised a shaking hand to the fence and swallowed hard. It was time to go down the rabbit hole.

CHAPTER 27

Everything was burning. EVERYTHING, and it was glorious. *Burn, burn, burn! Fire, fire, fire!*

I giggled with glee, but NO. This was not me. These thoughts were those of a fire imp, the one whose blood I'd touched in the alley. I was Ivy G-g-granger...

I felt myself slipping, drowning beneath the tide of flames...losing my sense of self...becoming a demon.

Fire, fire, fire, fire! Who that? Witch with bad magic. Nooooooooo! Darkness, stuck, bottled up with brothers. Bored. No fire, no fire, no fire, no fire. Whoa! Falling, tumbling, FREE!

Girl with purple hair? Witch! Run, run, run. Hide, hide, hide.

Tall buildings. No darkness. No masters. No witch. Make fire. Fire, fire, fire!

I groaned, drool leaking past my lips. I struggled to breathe, but the cloying scent of smoke and unwashed demons lingered. I turned my head to the side, pulled the mouthguard from my mouth, and puked my guts out in the alley.

I heaved until there was nothing left, body wracked with the shakes. My muscles cramped as spasms sent fingers of pain throughout every nerve, but it could have been worse. I'd survived the vision. Thankfully, fire imps were simple creatures obsessed with fire, flame, and smoke. Not much else left an impression on them—except being bottled up by a witch.

Oh shit. Images from the vision came back to me and I began to make sense of them now that I wasn't trapped inside a fire demon's puny brain.

Kaye had rounded up these little mischief makers before. She used her magic to keep them contained in a small, arcane vessel—an artifact that Arachne had disturbed in Kaye's office.

Now I understood the kid's nervousness on the phone. Arachne was the girl with purple hair from my vision.

Intentionally or not, she was responsible for the fires raging through Harborsmouth. Arachne had set the fire imps free.

Arachne had offered us the artifact to help lure the fire imps to the carnival grounds. So she knew that the magic item must have been a demon vessel, she'd figured that much out. If her nervousness was any indication, she also knew that she'd screwed up. But did she realize exactly what she'd done? Probably not.

I sighed and rubbed my face. The kid was about to learn about facing the repercussions of her actions. I knew from my own experience that it was a hard lesson to take.

I pulled on my gloves, glad they hadn't ended up in the line of fire. I didn't want to be smelling puke all day. In fact, I could really use some gum.

I turned to where I'd left my other things, and gasped. There was a note folded and set on top of the bag. Someone had been here in the alley with me while I was incapacitated by the vision.

I sighed and plucked up the note with two gloved fingers. I wasn't sure who had left it, but judging by the smell of tuna and the fact we were in a shadowed alley, I was guessing it was from one of Torn's minions.

I unfolded the note, reading it quickly. There wasn't much to read. *You're in danger, princess. The courts know about you, and they don't tolerate traitors. Watch your back.*

I squeezed my eyes shut and let my chin rest on my chest. Traitor. I'd never even been to one of the fae courts, had only known about my fae blood for a few months, but they'd labeled me a traitor just the same. I couldn't control my wisp powers, not without my father's help, and someone had found out. I'd screwed up, and now I was on their hit list.

As if this day wasn't bad enough already.

I retrieved my sack of belongings and began the methodical task of strapping on weapons. My muscles began to ease with the routine task and my breathing slowed. As I pulled on my leather jacket, my phone vibrated.

I checked the screen and sighed. It was Forneus.

"About time, demon," I croaked.

I coughed, throat raw from those last dry heaves. Puking sucked, but dry heaves always seemed to flay the flesh from my throat.

"A pleasure as always, Granger," he drawled. "I suggest we plan to meet."

"Fine," I said. I rubbed the back of my neck and sighed. I didn't want Forneus to see me like this, but I could use his help. If we met up at The Emporium, I'd at least have a chance to get the shakes under control. "Meet me at The Emporium in twenty minutes."

"You do realize that the witch's abode is one of the few places in this city that I cannot enter," he said.

"Yeah, yeah, I'll take care of it," I said. "Just meet me there."

"As you wish," he said. "If it will aid in Jinx's recovery, then I will attend you outside The Emporium."

I thumbed off my phone, changed the ringer to full, and shoved it inside a jacket pocket. I let out a shaky laugh and stumbled out of the alley. I wasn't looking forward to explaining things to Arachne. The kid was probably going to take things hard.

I tugged at my gloves and closed my eyes, surprised at the relief that washed over me at the realization that I wouldn't be doing this solo. When it came to hurting my friends, I was such a coward. But I needed to face Arachne and make sure she understood the full ramifications of her actions. With Forneus going with me to The Emporium, at least I wouldn't have to do this alone—even if he was a demon.

CHAPTER 28

Forneus said he'd meet me at The Emporium at the turn of the hour, which gave me plenty of time to hoof it back downtown. In fact, if I was speedy about it, I could check in with my *cat sidhe* allies and see if Torn had seen or heard anything else that was useful. Maybe his network of cat spies could shed some light on Kaye's whereabouts.

At least now I didn't also have to keep an eye out for Hell gates. Touching the fire imp's blood had sucked, big time, but now I knew there was no portal to Hell in my city. Normally, that would be reason enough to celebrate, but not today.

There was still the matter of cleaning up the demon pest problem for the people of Harborsmouth and the fire-phobic vamps. I also needed to find Kaye and convince her to let me kill her, and—fingers crossed—bring her back. And while I'm resurrecting my witch friend, I also had to find the incubus feeding on Jinx and break his hold on my friend, dodging fae assassins all the while.

Yeah, I wasn't really feeling much like celebrating.

The *cat sidhe*, on the other hand, seemed to be having a freaking party. Cats bounded toward the mouth of the alley, ears and tails twitching in excitement, as I approached. The alley where Sir Torn held court was completely filled with cats of all shapes and sizes.

I tiptoed carefully through the sea of cats toward Torn's leather clad body. Thankfully, the *cat sidhe* lord was in his human form, or I'd never have found him. Every surface was covered in felines, more so than usual.

I kept my gloved hands in my pockets and shoulders hunched. I'd had my fill of visions for one day, thank you very much.

As I approached, Torn turned and pulled a face. He didn't look happy to see me. Go figure.

"Hey Torn, sorry to interrupt your party," I said, waving a hand at the lively cats lining the alley. "I won't stay long.

Just wondered if you or any of your cats have seen Kaye. Maybe out on the edges of the city?"

Torn wrinkled his nose and looked me up and down.

"What have you been up to, princess?" Torn said. "You smell like troll farts."

Troll farts? I'd showered when I returned from working the fae pest control case, but there wasn't enough soap in the world to wash away the stink of jincan guts, not from the sensitive noses of *cat sidhe*. My time in the alley probably hadn't helped either. I blushed, but shook my head.

"Stop changing the subject, Torn," I said.

He shrugged and made a series of growling purr-like sounds in the back of his throat. Heads turned and ears perked up.

"No, we've been busy," he said. "No one here has seen your witch friend, but I can send word through the shadows— for a price."

Mab's bones, the cat lord was infuriating. We may be allies, but the *cat sidhe* dealt in information and that information rarely came cheap. I'd used up my one freebie when Torn sent me that note, vague as it may have been.

"Fine, what do you want in return?" I asked.

"A date with Jinx," he said, a slow grin lifting his scarred lips. "Though she should be paying me for the honor, not the other way around."

I ground my teeth. Cocky, son of a female *cù sìth*. He was right, of course. The cat lord was Jinx's type. He was a mysterious bad boy who exuded sex appeal. That was the problem. If my best friend survived her incubus encounter, the last thing she needed was a date with Torn. The guy was trouble with a capital T.

"That's not mine to give," I said. "Ask again."

Torn sighed and rolled his eyes.

"Fine, fine," he said. "Help us rid the city of fire imp vermin and we'll be even. I'll call if we get word of the witch's whereabouts. Deal?"

"Deal," I said, grinning.

That was one bargain I could happily make. I was planning on taking care of the fire imps anyway.

"Anything else you can tell me about that note you sent me earlier?" I asked.

"The courts want you dead," he said, shrugging. "I owe no court my allegiance. So long as the *cat sidhe* abide by the one rule that all fae must follow, then we are left alone, all but forgotten by the courts. You too may have remained beneath their notice if you hadn't flaunted your powers where humans could see. You broke the one rule, and now you must pay with your life. It is our way. I won't do the court's dirty work for them, but there is nothing I can do to protect you, princess. My people will not raise arms against the Moordenaar."

"Okay, um, thanks," I said. "These Moordenaar, they're tough I take it?"

"The Moordenaar are handpicked from the time they are infants and raised as killers," he said. "They live only to obey the courts. They are the keepers of the law, and they will dole out their punishment with no remorse. My condolences, princess. It was nice knowing you."

That was my cue to make a hasty exit. Torn had already lost interest in me being here. Either that or he didn't want to be in the Moordenaar's line of fire. I could take a hint.

But as I turned to leave, I looked past Torn and froze. There was the usual sea of cats, but this time they were playing with their food—food that was pint-sized and crying.

Judging from the red skin and diminutive size, I guessed that this might be another fire imp, though this one looked different from the ones I'd seen earlier today. But that may have had something to do with the way he dangled from the claws of a huge tabby cat.

The imp's long, thin ears drooped so low that the tips touched the ground and his pointy nose quivered with each gasping sob. His fingers twitched together repeatedly, but all they managed were harmless sparks. The little guy was shivering, skinny tail tucked between his bony legs.

I knew how he felt. I was being hunted by highly skilled fae assassins and being bossed around by powerful vampire and faerie leaders with nothing better to do than mess with me and those I loved. Something inside of me snapped.

"Put him down!" I yelled.

My hair danced around my head, tickling my ears, and the alley filled with light. I knew without checking my reflection that my skin and eyes were aflame. But it didn't matter anymore, did it? My secret was out. The fae courts knew that my wisp powers were out of control, so why not set it all free?

The cat flicked an ear in irritation and turned its head to Torn. With a sigh, Torn waved a hand.

"By all means, let the creature go," he said, voice thick with sarcasm. "We wouldn't want to upset the princess."

"You were torturing the poor thing!" I exclaimed, hands on my hips.

"That *poor thing* as you like to call it is probably one of the foul creatures setting our fair city on fire," he said.

"I've seen the other fire imps and this little guy isn't half their size," I said. "Look, he can't even make fire."

I pointed to the thing's fingers sparking together impotently like an empty lighter. Even though the imp's skin was red, he somehow managed to blush as he moved to hide his hands behind his back. The movement made his tiny belly stick out like the starving kids on television and I had the craziest notion that I could save the thing for the price of a cup of coffee.

"He is a demon," Torn said, rolling his eyes.

"He's a runt," I said. "Sorry little guy, but it's the truth."

"Runt or not, he's a menace," Torn said.

I snorted.

"Now who's calling the cauldron black?" I asked.

The imp shifted from foot to foot.

"Pretty," he said, pointing at my eyes.

Mab's bones, but he was cute. Gah! Stop it Ivy. He's a freakin' demon. Demons are not cute.

"Um, thanks," I said.

I fidgeted with my gloves. I didn't like my glowing eyes. They were just one of the many things about my wisp magic that I couldn't control—one of the reasons that the faerie courts had labeled me a traitor to our kind and sent assassins to put me down like a rabid animal. But it was kind of sweet that the little critter liked them—at least someone thought they were pretty.

"Thankyouuuuuuuuuuuuuuuuuu!" he cried.

Before I could react, the little imp launched himself at me, a mewling sound coming from where he nestled at chest level and wrapped his spindly arms around my neck. The imp was giving me a hug, which might have been cute if I hadn't been born with the gift of psychometry. Thing is, there's a reason I don't give hugs, and the imp now had himself pressed directly against my bare skin.

Oh, shit.

I barely had time to brace myself before the vision ripped me from my body. With a gasp, I was suddenly a few inches from the ground. The alley was the same, but I was quivering with terror as cats with pointy teeth and sharp claws herded me toward a bored looking man dressed in leather clothing.

A big, scary cat hooked its claws around me and lifted me into the air. The cat shook me and the alley filled with the scent of urine. I was going to die. I just hoped that I hit the cat with my pee. He was mean. *Stupid cat.*

Someone yelled and the alley filled with a bright light, like beautiful flames. The cat dropped me to the ground, thankfully not in the puddle of pee, and I stared at the glowing angel. In Hell, they say that angels are bad, but this angel was good. She saved me. My heart swelled. She was my new friend...

I sucked in air as the vision dumped me back into my body. I blinked at the little imp clinging to my neck as he rifled through my pockets.

"Okay, buddy," I said. "That's enough of that."

I tried to put the imp down, but he clung to me like a spider monkey. A laugh came from Torn and I grimaced.

"You never cease to surprise me, princess," he said.

I knew that boredom plagued the fae. I guess it's hard to find something amusing when you've lived hundreds of years. It was the downside of being immortal. Combine that with the curiosity of a *cat sidhe* and you had Torn. I had a knack for drawing Torn's attention. It was how we'd met. Too bad I didn't like being the source of the *cat sidhe*'s amusement.

"Whatever," I said, trying futilely to put the imp down.

I gave up and pulled a sparkly pencil from my utility belt. The imp's eyes widened at the glittery object, just out of his reach.

"Want it?" I asked.

He nodded and reached for the pencil, letting go of my neck. I handed the little guy the pencil and set him on the ground with a pat on the head. I didn't know what I was going to do with the imp, but I'd worry about that later. For now, I'd keep the *cat side* from toying with him. I didn't like bullies, never had.

"He's off limits," I said, eyeing the cats who sat licking their lips.

"Off limits," the imp said, parroting me. He snapped his fingers, creating sparks. With his other hand, he held the pencil against his shoulder like a toy soldier.

"You tell 'em, Sparky," I said.

Torn's eyes widened and a genuine smile crossed his face.

"You named him," he said.

I blushed and looked away.

"Yeah, what of it?" I asked. "It suits him."

"You're right, princess," he said. "It does."

I turned back to see if Torn was mocking me, but his face looked serious as he watched the little imp marching around my feet. Mab's bones, I think the little guy was trying to protect me. If he only knew what an impossible job that was, he wouldn't be so eager to play soldier.

I just hoped being around me didn't get him killed. Sparky thought I was his friend, but being my friend came with consequences. Just ask Jinx.

"Come on, Sparky," I said.

The sea of cats parted and we made our way out of the alley without any trouble from the *cat sidhe*. Sparky marched along at my feet, brandishing his glitter pencil like it was a weapon. But I knew the real reason the cats let us pass was that we had Torn's permission.

An itch burned between my shoulder blades, but I didn't look back. I'd done it again. I'd landed squarely in the faerie cat's sights, and it wasn't a pleasant place to be. No, being Torn's new curiosity was about as comfortable as a pixie rash.

CHAPTER 29

Sparky and I made it to Wharf Street with two minutes to spare. I yawned and rubbed a hand over my face. Oberon's eyes, I was tired.

My eyelids drifted closed for a second, but the scrabbling of claws on stone woke me from my near-nap. God, I was stupid. I couldn't let my guard down, not in this city, not with Moordenaar hot on my tail.

"Humphrey?" I asked. A growl from behind me lifted the hairs on my neck. "That you, big guy?"

I turned to see the gargoyle baring its fangs at Sparky. The imp, to his credit, stood at my back, pencil at the ready. Though what he thought it would do to a stone gargoyle was anybody's guess. I suppose he could get in some graffiti before Humphrey crushed him. Not much of a consolation prize that.

Guess it was up to me to make sure that didn't happen.

"Um, Humphrey, meet Sparky," I said. "He's with me."

"He's a demon," Humphrey hissed.

"Well, yeah, I know," I said. I ran a hand through my hair and sighed. I should have thought about the gargoyle's reaction sooner. "Actually, there's another demon coming too."

Unless the bastard stood me up. Forneus was late.

"Not inside," Humphrey said. The gargoyle cracked his knuckles, which was just damn creepy. "Not without Madam Kaye or Mistress Arachne's permission."

I held up my hands.

"Okay, okay," I said. "Let me call Arachne."

The gargoyle and imp stared each other down while I grabbed my phone and dialed the witch.

"Ivy?" she asked. "Everything alright?"

"Um, not exactly," I said. "I'm outside with Humphrey and I've got a demon with me...and another one on his way. I was hoping you could give us all permission to enter."

"You're kidding, r-r-right?" she asked.

"No, I wish I was," I said with a sigh.

"But Kaye's still not here," she squeaked.

I lowered my head and massaged my temple. I'd held out a slim hope that Kaye might be here when we arrived.

"Yeah, I figured," I said. "But you and I need to talk, and Forneus might be able to help us figure out how to fix Jinx."

"Forneus?" she asked. "Isn't he the demon Kaye rages about?"

"Um, yeah," I said.

Arachne let out a laugh.

"By the Goddess, Ivy," she said. "You don't ask much, do you?"

Yeah, I was a shitty friend. That wasn't news to me.

"Sorry, kid," I said. "Kaye's gone and it's up to you to make the call. I can leave the demons outside, but I'd rather have them where I can keep an eye on them. And, for what it's worth, Forneus has helped us in the past...and he cares about Jinx."

I left it at that, letting the silence hang between us. Either Arachne would let us in, or she wouldn't. There was nothing left to say, and begging wasn't my style.

"Fine, whatever," she said with a sigh. I heard the girl set down the phone, mutter something unintelligible, and come back on the line. "There, it's done. You can pass through in the company of two demons. But if they do anything I don't like, I'll let Humphrey eat them for breakfast."

"Thanks," I said. "I'm just waiting for Forneus and we'll head on in. Think you could put the kettle on for me?"

"I just gave you permission to enter with two demons and you want me to make you tea?" she asked. "How does Jinx put up with you?"

"No idea," I said. "But thanks."

I could practically hear the eye roll as Arachne hung up.

"You catch all that, Humphrey?" I asked.

"Get to eat demons for breakfast," he said with a grin.

"Hey, only if they misbehave," I said.

"Demons always do," he said, licking his lips.

I had a sinking feeling that the gargoyle had a point. I just hoped that Sparky and Forneus stayed on their best behavior while in The Emporium. That wasn't too much to ask, right?

I heard a throat clear and spun to see Forneus dabbing at his face with an honest-to-god lace handkerchief. Someone really needed to bring that man into the correct century.

"Where have you been?" I asked.

"A pleasure to see you as well," he said.

"That's not an answer," I said. "I called. You didn't call me back—for an entire day."

The demon tugged at his white gloves, not meeting my eyes.

"Yes, I was...detained," he said.

I was sure there was a story there, and I wanted to know what it was. What would keep him from helping Jinx? If it was something petty, I might just kill him. I stepped into his line of sight, cocked a hip, and made a rolling gesture with my hand.

"Get on with it, Forneus," I said. "What was so urgent that it came between you and your search for information that could help Jinx. This I've got to hear."

Forneus gave a long suffering sigh and I held my breath against the smell of sulfur. Damn that guy needed some Tic Tacs, and this from the girl with puke breath. I took a step back, careful not to step on Sparky. The pipsqueak was sticking close to my heels.

"Apparently, my adversaries in Hell are jealous of the fact that I am currently in the Dark Lord's favor."

"Yeah, yeah, I'm sure they're forming their own fan club," I said. "And did you just say, Dark Lord? 'Cause that's just cheesy."

Forneus tensed, his hankie gone, replaced by his walking stick. He'd gone dead serious.

"Trust me, it is best not to say His name," he said. "Being in his favor does not mean I wish to draw His attention."

"Noted," I said. "So why the delay?"

"Contrary to popular belief, we demons do not all sit around and drink tea together while roasting human souls on a spit," he said. "Hell is too large a place for us to know every other demon that those fiery pits have spawned."

I nodded and rolled my hand for him to get on with it.

"I did not have any first-hand experience with the incubi, only their sister race, so I journeyed to Hell to learn more about the incubi in hopes of discovering ways to break the spell on Jinx," he said. "Unfortunately, while I was there I was set upon by over ambitious demons looking for an expeditious way to advance through the ranks. Hence the delay."

"I take it you set these guys straight?" I asked.

I didn't care much about demon politics, but if Forneus' enemies started popping up on my city streets, things could get messy. Even without a Hell gate, there was a chance that powerful enough demons might enter the city, especially with Kaye's magic waning. Our current plan was dicey enough as it was without throwing angry, vengeful demons into the mix.

"Oh, I put those wastrels in their proper place, posthaste," he said, an evil grin crawling across his face.

A shiver ran up my spine, and I was suddenly glad that Forneus was on my side. Demons? Kings of the evil grin, let me tell you.

At least I wouldn't be facing off with Forneus' enemies. Just a couple dozen fire imps and a pissed off glaistig. Yeah, no big deal. Right.

"So, when you were done comparing pitchforks, did you find out anything useful?" I asked. "Please tell me you know an easy way to sever the incubus' hold on Jinx."

"The simplest way is to kill the man, which is what he deserves for touching Jinx and sullying her reputation," he said.

"That's on my to-do list, but I was hoping for an easier option," I said. "As in, something we can pull off from a distance."

"You could attempt to reason with the man," he said, rolling his eyes and flapping his hand as if to dismiss the idea. "But what can you offer him in exchange for Jinx's freedom? No, even if he was acting outside of The Green Lady's orders, which would be foolish to assume, there is nothing you could do to persuade him from feeding off from Jinx."

"Both of those options depend on getting close enough to either kill or reason with the man," I said. "I have a plan for storming the carnival and getting to the incubus, but it relies on a shitload of things to go right if I'm to pull it off." And a lot was riding on Kaye turning up soon and agreeing to something so insane I didn't even want to think about it. *Damn.* "I was hoping for something simpler and less messy. Complicated plans have a way of going sideways."

"I cannot change the facts," he said. "Kill him or reason with him. If you wish to do so from afar, then use that phone contraption you are so fond of. Reason with the man. Though the Dark Lord only knows what you could offer him."

I lowered my voice, hands clenched into fists.

"What if I gave myself in exchange?" I asked. "Would the feeding kill me, the way it would a human?"

For once, I was glad that Ceff wasn't here. I wouldn't have to see the pain written on his face.

Forneus raised an eyebrow.

"Yes, it would kill you," he said. "Not that the incubus would accept that bargain. His mistress would gain nothing by your death and an incubus would never trade a sexy human for a prudish half-breed. No offense."

I stiffened. Prudish half-breed?

"I'll have you know..." I said.

"Yes?" he asked. He leaned forward, rolling his cane between his hands.

"Never mind," I said, throwing my hands up in the air. I was not going to defend myself by sharing details about my sex life, not with Forneus. Not ever. "What is it with all demons being perverts?"

Sparky let out an indignant squeak and I reached down and patted his head with a gloved hand.

"Okay, all except for you buddy," I said.

Forneus' eyes widened as he noticed Sparky for the first time. A ripple of magic flared in his eyes and raced across his skin.

"What is a Tezcatlipocan demon doing in your presence?" he asked. "Alive, that is."

"I don't know what a Tezca-whatever is, but his name's Sparky," I said. The name sounded familiar, but my head was killing me and I couldn't place where I'd heard it before. "And he's with me."

The last I said with narrowed eyes, letting Forneus know where I stood on the issue. Sparky had experienced enough trauma for one day, no matter what kind of unpronounceable demon he was. I did feel smug though, I just knew he wasn't a fire imp.

"Your ignorance never ceases to amaze me, though in this case it may be justified," he said. "Tezcatlipocans are rare, and often misunderstood on this plane. Let me see." He tapped his chin with his cane, brow furrowed. "You have heard of Nephilim?"

"Yes," I said, nodding. Father Michael loved to go on and on about stuff like that. "Nephilim are the offspring of fallen angels and humans. They were all wiped out in The Flood."

"Not all," he said. "Though yes, many of the Nephilim were wiped out during that time. Their great strength was often unmatched by one creature alone, but many believed their existence to be a blight on the earth. They were hunted, and their gigantic size became a disadvantage as men banded together against them. There are some who hide in the mountains, waiting for man to forget their existence."

"Okaaaaaaay, so what does that have to do with Sparky?" I asked.

"Your...pet, ahem, is the offspring of a fallen angel and a demon," he said. "Such a demon is extremely rare. It is nearly inconceivable that this one was cast out of Hell to fend for himself as a newling. Yet here he is."

"Yep, and I sure didn't take a trip to Hell," I said. Though I felt like I had. Oberon's eyes, I was tired. "I found him here in the city, being toyed with by the *cat sidhe*."

"They would have killed him?" he asked, incredulous.

Sparky whined and tucked himself in closer to my leg. I probably should discourage that kind of thing, but I couldn't help but feel sorry for the little guy.

"Yes, after they'd tortured him for awhile," I said. "The *cat sidhe* like to play with their food."

I grimaced. The *cat sidhe* may be my allies, but that didn't mean I had to approve of their hunting practices.

"In their defense, I don't think the cats knew that Sparky was the son of a fallen angel," I said. "They were hunting fire imps."

"Fire imps?" he asked. "Here in Harborsmouth?"

I rubbed my face.

"Yeah, it's a long story," I said. "How about we take this inside and I'll explain over tea. I have a faerie bargain hanging over my head and it's giving me a headache."

There was also a pack of faerie assassins out looking for me, and when they found me, I had no doubt I'd be in big trouble. The back of my neck itched just thinking about it.

I moved for the door, but Forneus stayed as if rooted to the sidewalk. I followed his gaze to see Humphrey glaring down from where he crouched on the stone lintel above the entrance. Dust trickled from Humphrey's mouth onto the ground.

"What, him?" I asked, pointing my thumb toward the drooling gargoyle. "Don't worry about Humphrey. He's cool. Right, Humphrey?"

Humphrey just glared at us, the snick of claws the only sound. I sighed and tried another tactic. The gargoyle always liked my jokes in the past, so why not give that a try?

"We get it, Humphrey," I said. I waggled my eyebrows. "You're a stone cold killer. You gonna let us pass?"

The gargoyle fought a smile, but I caught the twitch of his lips as he waved us through. Guess that was our cue.

"You are forgetting about the witch," Forneus said.

He'd moved up behind me, his sulfurous breath hot against my neck. Too close for damned comfort. I shook my head and opened the door, stepping out of his reach.

"No, I didn't," I said. "We've got permission to enter, but no funny business, or they'll feed you to Humphrey here. You too, Sparky."

The gargoyle grinned from his perch, showing off a mouthful of bone crushing teeth. Forneus muttered something, but I didn't quite catch what he said. I was too busy gaping at Sparky.

The little demon had reached up and placed his tiny hand in mine. I took a steadying breath and closed my hand over his.

"Okay, kiddo," I said. "But no touching my skin. Got it?"

Sparky nodded, a serious look on his face. I told myself that holding his hand was a good way to keep the demon from getting into trouble while we were inside The Emporium. But who was I kidding?

Now that we'd already gotten the obligatory vision out of the way—one that wasn't all that bad as far as visions go—I didn't have much to worry about. I knew I'd survive if we accidentally touched again, and his presence was a comfort.

Sparky was a reminder of the one good thing I'd done today. At least, I hoped I'd been right to save him. He was a demon, sure, but he was also just a kid. That had to count for something.

I squeezed his hand and crossed the threshold into The Emporium. I wasn't looking forward to my chat with Arachne. And if Kaye showed up, I'd need all the comfort I could get.

CHAPTER 30

"So," I said, dodging occult bric-a-brac. "You learn anything else that might help us with Jinx?"

Arachne may have given us permission to enter, but the magic workings that Kaye had instilled in the place were making navigating the shop a bitch. Every time we headed toward the back of The Emporium, some freaking display ended up in our way. I had a nagging suspicion it had something to do with my guests of the demonic persuasion.

Oh well, nothing for it now but to keep on trudging until we found Kaye's spell kitchen. I sure as heck wasn't going to force my way through. Arachne said we needed to be on our best behavior, and I was taking the kid seriously. The last thing we needed was for The Emporium to swallow us whole.

I eyed a rack of grinning skeletons, keeping my free hand close to my weapons, and turned left. Again. Yeah, there was no question about it. We were walking in circles.

At least the detour gave me time to catch Forneus up to speed. I filled him in on the day's events—fire imps, vamp lords, and Hunters, oh my—as we walked, but now I was trying to edge the conversation back to Jinx.

The skin around Forneus' eyes tightened, as did his grip on his fancy cane. Apparently, the direction of my questions had pissed him off. Oh well, I was used to that. Pissing people off was like my super power.

"Nothing of import," he snapped.

"Come on, Forneus," I said. "Out with it."

He let out a theatrical groan and I smiled.

"You are the most persistent, troublesome, vexatious..." he said.

"Yeah, yeah, so what did you find out?" I asked.

He stopped, staring at his hands, though I was pretty sure he didn't really see them. No, his mind was somewhere else entirely.

"Before I ventured to Hell, I visited with a few patrons of Club Nexus," he said. I leaned closer, his voice so low I could barely make out the words. "My inquiries provided clearer insight as to how the incubus lured Jinx from the club, nothing more."

I swallowed hard. Forneus may not want to talk about it, heck I didn't want to hear it, but we needed all the facts.

"What did he do to her?" I asked.

"That is just it, the culprit was not a 'he' at all," he said. Well, that was confusing as hell. Jinx was fed on by an incubus, as in a half-fae half-demon who was totally, completely male. Forneus lifted a hand and waved off the questions forming on my tongue. "The incubus came later."

Normally, I would have snorted at the double entendre, but not this time. No matter how much my mind tried to reject the idea, this was Jinx we were talking about.

I tried to sort through what Forneus was saying and pieces of the puzzle finally clicked into place. Jinx may have made some bad choices when it came to men in the past, but she was smart, and tough as all get out. She never would have willingly left the club with an incubus. Even she knew better than that.

But she might have left with someone she trusted.

"Who was it?" I asked. "Who led Jinx out of the club?"

The words "like a lamb to the slaughter" hung in the air, unspoken. My mind raced with possibilities and I tried to prepare myself for who might be a traitorous bitch, but when Forneus broke the silence he still managed to surprise me.

"Delilah, the succubus," he said.

"Okay, that wasn't who I was expecting," I said. It wasn't that I didn't suspect that Delilah had the capability of deceit. No, it was that the succubus wasn't exactly in our circle of friends. Sure, she'd helped me survive an *each uisge* attack, but that was while she was under orders from The Green Lady to protect the carnival. It wasn't like we were best buds or anything. I mean, I hoped that Delilah would be an asset when I stormed the carnival, but I didn't count on it. Something about this whole scenario was hinky. "Why would Jinx trust Delilah?"

"From what I could gather from my informants, I do not believe her trust went so far as leaving the premises with the succubus," he said.

"But you said..." I argued.

"I know what I said, but listen," he said. "Jinx left with Delilah after trusting the succubus in as far as having a drink with her."

He watched my face, waiting for me to catch up. When I did, rage poured off me in waves of light, literally. The Emporium seemed to bristle and I took a deep, calming breath. Kaye's magic was not something I wanted to tangle with, but damn I was pissed.

"Delilah slipped her Ice, didn't she?" I asked.

It explained Jinx's loss of memory. It explained everything.

"Yes, it would seem so," he said with a curt nod.

Mab's bloody freaking bones. Ice was a nasty drug that had recently made its way through Club Nexus, until I'd put a stop to Puck's depraved side business. I'd assumed that with Puck out of the picture, Ice was off the streets. I'd been a fool.

The thing with Ice is that it made the perfect date rape drug. It was like a roofie on steroids.

And the succubus had given it to Jinx.

Delilah led a drugged Jinx out of the club, to her friend the incubus, and patrons of Club Nexus wouldn't have suspected a thing. It would have looked like two girls out having a good time—one just having a little too much of a good time.

Now that we knew the how and the why, I guess all that was left was to kick some ass. I wasn't going to negotiate—not with manipulative pricks willing to slip my friend a date rape drug in order to force me to do their bidding. The Green Lady, the incubus, and Delilah were securely on my shit list.

They were going to pay.

"She would be safer with me in her life," Forneus said, pulling me from my murderous thoughts.

Oberon, forgive me, but I was starting to agree with him. I couldn't be in two places at once, and with my search for my father, that meant a lot of time out of the office and away from Jinx.

I gave a noncommittal shrug and turned my attention to saving our asses in the present. If we survived the future, I'd have to consider making some changes in my life. Finding someone else to watch Jinx's back was one of them.

I didn't like that idea, not one bit, but I had to admit that so far I hadn't been able to keep my friend safe. Hell, I wasn't doing a stand-up job of surviving myself.

I blinked, surprised to see the door to Kaye's spell kitchen just ahead. Now that we'd finally made it to the back of the shop, I was questioning the wisdom of this visit. I rubbed the back of my neck, trying to ignore the rolling in my gut.

I was going to give an impressionable teenage witch advice? Yeah, that was bound to go well.

CHAPTER 31

"**U**m, hi," Arachne said, glancing at Forneus nervously. "Here's your tea, Ivy. I made some sandwiches too. Thought you guys might be hungry."

My stomach growled in reply, but I kept my eyes on the kid. She was babbling, overcompensating, and jumpy as hell—and it wasn't because of the demons in her kitchen. Yeah, the kid and I needed to have that chat.

"Thanks," I said.

I took the cup in both hands, heat leaking through my gloves. Oberon's eyes, where to start?

A strangled utterance pulled my attention to Forneus. He'd stepped further into the room, the stone topped island no longer blocking his view of the spell circle—and Jinx. She lay there unmoving, and for a second I feared the worst.

"Arachne, is Jinx okay?" I asked.

I jostled tea and set the mug down with a clatter.

"What?" she asked. "Oh, yeah, she's just sleeping. By the Goddess, Ivy, I would have called you if something happened!"

She sounded defensive, and more than a little angry. Good, she'd need that anger to give her strength. At least, that's how I cope.

"She...she is dying," Forneus said.

I tried to ignore the tears in his eyes and turned to Arachne. But what I saw there wasn't much better. I sighed and ran a hand over my face.

"Give it to me straight, kid," I said. "She's slipping, isn't she?"

Arachne had grabbed a towel to mop up the sloshed tea and now wrung it in her hands.

"My circle isn't as strong as Kaye's," she said. "I'm keeping Jinx comfortable, but the incubus is still feeding from her. I'm blocking m-m-most of it."

"But not all," I said quietly.

"No, not all," she said, lip quavering.

Shit, I did not need everyone to start crying. Not now.

"It's alright," I said, forcing a smile. "You've done good, kid. Leave the rest to me."

I pulled out a chair and starting dishing out sandwiches. I set Sparky's on the bench next to me and he dug into it with glee. At least someone was happy.

"Come on Forneus," I said, slapping a hand on the chair. "We have a battle to plan."

He pulled himself away from the spell circle and dropped into the chair, but kept his gaze on Jinx.

"Where's Hob?" I asked.

Not that I was disappointed that the brownie hadn't greeted us on arrival, but it was odd he wasn't out here demanding his gift. I was worried that I didn't have a gift suitable for this visit. What do you give a grumpy brownie for defiling his home with two demons? I eyed the hearth, skin already beginning to itch in anticipation. I hated being pixed.

"He left right after Kaye, singing something about pie," she said, rolling her eyes.

I snorted. Pie? Hob must be off to visit Olga, the female gnome he was crushing on. What was it with everybody lately? I was surrounded by lovesick puppies. Was there something in the air?

I shook my head. At least Hob was safe in the suburbs, and I was off the hook as far as the proper gift went. Maybe Fate wasn't such a bitch after all.

I narrowed my eyes at Arachne, and around a mouthful of sandwich, asked, "So, how'd you break Kaye's demon vessel?"

The witch choked on her tea, sputtering and gasping for breath. But she wasn't getting off that easy. Even Forneus broke his vigil long enough to turn a questioning eye her way.

"Yes, witch, just how did you release a plague of fire imps on this city?" he asked.

"I d-d-didn't," she stuttered.

I cocked an eyebrow at her over my sandwich.

"Come on, how else would you know about that artifact?" I asked. "Seems like way too much of a coincidence."

I'd come to learn that coincidence usually just meant that there was a piece of the puzzle that needed putting into place—and there was a witch sized piece sitting across the table from me. Plus, I had seen the kid in the fire imp's memories.

I waited while Arachne picked at her sandwich, covering her plate in bread confetti. She'd break, I just had to be patient.

I was giving her the eye, so was Forneus. Heck, Sparky had finished his snack and was peering over the table at her—though he could have been eyeing her sandwich. I wasn't keen on the mayo and mustard sandwiches, but judging by how fast Sparky ate his, he sure liked them. Damn the little guy could pack away the food.

Arachne pushed her plate away and folded her arms across her chest. Sparky pointed at the plate and then at his chest and I nodded.

"It wasn't on purpose," Arachne said, scowling.

"I never said it was," I said.

She flicked her eyes to Forneus and then down at her lap. Her face flushed and I realized that the kid was embarrassed. Crap, I couldn't deal with another friend having a crush on the demon. One was bad enough.

At least Jinx was likely to ram him through with a letter opener now and then.

Forneus, to his credit, hadn't even noticed. He was too busy watching Jinx, as if mesmerized by the rise and fall of her chest.

"Look, this can go one of two ways," I said. "You can tell us, like an adult. Or you can keep it to yourself and live with the fact that not telling us might put us all in danger."

Her eyes widened, but she nodded, finally making eye contact.

"I never meant to hurt anyone, Ivy, I swear," she said.

"I don't doubt that," I said. "But one thing you learn in our world is that we're bound to hurt someone someday. It's part of growing up. What matters is how we handle the fallout."

She swallowed hard, and placed her hands flat on the table. Yeah, she was growing up alright. There was a darkness in her eyes that hadn't been there before today—a shadow of pain that would never fully go away.

"It's bad, isn't it?" she asked. "I've heard sirens, but...I tried to ignore it. Up until now, it didn't seem real. Like it was happening to people on television, or a video game."

I'd always treasured Arachne's innocence. It was something I hadn't had the luxury of experiencing in my teen years. My psychic gifts had blossomed way too soon for that. But this wasn't a time for treading lightly. Some lessons were best learned hard.

"This is no game, Arachne," I said. "Whatever you did, those fire imps are making a mess of this city. People have lost their homes, their jobs. Before this is over, some may lose their lives."

She sniffed, eyes red and full of unshed tears, but she didn't look away. Maybe she was tougher than I gave her credit for.

"What can I do to make it right?" she asked.

That was the million dollar question, one that gnawed at me in the dead of night. I clenched my jaw and narrowed my eyes.

"You can help us plan the upcoming battle," I said. "Tell us everything you know, and help us with any magic that you can. Are you in?"

"I'm in," she said, steely resolve stiffening her shoulders. "And there's something you need to see."

She got up and strode over to the wall where a backpack hung from a hook. She pulled out a sweatshirt wrapped bundle and carried it to the table.

"I went into Kaye's office looking for a book," she said. Her eyes flicked to Forneus and she blushed again. "It was for a love spell. It was stupid."

"Love spells never end well, you know that," I said.

Damn, how could she be so foolish? She'd grown up around magic. She should have known better than to dally in that shit. Some forces are best left alone.

"In my many years of existence, I have never known that knowledge to stop humans from trying," Forneus said. My mouth fell open as the demon rose to Arachne's defense. I hadn't even been sure that he'd been listening. He'd been so wrapped up in watching Jinx. Apparently, he could multitask. "You would not believe the quantity of souls collected in the name of love. It can be a great strength, but an even greater weakness. None of us wish to be alone."

"Point taken," I said.

"So, um, when I tried to open the book of love spells, I knocked this over," she said.

She removed the sweatshirt from a brass artifact similar to the censer that Father Michael used for burning incense in his church. She set the item in the center of the table with a thunk. It didn't look like much really, but apparently, it was the real deal.

Sparky let out a shrieking wail that sent goosebumps skittering up and down my neck. He pulled his long ears over his eyes like a blindfold and burrowed into my jacket. I didn't push him away. My skin was covered, and the little guy was terrified.

"They all came pouring out so fast," Arachne said, voice shaking. "I didn't even react. By the time I ran out of the office, they had already gone to ground. There were just too many places for them to hide."

"Wait, the shop didn't fight back?" I asked. The Emporium often gave me grief. It seemed unfair that the shop's magic hadn't attacked the fire imps.

"No," she said. "I don't think it understood an invasion coming from within. It just...tried to push them out."

"If that is the case, then it would have hastened their escape," Forneus said.

Arachne gave him a grateful look, but when she turned back to me there was steely determination in her eyes.

"Help me make this right," she said.

"Fine," I said. I nodded. "Put that thing away before Sparky has a heart attack. We have a battle to plan."

CHAPTER 32

Whoever said planning a battle was the easy part, never had to deal with a vengeful demon and a guilt-ridden teenage witch.

"You're going to lure the fire imps to the amusement park where the carnival fae reside?" Arachne asked.

It wasn't the first time she'd asked.

"Yeah, I'm going to sick their fiery little butts on The Green Lady, just as soon as you show me how to use that magic artifact," I said.

"Innocent carnival fae could be injured," she said.

It was a reasonable concern, especially since the kid was somewhat responsible for this clusterfuck. Heck, the idea of someone else getting hurt made my stomach twist into painful knots, but The Green Lady had put her people in the line of fire as soon as she attacked my vassal. According to fae law, her subjects were an acceptable loss—no more than collateral damage in our power struggle.

I wasn't so callous, but I would grasp the opportunity to create enough mayhem to cover my entrance into her territory. In the ensuing chaos, I hoped to find the glaistig's incubus and break his hold on Jinx—with my blades. If it gave the faerie queen a headache, then all the better.

"That's why Ceff's people will be on fire duty," I said. "The carnival grounds are on a jetty that juts out into the harbor, which means the place is surrounded by water. With the kelpies there with their water magic, we can minimize the damage."

"Um, okay, I guess," she said. "If you think Ceff will get the kelpies to help."

"Of course he will," I said. "He's Ceff."

"Yes, yes, we have all been dazzled by your suitor's heroism," Forneus said, feigning a yawn. "Can we get on with the killing?"

I sighed, damn that demon. He wasn't helping.

"No, not yet," I said through clenched teeth.

Forneus was as bad as a sugared up kid on a road trip. *Are we there yet? Are we there yet? Is it time to flay the incubus' flesh from his bones?* Thank Mab, I never planned on having rugrats. I didn't have the patience.

"Not yet, not yet!" Sparky chimed in.

Forneus shot the tiny demon a glare and I covered my laugh with a cough.

"I still cannot fathom what possessed you to take a Tezcatlipocan demon as a pet," he said.

"Tezcatliwhatchamacallit demon?" I sputtered.

Eyes bugging out of my head, I stared down into Sparky's smiling face. Maybe it was the mayonnaise sandwich or the healthy dose of caffeine that helped to clear the brain fog, but I realized where I'd heard that name before.

According to Father Michael, Tezcatlipocan demon lords were the powerful masters of smaller demons. I also remembered that the Tezcatlipocan demons were also supposed to be huge, as in bigger than a super-sized bread basket. There was no way this little runt was Tezcatlipocan. Forneus was just messing with me.

"Stop yanking my chain, Forneus," I said, rolling my eyes. He'd had me there for a second, damn him. "Tezca-whatevers are giants. And this kid is no giant. Even I can tell that much."

"No, he is not a giant, *yet*," he said.

"You mean he'll get big…like a Saint Bernard?" Arachne asked.

"I mean, young witch, that if Sparky here were a puppy, he would grow to become a wooly mammoth," he said.

My gut tightened and I tasted bile. There was truth in Forneus' words, much as I loathed to admit it. If I stopped and gave it some thought, it made sense. I knew there was something different about Sparky. Though there were similarities, he wasn't quite like the fire imps I'd chased earlier. My subconscious had already placed him in a different category altogether. Forenus was just giving it a name—one that I'd like to forget.

Fatigue and stubbornness had allowed me to ignore Forneus' earlier comments, but maybe he was right. Or not.

"Wooooly mammoth!" Sparky exclaimed, gleefully crawling on the table holding two pickles to his face like tusks.

Oh yeah, he was an evil demon lord. I was trembling in my boots.

Forneus had to be mistaken. And even if he wasn't, and Sparky really was a Tezcatlipocan demon, I just couldn't believe that the runt was evil.

"Come on, Forneus," I said waving a hand at Sparky's antics. "Does this look like an all mighty master demon to you?"

"Well, he is a bit *unusual*, but with enough training..." he said.

"Exactly!" I said. "Demon lords aren't necessarily born evil." Oberon's eyes, did I just say that? "It's that nature vs. nurture thing. If he grows up with me, instead of in Hell, then he's got a chance, right? Everyone deserves a chance."

Okay, some people would say that growing up with me would be just another kind of hell, but I wasn't asking them. If Sparky wanted to stay, he was staying—come what may.

"Be still my heart," Forneus said, hand to his forehead, feigning to faint. "Are you saying that demons are not inherently evil? You? I can scarcely believe my ears. What did you put in our tea, witch?"

"N-n-nothing," Arachne stammered.

"Stop messing around, Forneus," I said. "Yes, I might have been a bit...prejudiced before. Can you blame me? My own father was tricked by the big S man himself, and it's not like you weren't a manipulative prick on our first meeting."

He raised an eyebrow, but a slow grin slid across his face.

"A manipulative prick?" he asked. "How gauche of you. It is not like I call you a stubborn prude with daddy issues, not to your face."

My face flushed hot, but I just shrugged. Sticks, stones, whatever.

"He's staying," I said. "Get over it."

To make my point, I picked up Sparky from where he was now sprawled out on the table and carefully placed the sleeping demon in my lap. I slid a throwing knife from its sheath and used it to clean my nails. The message was clear; mess with Sparky, mess with me and my collection of pointy things. The demon runt was now part of my ragtag family, such as it was.

Arachne's eyes widened, but she gave me a thumbs up. It was nice to have the kid's support, even if she was obviously freaked out by the fact that I was willingly touching someone other than Ceff or Galliel. Oh well, she'd get over it. We all would. Everything was changing, even this.

"Soooooo," Forneus said. "Can we go kill the incubus now?"

"No," I said. "First I need to know more about how this artifact works. If we lure the fire imps to the carnival, can we force them back inside the vessel—after they've caused the glaistig some misery and provided our cover diversion—and put a cork in it?"

Arachne bit her lip, tugging on a chunk of purple-streaked hair.

"I can try to compel the imps to follow the artifact, since that's the vessel they came from, but I can't actually stuff them back inside," she said. "I don't know the original spell."

"It's a good thing then, child, that I do," a voice said from the door. "I cast it myself."

Oh, shit. Kaye was back.

CHAPTER 33

Kaye's hands were moving, tattoos slithering and I was sitting in her kitchen with two demons. We were so screwed.

I cursed myself for my stupidity. I had my back to the door, leaving myself vulnerable. The fact that I had brought two demons into Kaye's spell kitchen also wasn't smart. She was going to be angry as hell, and pissing off a witch as powerful as Kaye was never a good idea.

I cradled Sparky in my lap with one arm and held up the other gloved hand toward Kaye.

"Kaye, wait, I can explain..." I said.

Black tendrils of magic sprung across the kitchen to stop within inches of Forneus, Sparky, and me. I licked my lips, heart racing. I had no doubt that the black mist could claw through our bodies, knocking us out of this fight, or killing us dead. Everything depended on what we said and did next. I just hoped that Forneus kept his sulfurous trap shut.

"You let DEMONS inside my spell kitchen?" she seethed, glaring at Arachne.

The young witch blanched and swayed where she sat. I was pretty sure the kid was going to faint, but there was nothing I could do. If I moved to hold her upright, I'd be in the clutches of Kaye's magic talons.

The air in the room changed and I heard a moan from the spell circle. *The spell circle.* Mab's bones, Arachne had lost her concentration. The circle no longer held and Jinx was awake.

No, no, no, this could not be happening.

"What the...?" Jinx mumbled. Jinx groggily shook her head and sat up on the cot, eyes narrowing as she caught sight of Forneus. "You! You goddamned son of a..."

Jinx lunged toward Forneus. Thankfully, she was half asleep and tangled in a blanket. But she looked determined to kill him all the same.

That probably had something to do with the fact she'd been violated by a demon. It hadn't been Forneus—wrong

demon—but Jinx didn't know that. I was working on finding
the bastard who did this to her, and now I was here with
Forneus. That was enough proof for Jinx.

"Yes, yes, I'm a damned son of a demon whore," he said.
"You know how I love it when you talk dirty, darling, but now
is not the best time. Sensitive ears and all that, and I do think
you're supposed to be safely ensconced inside that spell circle."

He waved his hand to encompass Kaye, Arachne, and
me, but Jinx only had eyes for Forneus. It was as if the rest of
us didn't exist, which was very, very bad considering that Kaye
was poised to kill us all and be done with it.

"Kaye, Arachne, the spell circle," I said. "It's the only
thing keeping Jinx alive!"

Arachne trembled, barely staying upright, her eyes
rimmed in red—no help there. The kid was too upset. I turned
to Kaye, still managing to hold Sparky who, thank Mab, was
still asleep in my lap. The witch's tattoos writhed up and down
her arms and neck, her magic ready to be unleashed.

"Not yet," she said her tone sharp.

Her eyes flicked to Jinx and I followed her gaze. Jinx
was reaching for an athame that was on the altar beside the
edge of the spell circle. Kaye was going to let my friend have
her revenge.

"Jinx no!" I screamed. "The incubus marked you, not
Forneus. He's here to help!"

But I was too late. Jinx's eyes widened, my words
sinking in at the same time as the blade.

"Lucifer's fiery prick, that hurts," Forneus said. He
looked down at the hilt protruding from his chest. "Is that a
blessed ritual dagger?"

He cast a questioning gaze around the kitchen, and I
shrugged. How should I know? Knowing Kaye, it probably
was. I was guessing from the look on his face that blessed
daggers hurt, a lot.

He turned back to Jinx who was now scrambling to
extract herself from his lap. They'd tumbled to the floor in a
bloody heap of blankets and tangled limbs.

"We really must do something about that memory of
yours," he said.

He raised a hand to cup Jinx's face and she went rigid in
his arms. Oh crap. Forneus was going to retrieve Jinx's

memory of their first kiss, now? Could this situation get any worse?

"Ivy, what's going on?" Jinx asked, her dark-circled eyes meeting mine from across the room.

"Forneus is here to help and..." I said, letting out a strangled groan. "And he obviously wants to give you back a memory...from the night we fought Puck."

"Will it help?" she asked.

Oberon's eyes, she looked tired.

"If this is our last moment together, I would have you remember," Forneus said, his hand still gently cupping the side of her face.

I nodded and Jinx gently bit her lip, turning to lock eyes with Forneus.

"Okay," she said.

Would she hate me for what I'd done? I thought I was protecting her by never telling her about that kiss she shared with Forneus. But now, I wasn't so sure. Maybe if I hadn't run interference with those two, they might be dating and she wouldn't be in this mess now, fighting for her life.

"Thank you," Forneus said.

I don't know if he was thanking me or Jinx. It didn't really matter. He slid an arm around Jinx's waist as she shuddered, eyelids fluttering closed. When they opened again, I could tell that everything had changed.

Her hands slid along his chest, his neck, and into his hair as she devoured him with her eyes. She may be human, but there was magic in that look and Forneus was a man bespelled. He gathered her into his arms, pulled himself to his knees, and stood.

"May I enter your spell circle?" he asked, bowing his head to Kaye.

As he broke their soulful gaze, Jinx turned to me and scowled. Her eyes narrowed and I knew what that look meant. When this was all over, we were having a talk. I wasn't looking forward to that chat, not one bit. I just hope I didn't end up with an athame to the chest.

Kaye nodded to Forneus, her magic pulling back into her body. He laid Jinx gently on the cot that Arachne had set up for her and settled the blanket up around her shoulders. He kissed her forehead and stood. Her eyes fluttered closed, a smile on her lips.

"Kaye?" I asked.

The familiar tingling sensation of magic rippled across my nerve endings and I knew that the spell circle had been reinvoked. Unfortunately for Forneus, the spell singed his boot heels as he was just crossing the silver circle laid into the kitchen floor. He yelped and Kaye winked.

At least some things never changed. Kaye was a prankster through and through. And she hadn't killed any of us, yet. That was something to celebrate.

Forneus staggered to the table and dropped into his chair.

"You okay?" I asked.

"Yes, so long as your witch friend doesn't send me back to Hell," he said. "My enemies would love to have another chance at me, especially in my injured state."

He grabbed the hilt of the athame, trying to pull the blade from his chest, and hissed. Kaye laughed and came forward in a rustle of skirts and tinkling bells. I let out a relieved sigh. If Kaye was letting us hear her coming, the danger had passed. For now.

"Don't be daft," she said, pointing to Forneus' chest. "You don't want to touch that, demon. That's an athame, blessed by the Goddess under a full moon. Allow me."

She reached down and yanked the blade from Forneus' chest with a sucking, grating sound that made me wish I hadn't eaten that sandwich. Judging from the sickly sheen of sweat on his face, Forneus was wishing the same thing. But he already looked better, now that the blade was out.

Kaye carried the blade over to the stove and held it vertically over a large cauldron. Forneus' blood dripped into the pot with a sizzle.

"Do I even want to know what she is doing?" he asked.

"No, probably not," I said.

Arachne shook her head and swallowed hard. Yeah, that couldn't be good.

"Now," Kaye said, coming back to the table to loom over us. "Tell me what you're all doing in my kitchen."

No, not good at all.

CHAPTER 34

We told Kaye all about the fire imps, which she took pretty well all things considered, and what we'd learned from The Green Lady. It was the part about Kaye's pending death that I was getting hung up on.

"We were thinking that we could pull a Romeo and Juliet..." I said.

My heart raced and I started to sweat. God, this sounded so much better when Ceff had said it.

"You want to fake my death?" she asked.

I fidgeted with my gloves. What are the right words for telling the most powerful witch in the city that you don't just want to fake her death—you need to kill her and, fingers crossed, bring her back to life?

"Ah, sweet Goddess, dear," she said. "You really do intend to kill me."

"Not...exactly," I said. I cleared my throat, and studied the pattern of tattoos that traced their way along Kaye's hairline, not able to meet her piercing gaze. Mab's bones, why did this have to be so hard? "Not permanently, I mean."

"You wish to kill me truly, but not permanently?" she asked, eyebrows reaching up into her headscarf. Oh yeah, I was making a total mess of this. I shot Forneus a pleading look and he, thankfully, came to my rescue.

"Mistress Kaye, it was our hope, Ivy's hope, that in your great wisdom you may possess the knowledge of a potion that would kill you...temporarily," he said. "In order to fulfill the faerie bargain, you must experience a true death, but there is no rule that says you cannot be revived, either my magical or physical means."

"Yeah, what he said," I said. "I could get my hands on a cardiac defibrillator if, for example, you had a potion that stopped your heart."

I winced and looked down at the well-worn table. That sounded callous, even to my ears. I sucked at trying to negotiate killing someone. Though, if I ever got good at it, I'd really start to worry.

Kaye tapped her chin with her wand, deep in thought. She'd pulled the wand from one of the many pockets of her voluminous skirt, and had a tendency to wave it around and punctuate her words by pointing it at us as we talked. She may not need the wand to cast a spell, but the threat was there all the same. Behave or get turned into a toad—got it.

If only I didn't have to ask for her death. Rock on one side, hard place on the other—story of my life.

"If I agree to this lunacy," she said, pointing her wand at me. "And that's a big if, dear, then I would want to use the most effective means possible of revival. But fetching the item that I need will not be easy. It will require a hero's journey."

That sounded about as fun as rolling around in a pixie nest, but I nodded.

"What do you need me to do?" I asked.

I wasn't being overly presumptuous. These days, I was the hero in the room. Trials and tribulations, that was my life.

Years ago, that person would have been Kaye. Someday, when she's older and better trained, Arachne might even step up to the plate. Forneus? Not so much, though the jury was out on Sparky. I was still trying to get over the fact that the cutie was a Tezcatlipocan demon. Try saying that three times fast.

"You must travel to Emain Ablach," she said.

A trip to the Otherworld? To Emain of the Apples? "Just peachy—apple-y, whatever.

"Okaaay, that's doable," I said. "I've been to Mag Mell and back and survived."

"Once there, you must pass Manannán mac Lir, guardian of the sacred isle, and retrieve one of the apples from the silver tree that grows from the grave of his tragic love, Ailinn," she said.

"This Manannán guy, I take it he's no marshmallow?" I asked.

"No," she said. "He is a powerful sea deity. "

"Of course he is," I said. I rubbed my face. "Fine, how do I get to Emain Ablach? Might as well get this party started. We need to converge on the carnival tonight, after it closes for business."

I didn't want to have to wait another full day. Fire imps could do a lot of damage in that amount of time, and I didn't know if Jinx and I had that long.

Kaye narrowed her eyes at me and skewered me with a look.

"Don't be so hasty, Ivy," she said. "There is more you must know."

That's what I was afraid of. Hadn't she ever heard that ignorance is bliss?

"Manannán mac Lir wields Fragarach, The Answerer," she said. "Fragarach can slice through any armor as if it was marzipan, and with the sword at your throat the sea god can force you to tell the truth."

Apparently, they didn't call it The Answerer for nothing.

"Great, sea deity guardian, magic sword, pluck an apple from some dead girl's grave, got it," I said. "Anything else?"

"Manannán mac Lir has the ability to control the mists of Emain Ablach," she said. "Do not believe all that the eyes see."

Yeah, that wasn't cryptic or anything.

"And how do I get to this Emain Ablach?" I asked.

"The ways to the Otherworld are hidden," she said. "You will need a guide to take you."

"You mean Torn, don't you?" I asked.

Kaye nodded and an evil grin spread across Forneus' face. Torn had been flirting ruthlessly with Jinx lately. I'm sure that Forneus had a little payback planned. Too bad I had something else in mind for the demon.

I lifted Sparky from my lap and sighed. It looked like I'd have to hit up my least favorite *cat sidhe* lord for a roundtrip ticket to the Otherworld. Oh, goody.

CHAPTER 35

I left Sparky with Forneus, who wasn't too happy to be on babysitting duty. Forneus would much rather have come with me, but I reminded him that this wasn't the time to get into a pissing contest with Torn. I needed the *cat sidhe* lord to get me safely to Emain Ablach, and back again. He couldn't do that while dodging hellfire.

Sparky hadn't been happy about the arrangement either. The little guy was mewling and clinging to me until I gave him a new glitter pencil and told him to guard Forneus until I returned. I meant guard, as in protect Forneus, but I'm pretty sure from the direction he was pointing his pencil that Sparky thought that the demon attorney was his prisoner.

I snorted and left the two on the corner of Water Street. Forneus was going to try to work reconnaissance while the witches brewed up spells and I went on a sightseeing trip to the Otherworld.

But before I went apple picking, I needed to call in backup. I punched in the number to my burner cell and Ceff answered on the first ring.

"Ivy?" he asked.

"That's my name, don't wear it out," I quipped.

"Oberon's balls, I was worried about you," he said. "Thank Mab, you are hale and whole."

He sounded out of breath, and I winced at the relief in his voice. I probably should have checked in sooner, but I'd been busy.

"I'm fine," I said, stretching the truth a bit. "How goes the battle?"

"The fires are now under control," he said. "I have enlisted the help of my guards and sent word for reinforcements. The humans are fortunate. They would not have fared as well without our water magic."

Yeah, and they'd never know about it either. That was the faerie way, though usually their magic wasn't being used to help the humans. I was proud of Ceff.

"Casualties?" I asked.

"No deaths, though many are being treated for smoke inhalation," he said. "Flynis and her family are safe."

I let out the breath I'd been holding. The *bean tighe* were safe. I smiled.

"Good," I said. "You up for a road trip?"

"Something tells me you do not mean a simple excursion where we ride in an automobile and argue over what radio station to listen to," he said.

"Um, no," I said, with a snort. "Different kind of road trip. More like a hero's journey in which I have to face down a sea deity and steal a magic apple."

"Sea deity?" he asked. "Yes, you will require my help on your quest. Where are you now?"

I gave him my address and cooled my heels while I sent messages to Torn and Master Janus letting them know I'd located Kaye, and in Torn's case, I gave him a heads-up that I'd be stopping by. I figured it was best to cultivate my assets, instead of my usual habit of being a thorn in their backsides. See, a girl can learn.

I felt Ceff before I could see him, a strange new blossoming of my faerie powers that I had yet to understand. It was as if our auras recognized each other and became stronger when intermingled. Ceff's presence buoyed me, and I felt a surge of much-needed energy.

A smile split my face, made even larger by the smell of coffee and the super-sized cups Ceff carried in each hand.

"Is that smile for me or the coffee?" he asked.

He drifted up, leaned against the wall beside me, and handed me the largest cup. I closed my eyes and took a swig of coffee and let the caffeine sing all the way down to my toes. A hot guy and a perfect cup of coffee, maybe this day wasn't so bad after all.

"Both," I said, opening my eyes. "How'd you know I was so desperate for a coffee?"

"You still haven't fulfilled either bargain, to The Green Lady or Sir Gaius," he said. "Which means you are likely beginning to feel the side effects. Delaying a bargain will sap you of your strength, and your symptoms will only worsen over time."

"Then I guess we better get this trip over with," I said.

I tipped my head back and drained the cup of coffee, then tossed it in the nearest trash bin. The caffeine jolt wouldn't last long, not with my half-fae metabolism, all the more reason to get our butts to the Otherworld, pronto.

I filled Ceff in on the details of our upcoming journey as we hoofed it over to the alley where Torn held court. To say he was worried was an understatement, but he never shied away from my request for him to come with me. Jinx may be my best friend and staunchest defender, but Ceff had become an extension of myself, a projection of my mental armor, shielding me from the darkness and pain that was so much a part of my life. Jinx was my sword and Ceff my shield—and I swore to never lose either one.

Too bad I had to keep putting their lives in danger.

Fifteen minutes later, I entered Torn's domain, Ceff's silent, solid presence behind me. It looked just like your typical alley in the city, graffiti-covered brick walls, overflowing trash bins, worn, overturned crates, and the obligatory cats, but people didn't stagger into this alley unless the *cat sidhe* wanted them to.

Humans experience a sense of dread when they venture too near this place, a foreboding that quickens their steps as they pass by. You have to be invited in or you'd never find this entrance to the alley—not unless the *cat sidhe* were looking for a new plaything.

Thankfully, I was on the guest list—and not on the menu.

CHAPTER 36

That didn't keep the bastard from toying with us.

"Ah, princess, I've been expecting you," Torn said, slinking up to me and draping an arm around my waist. "Just couldn't stay away, eh? I do get that a lot. From what I hear, I'm like catnip. Want to roll around and find out?"

With a flick of our wrists, Ceff had his trident aimed at Torn's throat and I had one of my knives pressed against the most precious part of the sidhe lord's anatomy.

"You know the rules, Torn," I said through clenched teeth. "No touching."

"You heard her," Ceff said. "Back off. Now."

I risked a glance at Ceff whose eyes had gone completely black. Oh yeah, he was pissed.

"Fine, fine," Torn said, stepping gingerly away. "It wasn't skin—I don't think you could handle me, princess—but it's not like we haven't touched before. Remember sweetheart?"

Ceff stiffened and I shook my head.

"That was to travel to the Otherworld, not an invitation," I said.

"Ah yes, Mag Mell," he said, with a wink. "Good times."

Actually, it had been downright terrifying. Apparently, my definition of fun and Torn's weren't even close to the same. But I nodded, a slow smile sliding onto my face.

"Ready for another Otherworld adventure?" I asked.

Torn's eyes sparkled and I knew he was interested. Now, I just had to sell it.

"What do you have in mind, princess?" he asked, licking his lips.

"Emain Ablach," I said.

"Ah, if you want to escape to a tropical island, I can think of better places," he said. "There's this one off the coast of Brazil where the women sunbathe nude and..."

"It has to be Emain Ablach," I said. "I hear the apples there are great this time of year."

Torn sighed and crossed his arms.

"This isn't a titillating trip of seduction, is it?" he asked.

"No, nor will it ever be," Ceff said, stepping forward.

"Hey, yeah, we're not going there for the nude sunbathing—obviously—but that doesn't mean this won't be fun," I said. "Just think of all the danger, the peril, the...the..."

"Fine," he said. "You had me at danger. When do you wish to leave?"

I checked my weapons and nodded. "I'm good to go."

"Excellent," he said. Torn tugged a shadow from a crevice in the wall and pulled it out with a flourish.

An arrow buried itself deep in the same wall, inches from my head and I gasped. The fae assassins had found me, and apparently, their orders were to shoot on sight. So much for a trial.

"Hurry up Torn!" I yelled.

He stepped between me and Ceff, an evil grin on his face. "Hold on tight. We're in for a bumpy ride."

That was an understatement.

CHAPTER 37

My first impression of Emain Ablach was that it was wet. Very, very wet. But I didn't have much time to think about that fact. I was too busy drowning.

I struggled to swim to the surface—wherever the hell that was—the weight of my clothes, leather jacket, and weapons weighing me down. My lungs burned and my brain screamed at me to find a way out of this wet torment. I needed air, badly.

I forced my eyes open, salt and whatever else was in the water burning like acid, but being able to see my surroundings didn't help matters. It did, however, make me glad for quick reflexes and muscle memory.

At the first sign of my assassin stalkers, back in a Harborsmouth alley, I'd grabbed one of my throwing knives. I may not be able to throw it now, not in this water, but the pressure of the blade in my gloved hand made it easier to face the grinning corpses smiling back at me.

There were hundreds of them.

Bloated bodies in every state of decomposition drifted at the ends of seaweed infested chains that rose up from the ocean floor. I would have assumed that the people on the ends of those chains were dead, a warning to anyone foolish enough to trespass here, except for the hands reaching outward and the curve of their rotting lips.

Grins like frightened, blue worms curled up toward vacant eyes. The eyes, or what was left of them, were coated with a white film and looked as though they'd been nibbled on by grazing fish. The chained corpses may not be able to see, but I had no doubt that they could sense my presence. Their hands clawed at the water and their faces were all turned in my direction. Perhaps they could scent me, like sharks on a blood trail.

Now that was a cheery thought.

I kicked away, trying to put more distance between myself and the grasping dead. I recoiled as my boot hit something squishy. Mab's bones, I didn't realize there was a chained corpse that close to where I swam. I did not want to touch these things or the chains that bound them. Those were visions I'd never survive.

The delay alone would kill me.

Heart pounding, I propelled myself upward, but I had a nagging suspicion that I wasn't going to make it. I'd sunk too deep into this watery hell. Already my lungs burned and dizziness sent my head spinning like a ride on an otherworldly merry go round. My limbs were cold and heavy and I could barely feel the knife in my hand.

How ironic would it be to die here, within spitting distance of a tree that grew magical apples capable of reviving the dead?

Air bubbles sprung from my nose and I fought not to breathe. Inhaling water would mean my death. I made one more sluggish stroke through the water and felt strong hands grip my waist and haul me upward. I was sailing through the water, away from greedy hands and the hundreds of faces that grinned hungrily after me.

My rescuer was a strong swimmer and I doubted Torn would have gone to so much trouble to save me. I felt a tingle of energy zing through my system, helping me to hold onto the slippery tendrils of consciousness. Ceff, it had to be Ceff.

I gasped as my head broke the surface of the water, gulping air and choking on a mouthful of water. I coughed up phlegm and who knows what else—with those corpses steeping down below, I didn't want to think about it—and pushed wet, bedraggled hair from my face. I was alive, but it wasn't pretty.

I grimaced and pushed the floating evidence of my humiliating coughing fit away. Ceff had a grip on my jacket, still helping to keep my head above the water's surface.

"Are you alright?" he asked.

With his wet hair slicked back from large, dark green eyes and his chiseled jaw, he looked gorgeous. He was completely in his element here, unlike his half-drowned girlfriend.

"I just swallowed a gallon of salty corpse tea and sea monkeys," I said, a rueful grin on my face. "I've been better."

Shivering, I took in our surroundings. From the looks of things, we were in the ocean about half a mile off the coast of an island paradise. The sun was shining, the sky an azure blue that practically screamed for bathing suits and lazy days at the beach. A light breeze caressed my skin, smelling of apple blossoms and something earthier.

I scanned the horizon for threats, but so far there was nothing but me, Ceff, and a tropical utopia. But looks can be deceiving—a lesson I'd learned as a child when my second sight came online in all its nightmare-inducing glory. In fact, the corpses chained somewhere beneath my feet were a testament to that. I may not be able to see them, but that didn't mean they weren't lurking below, waiting for a chance to claw my eyes out.

Speaking of claws...

"Where's Torn?" I asked.

Ceff pressed his lips in a firm line and ran his fingers through wet hair. The movement showed off his chest and arms and I struggled to remain focused. Damn, we really needed a vacation. Maybe when we got home, we could sail down the coast to a real tropical island—one that wouldn't try to keep us as chained pets.

"Torn muttered something about this not being his quest, and cats disliking getting wet, and said that he would meet us on the island," he said.

The scowl on Ceff's face could fill volumes. He wasn't happy about Torn's disappearing act. Neither was I, but there was nothing to be done about it. Torn was a wild card, I'd known that from the beginning.

"So we're on our own," I said with a sigh.

"It would appear so," he said.

"Fine, us it is then," I said. I paddled in a circle, double-checking the surface of the water between us and the island. Nothing had changed since my last scan of the place. "So where's the sea deity who's supposed to guard this place? Think we caught him on vacation?"

The irony of a sea deity hanging up a "gone fishing" sign make me chuckle. Ceff eyed me as if he suspected I may have suffered brain damage from lack of oxygen, but his words were deadly serious.

"Manannán mac Lir will come," he said.

"Okay, then I guess it's time to storm the beach," I said.

The sand and palm trees in the distance looked warm and inviting. There were no gun turrets or razor wire, but that didn't mean this wouldn't get bloody. I eyed the distance to the island and grimaced. I was a strong swimmer, but I'd need to be physically at my best for when Manannán showed up.

"Think you can tow me along?" I asked, holding out the belt that was attached to my leather jacket. Being dragged along by my jacket wouldn't be comfortable, but it'd be better than dying because I was too worn out to fight.

"I have a better idea," he said.

Ceff clenched his jaw and closed his eyes. His muscles rippled and stretched, elongating and moving as a gray coat of fur sprung from his body. He arched his back, sunk beneath the waves, and reappeared as a gorgeous stallion—one with gill slits along its neck, just below the slightly webbed ears. He blew water from his nose and swam closer.

The kelpie bumped against my hip and I got the hint. Looked like my ride was here and ready to go.

I wrapped an arm around Ceff's neck, allowed my body to float as I positioned myself alongside him, and swung a leg over his back. With me astride his scarred back, Ceff rose up so that the top of his body was fully out of the water. Only his powerful legs were submerged.

"Hi ho, Ceffyl, away," I whispered into one of his ears.

Ceff snickered and, with a powerful kick of his legs, we were off. The speed with which we cut through the water was exhilarating and I couldn't help but smile as the breeze and Ceff's magic pulled the water from my soaked clothes.

I flexed my hands and rolled my shoulders. The leather of my jacket and gloves wasn't as supple as it should be, but it hadn't stiffened yet. The salt crusted clothes would likely chafe once I got walking, but I was no longer weighted down by waterlogged gear and I had only a slightly diminished range of motion. It was good enough.

I thought about what we knew of the island's guardian. Manannán mac Lir was a powerful sea deity who could call upon mist to hide his movements and who possessed Fragarach the Answerer, a sword that could cut through anything and force the truth from any throat it threatened. I wasn't too worried about the truth telling part—I didn't plan on talking the guy to death—but the sword that doubled as a Ginsu knife had me shaking in my salt crusted jeans.

That's why I reached for both of my throwing knives when a mist began to form along the surface of the water. It could have been the natural result of the afternoon sun striking the cold, ocean water, but I wouldn't bet on it.

"You see that?" I whispered.

Ceff nodded and kept swimming. The mist grew, becoming so dense that within seconds I lost sight of the island. I had to trust Ceff's sense of direction and hope that we were still headed the right way. I turned my head left and right, pivoting atop Ceff's back to see or hear any sign of Manannán mac Lir.

Sibilant voices seemed to whisper through the mist, and I spun around wondering where our attacker would rear his ugly head. It was like turning the crank of a jack-in-the-box, staring transfixed, knowing that eventually, the creepy clown will leap out. It's just a matter of time.

All around the Mulberry Bush,
The monkey chased the weasel.
The monkey stopped to pull up his sock,
Pop! goes the weasel.

I tightened the grip on my knives. This monkey wasn't getting caught with her socks down. I snuck glances out of the corner of my eyes, hoping that my second sight would give me a clue before the sea deity struck.

My skin began to glow and I cursed myself for thinking about clowns and jack-in-the-boxes. There's nothing like childhood terrors to weaken what little control I had over my wisp powers. But when another childhood thought followed, I invited it in. *Rudolph the red-nosed reindeer, had a very shiny nose...*

It was silly and outrageous and it might just paint a big target on our heads, but then again, it might just work. Or maybe I did spend too much time under the water. Either way, it was worth a shot. I focused on all of my fears, every single thing that had frightened me over the years.

Trust me. I had more than enough nightmare fodder to choose from. Heck, I could have alphabetized them and filled a multi-volume encyclopedia of terrors. Light sprung from my eyes and my skin glowed eerily, cutting through the mist.

There! Light glinted off metal, and I barely had time to duck before a blade sliced through the air where my head had been. Damn, this guy was fast.

Ceff dove beneath the waves and I held on tight, wrapping his mane around one gloved hand while I kept the blade in the other hand held out like a javelin—a very teensy, tiny javelin. I fought to keep my eyes open against the rushing water, using my wisp light to scan the waves for our attacker.

I caught movement to our right and lashed out with my knife, scoring the blade along a man's ribs. I tried for one more backward thrust before we were fully past, but Manannán mac Lir brought his sword up to block the blow and Fragarach split my knife blade as if it were made of wet paper.

I willed Ceff to swim faster, but Manannán spun again and raced toward us, hot on our tail. We broke through the waves and I gulped in air. The mist was gone and I smiled. The beach was there, just meters away. We did it.

Ceff's hooves hit sand and we went from a hard gallop to an abrupt halt so fast it had me tasting blood. But I didn't stop smiling, not until I felt the sword at my back.

CHAPTER 38

Fragarach pressed lightly against my jacket collar and a whimper escaped my lips. The leather collar of my jacket was reinforced with silver mesh, a trick Jenna had taught me to prevent vamp bites and glancing blows, but it would do nothing to keep the sharp edge of that particular sword from my skin. If Manannán mac Lir wanted to decapitate me, all he had to do was press the blade forward. Silver, leather, and bone were no match for the magical blade.

I just hoped he had a steady hand, and didn't sneeze.

I went completely still, even Ceff holding his breath for fear of the blade touching my skin, or taking my head off. I wasn't sure which would be worse. I was sure that a named magic sword would have spilled its fair share of blood over the years. Maybe a quick death would be preferable to the visions that a mere touch would bring.

Not that decapitation was high on my list of ways to go.

"Who dares to tread the path of the silver apple?" Manannán mac Lir asked.

I wanted to quip something from an old Monty Python movie, but they didn't call Fragarach "The Answerer" for nothing. I guess I was sticking with the facts and nothing but the facts.

"Ivy Granger, daughter of a human and Will-o-the-Wisp, and Ceffyl Dŵr, king of the north Atlantic kelpies," I said. "Oh, and our guide, Sir Torn, lord of the Harborsmouth *cat sidhe*."

That is, if the bastard hadn't already run off at the first sign of trouble, or something shiny. Torn leaving us here to die was a distinct possibility.

Manannán mac Lir circled me, never letting the tip of his sword leave my throat. From the sound of Fragarach slicing through leather and skittering along the thin layer of silver mesh lining, I was going to need a new leather jacket when this was over. That pissed me off. This jacket had more scars than I did, but it was mine and it didn't give me unwanted visions when I shrugged it on each day. Breaking in

a new jacket was going to suck and the clurichaun tailoring bill
was going to set me back a month's pay.

I focused on my anger, grabbing hold of the rage and
letting it grow. Fear may be a strong enough emotion to light
me up like an overcooked turducken, but anger would give me
the strength I needed to face Manannán.

The sea deity had made his way into my line of sight, all
eight feet of him. Even riding atop Ceff's back, Manannán mac
Lir managed to tower over me. He was a giant of a man with a
long white beard that would have made him resemble Santa
Claus if he wasn't sporting six pack abs. That was no bowl full
of jelly, that's for sure. He had wide shoulders, a barrel chest,
and arms the size of oak trees. He was naked from the waist
up, except for a cloak draped over his shoulders, and covered in
fish scales to the knee. I suspected that, like mermen, his
lower half probably took the form of a tail when he wasn't on
land. It would explain his speed in the water.

"Why have you come to Emain Ablach?" he asked.
"What do you seek?"

"I need a magic apple to bring my friend back to life," I
said.

Something wistful shifted behind his expression,
replaced quickly with a scowl.

"If your friend is dead, then you are already too late," he
said. "Abandon your quest and leave this place."

"Um, she's not dead yet," I said.

I put a stranglehold on the giggle that tried to force its
way up through my body. Now was no time to lose my head.

Manannán mac Lir's green eyes widened, white
eyebrows reaching up to disappear into his hairline.

"Are you a Seer?" he asked.

"Nope," I said.

"Then how do you know that your friend will die?" he
asked.

"Because I'm the one her enemies sent to kill her," I
said.

His eyes narrowed.

"You would take the life of a friend?" he asked.

"Not if I can help it," I said. "And if I can't, then the
least I can do is bring her back to life. Apparently, your silver
apples can make that happen."

He knew that I was telling the truth. With Fragarach at my throat, I was unable to lie.

"And the kelpie king and *cat sidhe* lord?" he asked

"Ceffyl Dŵr is my official suitor…I love him and he loves me," I said. I blushed, knowing that Ceff could hear every word. Pesky magical sword. "And Torn is an official ally, though I suspect he's here out of boredom rather than obligation."

"A half human, wisp princess bound by love to a kelpie king and in the company of a *cat sidhe*?" he asked. "Never has such a party of adventurers graced these waters."

"Perplexing, isn't it?" a voice asked.

Torn emerged from the shadow of a palm tree, empty hands spread wide as he swaggered toward us. His expression was all innocence, but I knew better. The *cat sidhe* lord had been up to something, I just wasn't sure what. I probably didn't want to know since at least then when the shit hit the proverbial fan I could plead plausible deniability.

With Fragarach the Answerer at my throat, that was likely the best strategy.

I gasped as Manannán swung Fragarach from my throat to Torn's. Mab's bones, I was happy to have room to breathe again, but a little warning would have been nice.

"Who are you to trespass on this isle?" he asked, frowning at Torn.

"Sir Torn, king of cats, lord of the *cat sidhe*," he said.

King of cats? That title was new to my ears. I wondered what it meant, but I wasn't the one asking the questions. I filed it away for later, if there was a later.

Manannán gave Torn a dubious once over. We were probably a sore disappointment for the guardian's expectations for fae royalty.

"Why do you seek the silver apples of Emain Ablach?" he asked.

"I don't," Torn said, shaking his head. "I'm not the hero in this adventure, just the ruggedly handsome guide."

"If you are their guide, as you say, then why did you not take part in the trial of water?" he asked.

Torn shook his head ruefully.

"Cats don't like to get wet," he said with a shrug. "And have you seen what sea salt does to leather?"

Torn waved a hand at his leather pants.

"Why did I not see you on the beach before now?" he asked.

"The beach isn't really my style, I'm more of a shadows kind of guy," Torn said. "Plus, I'd rather not get sand in my trousers. So I went to see Ailinn. The island's defenses are set to deter those seeking the apple, not bored *cat sidhe*, so it was an easy trip. But apparently, Ailinn only shows herself to heroes. So I came back to wait here for these two."

"Ailinn was not at her grave?" he asked, tilting his head to the side.

"No, but like I said, I don't think she appears without a hero present," Torn said.

"I am no hero," Manannán muttered. He looked longingly up the hill in the direction Torn had come. "But I protect her grave in hopes that some day she will appear to me."

"Do you have a message for Ailinn?" I asked.

I was grabbing at straws, but the pain on Manannán's face was real. Love can make a person do crazy things. If the sea deity had taken on the role of guardian to this place in hopes of someday being worthy of a glimpse of his beloved, then maybe he'd be willing to let us pass if we carried a message to her.

Fragarach was back at my throat, but this time I was ready. I suspected that Manannán didn't believe any words spoken without the sword's compulsion. This guy had bigger trust issues than I did, and that's saying a lot.

"You would carry my words to Ailinn?" he asked, a sanguine smile on his lips.

"Yes, if you let us pass," I said. "All I need is your message."

"Tell her...that someday I will be worthy of her forgiveness," he said. "Those exact words."

"I swear it," I said.

Manannán lowered his blade and I slumped forward as the bargain settled heavy on my shoulders.

"Then I wish you luck on your quest," he said. "Safe travels."

"Safe travels," I gasped.

The guardian sheathed Fragarach, spun, and leapt into the ocean at our backs. With the flip of a shimmering tail, the sea deity was gone. Manannán mac Lir was letting us onto the island. I smiled and shook my head. He'd even wished us luck on our quest.

Well, how's them apples?

CHAPTER 39

I upended my boot, dumping sand onto the rocky path, and swore an oath to never wear leather to the beach again. My boots, gloves, and jacket were stiff from my little swim with the corpses and my jeans were caked with salt and sand. My skin was rubbed raw in more places than I could count and we'd only just made it off the beach and onto a path that plunged us into the false night of a thick forest.

Unlike the sunny, tropical beach dotted with palm trees, this place was filled with old growth trees that blocked out the sky as they leaned together in their death throes. I scowled at the murky path ahead. It was hedged in by a wall of writhing brambles, some with thorns bigger than an ogre chieftain's tusk.

Going through the wall of thorns was not an option. There was nowhere to go except to follow the path ahead—a path choked with webs. Spiders, why did it have to be spiders?

"Torn, what the hell?" I asked. I yanked on my boot and pointed one of my blades at the webs that crisscrossed our path. "I thought you came this way already. What could weave those webs that fast?"

Please don't say spider fae. Please, please, please.

"Like I've been trying to tell you, princess," he said. "I wasn't here for the apples, so the island wasn't hostile to me. There was a different path that led right through those briars."

I narrowed my eyes at the wall of thorns, but the path was no longer there. Neither was the one leading back to the beach. Well, fuck a duck.

Ceff—who had changed back to his humanoid form once our encounter with the sea deity was over—went over to the twisting vines and poked at them with the tip of his trident. A thick tendril lashed out in a blur of motion, snapping its thorns within an inch of Ceff's retreating hand.

"Avoid the local flora," he said.

"You think?" I asked, rolling my eyes.

I hadn't planned on touching anything in this godforsaken place anyway, but I inched closer to the center of the trail.

"As for the webs," Torn said, licking his lips. "I'm thinking spider fae."

Crap, I knew it. I may have taken up moonlighting as fae pest control lately, but so far I hadn't been asked to clear out any spider fae nests. I'd counted myself lucky that the urban jungle I call home wasn't their favorite nesting grounds. Judging from the webs that clung to every surface, I was guessing creepy, old forests were more to their liking.

"That's what I was afraid of," I grumbled.

I slid one of my throwing knives back into its wrist sheath and pulled a machete from where I kept it nestled in the small of my back. It was a new addition to my utility belt, one I'd rather not have to use. I preferred throwing knives, since they allowed me to keep a safe distance, but if I had to get up close and personal, the machete was a better option than one of my daggers. The blade was too long to be street legal, heck it handled like a sword, but it had a better chance of keeping my enemies at arm's length than my daggers did and the iron in the blade would be effective against fae.

It also was a useful tool for chopping through the threads of spider webbing as big around as my wrist. With a throwing knife ready in my other hand, I began hacking a path.

We'd cleared a couple hundred yards of web when I felt the first drops hit my leather jacket.

"Rain, seriously?" I asked. "How can this get any worse?"

"You just had to ask, didn't you, princess?" Torn asked, voice thick with sarcasm.

"That is not rain," Ceff said, pointing to a hole in my jacket. "Last I knew, even the poisoned human world does not have acid rain that destructive."

They both looked up and I followed their wide-eyed gaze to the trees thick with web above our heads. I wished I hadn't. I tightened the grip on my knives as eight beady eyes stared back at me.

Apparently, whacking at the spider fae's web had rung the dinner bell. If I'd taken the time to think about how spiders hunt their prey, I wouldn't have been surprised. Not

that we'd had much choice. The island knew we were here for
the silver apples and now we were the flies in the spider's web.

Yanking our weapons from the sticky strands we'd been
cutting, we each took a step away from the web until we stood
weapons out, back to back. Before the web even stopped
vibrating, ten more spiders crept toward us. The largest
spider, still hovering over our heads, descended further down
its thread. We were surrounded.

"Anybody got any ideas?" I whispered.

"Besides run like hell, not really, princess," Torn
muttered.

"What do we know of the spider fae, any weaknesses?" I
asked.

"It depends on the type," Ceff said. "As with regular
spiders, the spider fae are varied. At a guess, I would say these
are similar to black widows."

As we talked, the spider fae converged on the area of
disturbed web, but they didn't attack. Not yet.

"Okay, I have an idea," I said. "Whatever you do, don't
move."

Slowly, I shifted my blades to one hand and detached a
water balloon from my utility belt. The holy water inside the
balloon wouldn't harm the spider fae, it was loaded for demon,
but I was testing a theory. I palmed the balloon, raised my
arm, and lobbed it to our left.

Spindly legs skittered along the sticky web, carrying the
orb-shaped bodies of the spiders at astounding speed. The
spider fae chased the balloon, rearing up and pouncing on it.
They tore the balloon to shreds, fighting over the measly
meal—all except for the giant spider above our heads.

"How did you know they'd go after it?" Torn asked.

"Lucky guess," I said, remembering not to shrug at the
last second. "I figured if they hadn't attacked already, it might
be because they couldn't see us, or rather feel us."

"They hunt by following the vibrations in their web,"
Ceff said.

"Appears so," I said.

I carefully tugged a lighter and a lump of raw iron from
my pocket.

"On my mark, run as fast as you can, weapons out," I
said. I flicked my eyes to the giant spider that continued to
dangle over our heads. "I'll create a diversion behind us, but

we need to clear the web ahead. I'm guessing fire will work faster than cutting our way through, and it's too late to worry about pissing off the island. Ceff take the lighter and set as much of this on fire as you can. Torn watch his back. I'll take care of our drippy friend."

I pointed up and Ceff and Torn grunted their agreement. It wasn't a foolproof plan, but it was a start. I slipped the iron from its protective covering, took a deep breath, and heaved it with all my strength, throwing it as far behind us as I could.

Ceff and Torn sprinted forward, hacking and burning their way through the web. At our movement, the spider above us dropped further down the silk thread, its mandibles dripping venom onto the path at my feet. With a flick of the wrist, I threw one of my knives, striking the spider in a cluster of eyes. It shrieked and tore at its face, trying to dislodge the knife.

I took the machete in both hands, leapt up, and whacked the dangling spider, splitting open its abdomen like an ichor filled piñata. As soon as I hit the ground, I rolled to the side, away from the sizzling pile of goo.

The spider shrieked again, its cries mingling with the hisses and squeals of its friends. The other spider fae were learning the hard way not to eat cold iron. But after seeing the effects on the first few, the other spiders were getting savvy to my trick—and were spinning this way.

"They're coming!" I shouted.

"It is burning too slowly," Ceff said. "We will have to stand and fight."

"You make that sound like a bad thing," Torn said, a predatory look on his face.

Ceff and Torn may be ready to fight, but we were seriously outnumbered. I'd been lucky with the first spider fae, having the element of surprise on my side, but that advantage was long gone and I was pretty sure that none of us would survive a single spider bite. If only the web would burn faster.

Burn, damn you, burn! Heart racing, skin glowing, my power raced up to the surface and the small fires that Ceff had set with my lighter exploded into balls of flame.

"What in the shadows?" Torn yelped, brushing at a singed patch of fur that dangled from his ear.

Wide-eyed, I reached for the power that poured from me and focused on the web choked path ahead. *Burn, burn it all, burn it to the ground.* Flames leapt, heat knocking me to my knees. I pulled my shirt over my nose and mouth and crawled forward. Tears blurred my vision and smoke choked the air.

I looked behind us to see the spider fae waving their legs and chomping their mandibles at the shimmering air. The flames were keeping our attackers at bay, but that wouldn't last. We had to get out of here. I scrambled forward, letting out a shriek of my own when a hand grabbed my jacket and pulled me forward.

"Come, we must hurry," Ceff said.

"Wha..." I nodded, a cough cutting off my words. I pointed to the spider fae behind us and Ceff shook his head.

"Leave them to Torn," he said.

I raised an eyebrow, but he just shook his head and pulled me to my feet. My lungs screamed at me as we ran, spots forming before my eyes a sure sign that I wasn't getting enough oxygen.

We made it to the top of a shallow rise, above the worst of the smoke, when I heard the groan and snap of wood. We ran faster, Torn close on our heels as a huge tree fell behind us, blocking the trail. As the first spider climbed onto the fallen tree, the dead wood burst into flames. That should keep them busy for awhile.

As I watched, the silhouette of the injured spider fell onto its back, legs curling inward. That was one opponent we wouldn't have to deal with later. As I turned to go, I saw the legs of the other spiders reaching for it—not to rescue it from the flames, but to devour its corpse. I don't imagine that spider fae woke up this morning wanting to become dinner for his brothers, but I knew better than most that you don't always get what you want.

But if you try sometimes, you just might find...you get what you need.

CHAPTER 40

I bent down, hands on my knees and coughed, spitting out a mouthful of soot and phlegm.

"You going to be alright, princess?" Torn asked. "That won't hold them forever."

He pointed at the wall of flame rising up from the felled tree that blocked the path at our backs. I sighed, ran my tongue along my teeth and spit the last of the soot and ash from my mouth.

I needed the *cat sidhe*'s nagging like I needed a hole in the head. My head pounded with each word.

"Yeah, I'm fine," I said.

I kept my expression wry, but inside I was reeling. My wisp power had fueled the flames, which was something I didn't know was possible. It wasn't a bad skill, if I could ever figure out how to do it again. I shook my head. No time to worry about that now.

I straightened and surveyed the trail ahead. The worst of the sticky web had burned, leaving drifting piles of ash and puddles of sticky goo at our feet. The wall of thorns wriggled, forming sooty clouds as they shook off debris. The brambles may not have burned, but they looked like they'd been dragged through Hell and back.

My companions didn't look much better.

Torn's collection of feathers and fur, that normally adorned his leather clothes and hung from his scarred ears, were singed and smoking. Soot streaked Ceff's face and he'd lost his shirt somewhere along the way. We looked like soldiers limping into battle, and perhaps we were. We still hadn't faced Ailinn and her magic apples.

"Come on," I said, ignoring Ceff's sideways glance. "Torn's right for once. We need to get a move on."

Ceff took the lead with Torn bringing up the rear. That left me in the middle, a position I normally would have argued with. The middle was for the weakest link, but right now I had to admit that I wasn't up for more fighting. As the last of the adrenaline washed from my system, I felt all the aches, pains, and fatigue of the day's trials—and the weight of the faerie bargain that siphoned off what little strength I had left.

We walked for what felt like an hour, but was probably more like five minutes when Ceff called a halt. We'd found the spider fae's nest.

As Ceff and Torn scanned the area for threats, I took in the grisly scene. Apparently, this was where the spider fae kept their food. I shivered and rubbed my arms, surveying the larder full of tasty snacks.

Cocoon shrouded skeletons hung like macabre decorations from the branches of moldering trees. Some of the cocoon shrouded bodies had dropped to the ground in a heap, too much of a burden for the rotten, worm-eaten wood.

As I examined one such bundle where it protruded from the ground, leaves and mulch writhed and heaved, swallowing the body deeper into the earth. My stomach roiled and I looked away.

Okay, right, stick to the path.

Ceff waved me forward and we continued past the bodies. But just as we were about to turn the bend, I caught movement to our right. Ceff and Torn hadn't found any spider fae, but that didn't mean there were none here.

I strafed left, blades out and at the ready, but it wasn't a spider. It was one of the cocoons. It was moving.

"Ceff, wait!" I said. "I think this one's alive."

"Come on, princess," Torn said, bringing up the rear. "We haven't got all day. Time moves differently in the Otherworld, you know that."

I did know that from my experience in Mag Mell. If we dallied too long here, there was a chance that we'd return too late to save Jinx or the city. It was one of the things that I'd worried about since being plunged into this place, but it didn't change the fact that someone was trapped here. I couldn't just leave them like that.

"We can't leave them here to die," I said, testing the ground with the toe of my foot as I inched to the edge of the trail and toward the writhing bundle.

"Sure we can," Torn said, tossing his hands in the air. "Just keep walking."

Ceff gave Torn a glare and came to stand at my side.

"Here," he said. "I'll hold them still while you cut through the cocoon."

"Have you both lost your minds?" Torn asked.

"What would you have us do, leave them here to become spider food?" I asked.

"Yes," he said. "Yes, exactly. It's the cycle of life, a beautiful thing best left alone."

I shook my head.

"That could have been any one of us," I said. "Hold still, we're here to help!"

The last I yelled at the cocoon. I didn't know if the person inside could hear me, or how far gone they were if they could, but I had to try to comfort them. Plus, I really didn't want to risk maiming the person I was trying to save.

"You have no idea what kind of monster is inside that thing," Torn said.

I scowled at Torn. No one deserved to be hung out like prosciutto and gobbled up by some huge spider.

"This is a hero's path," Ceff said. "It is highly probable that they are honorable. If not, at least we tried."

Torn sighed and shook his head.

"Fine, it's your funeral," he said.

"Ready?" Ceff asked, holding the bundle as still as he could.

"I was born ready," I said, doing my best tough guy impersonation.

I carefully cut away at the tough fibers of the cocoon. Almost there...

Thousands of baby spider fae poured out of the cocoon, skittering in every direction. Except it wasn't a cocoon. It was an egg. I screamed—though I'd deny it if I lived long enough for Torn to tell anyone—and stumbled away from the horde of spiders. So much for my tough guy act.

I stomped on the spiders as I backed away, halting their progress. A brave one ambled forward and sank it's dripping mandibles into its nearest kin. The other spiders followed suit, joining in the feeding frenzy.

"Oh, look, aren't they cute?" Torn asked, pointing to where baby spiders were busy cannibalizing each other.

"Freaking adorable," I growled.

I inched further up the trail, relieved to see that most of the spiders were too busy attacking each other to notice my retreat.

"Perhaps we should have listened to the *cat sidhe*, just this once," Ceff said, whacking the more determined stragglers with his trident.

"I told you so, princess," Torn said.

I flexed my fingers, hands itching to wring the *cat sidhe*'s neck and wipe that smug look off his face. Instead, I stormed past him and around the corner. I'd had it with this place and its creepy inhabitants. We needed to find Ailinn's grave, grab a magic apple, and get the hell out of dodge.

CHAPTER 41

Judging by the eldritch glow coming from the burial mound in the clearing ahead of us, we'd come to the right place. The silver tree heavily laden with magic apples might also have been a hint.

"So what's the plan?" Torn asked.

"We walk up there and pick an apple," I said.

"Not much of a plan," he said.

I shrugged. It's hard to plan when you have no idea what the universe is going to throw at you, but going by my track record it was probably going to be something nasty.

"I will scout ahead," Ceff said. "If we use every caution, then we may be able to climb the hill unnoticed."

I doubted his assessment, but I kept my pessimism to myself.

"We're just going to sneak up there and steal the apple?" Torn asked.

"That's the idea," I said.

"Well, that sounds bloody boring," he muttered.

I snorted. I'd be more than happy if this was boring.

"Sorry it's not to your liking, Torn," I said. "If it's any consolation, there's always a plan B."

"And what's that?" he asked.

"Stab first, ask questions later," I said.

"I like that plan," he said, lips lifting in a grin.

I snorted and tiptoed forward to follow Ceff, but my good humor didn't last more than a step into the clearing. It should have been a relief to leave the wall of thorns behind. After we'd passed spider fae territory, the brambles had towered more than ten feet above our heads and the individual vines had become more aggressive. But as much as I was happy to leave the narrow tunnel of encroaching, carnivorous plants, I wasn't thrilled at climbing the path to Ailinn's grave.

A chill ran icy fingers up and down my spine.

"Well, that looks inviting," I muttered.

Ravens circled the mound while one industrious bird pecked at a bloated body that hung from the tree. Its attempts to pluck an eyeball from one corpse shook the tree hard enough that a second corpse fell to the ground with a meaty thud. The other birds descended with raucous cries and tore the body apart. They swallowed strips of flesh and tossed the bones to roll down the hill—to join the mass open grave of hundreds, perhaps thousands, of bodies.

"Not very homey, is it princess?" Torn asked, nudging a ribcage with the toe of his boot.

"Nope," I said, shaking my head.

I strode forward and cringed as bones crunched like cockroaches beneath my feet. But I kept walking, a throwing knife in each hand. Ceff was scouting just ahead, using his trident to check the footing before stepping gingerly through the maze of bones. I didn't know how he could stomach walking through this boneyard with bare feet. It was bad enough stepping on the dead while wearing thick soled boots.

I bit my lip and skirted around a skull the size of a boulder, not willing to climb over it like Ceff had done. I didn't want to touch anything in this place. I had a nagging suspicion that all of those who died here had experienced a horrible death and that was something I didn't need to share—not if I was going to make it out of here with my sanity intact.

I was so focused on dodging the skull that I didn't even see the femur underfoot. In fact, it was as if the ground shook with a mini quake that threw me momentarily off balance. I hooked the femur with the toe of my boot and tripped. Heart racing, I threw out my hands hoping to brace my fall, but I couldn't release the death grip I had on my knives. I was headed face first into the pile of nightmare infused bones...

"Whoa there, princess," Torn said. He grabbed the back of my jacket, holding me at an angle, mere inches from the ground. "I know you're tired, but it's not naptime yet. Not unless you want to end up like those guys."

Yeah, right, like I was just going to lie down and curl up with a bunch of skeletons. I scowled and got my feet under me, careful to touch as little as possible.

"Don't worry, Torn," I deadpanned. "I never lie down on the job."

I forced my fingers to release their death grip on my knives, slid them back into their sheaths, brushed off my pants, and took a shaky breath.

"Good," he said with a smirk on his face. The ground heaved again, not my imagination this time, and I spun to see what Torn was pointing at over my shoulder. "Because things finally just got interesting."

CHAPTER 42

"What the hell are those things?" I asked, palming my knives.

It had been foolish to put my weapons away, even if it had only been for a measly ten seconds. In my life, that's all the time it took for Fate to dump me in a handbasket and send me on a one way trip to somewhere fiery.

"Duergar!" Ceff yelled.

"Duergar?" I asked.

"Malicious, bloodthirsty goblins, princess," Torn said. His slit pupil cat's eyes flashed and his fingers extended into long, deadly looking claws. He licked his lips and grinned. "Like I said, things just got interesting."

Great, evil goblins, just what I needed. Three of the grey-skinned creatures crawled up out of the ground, coming from tunnels that emitted a faint, green glow. The tunnel entrances were cleverly camouflaged, hidden beneath piles of skeletal remains. But now that I knew they existed, I knew what to look for. I had no idea how many duergar lived in the warrens below—the barrow was large enough to house plenty of the nasty goblins—but I figured we'd better watch our backs.

"Uh, plan B?" I asked.

"Thought you'd never ask," Torn said.

Ceff sidled to the right, trying to flank the duergar. He held his trident out in front of his body and he moved with liquid grace. Torn, claws extended and arms hanging loosely at his sides, padded to my left. With a blood-curdling war cry, the duergar sprinted toward us, weapons held aloft.

I focused on the largest goblin, a grotesque creature with a protruding lower jaw and pustule covered lips, holding a spiked club caked with blood and gore. I breathed in and on the exhale tossed one of my throwing knives to spin end over end and sink deeply into his chest. He paused, looking down at his chest, giving Ceff the opportunity to skewer him in the back with his trident.

The duargar to my left howled as Torn raked his claws down the goblin's face with one hand. The *cat sidhe* plunged his second hand into the goblin's belly, disemboweling him in one stroke. My stomach twisted as ropey, pink intestines spilled to the ground, but I didn't have time to puke.

I hadn't forgotten about the smaller goblin, but he still managed to sneak up on me. He was damned fast. He grinned, close enough now to count his needle-like teeth. I tossed my second throwing knife, but it glanced off his shoulder armor without even slowing him down.

Heart racing, I grabbed a dagger from my boot and stood my ground. Running wouldn't do me any good, not with the tangle of bones underfoot. Beady, red eyes raced toward me and I shifted my weight onto the balls of my feet. The goblin lunged, sword nearly taking off my head, but I spun left and drove the iron and silver dagger into his hip.

The goblin shrieked and came at me again. Sweat dripped into my eyes, blurring my vision and I pulled my backup dagger from its spine sheath. I nearly fell when the hilt caught on the tattered collar of my jacket—damn Fragarach to hell—but I managed to keep my feet under me and the weapon in hand.

If Jenna had taught me one thing, it was never drop your weapon. The Hunter was a damned good teacher. But I couldn't keep this up, not for long. I was already too fatigued and I was running out of weapons. I raised my dagger to block the goblin's falling sword—and hit the ground hard.

The wind knocked out of me, I blinked trying to make sense of my new vantage point. I looked up into Ceff's blood spattered face.

"Wha, what happened?" I asked, gasping for breath.

"Thought you could use a hand, princess," Torn said, grinning over Ceff's shoulder.

I could barely hear him over the beating of my heart and the constant squawking of the nearby ravens. Throughout the entire fight, the birds never stopped their squabbling over carrion. Who knows, maybe they were cheering us on, waiting to eat whoever lost the fight.

"I was doing alright on my own," I said.

"Yeah, well, thanks for keeping this one busy," he said.

He held up a gore covered head. I shivered recognizing the red, beady eyes and needle sharp teeth of my attacker. I may not like to admit it, but that had been close. Too close.

Ceff stood and pulled me up with him, looking me over from head to toe. I couldn't help but do the same. His bare chest was splattered with blood, but it didn't look like any of it was his.

"You okay?" I asked.

"Yes, though you nearly gave me a heart attack," he said. "I did not think that I would reach you in time."

"I never doubted you for a second," I whispered in his ear.

He smiled and my stomach tightened, warmth spreading through my body. I shook my head and smiled back. Ceff was dead sexy, even covered in gore.

"Come on, let's blow this popsicle stand," I said, voice ringing loudly in the silence.

Panic spun up through me as the realization hit—the ravens had gone silent as the grave. I tilted my head up to see a woman beckoning to us from the top of the burial mound. This was it, the end of the line. I just hoped Ailinn would be more hospitable than the duergar. Ceff raised an eyebrow and I nodded.

I kept my eyes on the woman, Ailinn I presumed, retrieved my weapons, and hurried up the hill. With Torn at my back, I strode forward, following Ceff up the gore strewn path. I swayed on my feet, but I kept putting one foot in front of the other until we stood beneath the silver apple tree.

The ravens watched from where they'd perched on the hanging bodies and skeletal, silver tree branches and I stifled a shiver.

"The king and the would-be queen," Ailinn said. "As it was prophesied, as it was written, as it was seen."

This chick was the first ghost I'd ever seen—in fact, I thought ghosts were a fiction created by delusional humans with overactive imaginations—but she definitely fit the bill. Her spectral form wavered above the grave, eyes dark pits in a face sad and forlorn, and her words were creepy as hell.

"Are you Ailinn?" I asked.

The ghost nodded and tilted her head to the side. It wasn't a human gesture, not at all. She reminded me of old

vamps, the ones who had been undead so long that they'd
forgotten what it was like to be alive.

"Then I have a message for you, from Manannán mac
Lir," I said. She hissed, but I continued on. I'd made a promise
to deliver the message. I flicked my eyes to the bodies dangling
from the tree behind her and swallowed hard. I just hoped she
didn't decide to hang the messenger. "He said to tell you that
someday he will be worthy of your forgiveness."

Tears oozed down her face to hit the ground like clots of
congealed blood.

"He waits for me?" she asked.

"He's the guardian of this island…" I said. "I assumed
you knew that."

"You know what they say about assuming, princess,"
Torn said. "It makes an ass out of…"

"Shut it, Torn," I said with a growl.

Oberon's eyes, that cat would be the death of me.
Thankfully, Ailinn was too busy processing my message to take
offense to Torn's snarky comments.

"I thought…I thought he was dead," she said. "I could
not live without Manannán, so I took my own life, so that we
may join together in the afterlife. But I could not find him, he
did not come."

"I don't think he ever left," I said.

"I assumed he did not love me," she said.

I glared at Torn and he stifled a giggle.

"True love endures all things," Ceff said. "Even death."

A chill ran up my spine and I grabbed his hand. Even
with my gloves on, it wasn't like me to be all touchy feely, but
his words made me want to hold him close, and never let go.

The ghost smiled and began to fade.

"Hurry," she said. "Take the apples. You will need
them for the trials that lay ahead."

She held out her hands, pointing to the silver apples
hanging behind her. I pulled a drawstring bag from my jacket
pocket and held it open. I plucked an apple from the tree, and
as the apple dropped into the bag, Ailinn disappeared. But I
could hear her voice ringing in my ears.

Now go, leave this place and never return.

"Um, princess?" Torn asked.

The ground shook and the silver tree began to wither.
Apples rotted and fell to the ground as if caught on time lapse

film. Ailinn's ghost was gone, finally able to leave this place. I was happy for her, but I had a bad feeling that she had been the sustaining force of this island. Without her spirit here to hold it together, Emain Ablach was falling apart.

Torn reached for a shadow, plucking it from where it hid beneath a shifting pile of bones. On impulse, I grabbed one of the half rotten apples from the ground and tossed it into the bag. I didn't know if the rotten apple had any magic left, probably not, but it was worth a shot. You never know when you'll need an ace, or an apple, up your sleeve.

"Let us breathe this popsicle stand," Ceff said.

Torn pulled the shadow around us, preparing for our return trip to Harborsmouth, but I laughed hard, tears springing to my eyes.

"It's blow," I wheezed. "Let's *blow* this popsicle stand."

I wrapped an arm around my stomach, body shaking with laughter. Ceff and Torn looked at me like I was nuts, but, hey, with a life as crazy as mine, you take pleasure in the little things.

CHAPTER 43

We appeared in a different alley than the one we'd left from, thank Mab. That was good thinking on Torn's part. When we traveled to Emain Ablach, we'd left behind a firing squad of fae assassins. I was happy not to be going toe-to-toe with the Moordenaar, not while shivering from fatigue and a case of the giggles.

A glance at what was left of my leather jacket was enough to stop my laughter dead in its tracks. The leather was stiff and crusted with white rings of salt from my dip in the corpse-filled sea of Emain Ablach. The collar was sliced where Manannán mac Lir had held Fragarach the Answerer to my throat. There were holes big enough to put my fist through where the leather had been eaten away by spider venom and I was dripping goblin blood all over the cracked pavement at our feet.

A sound escaped my lips that sounded suspiciously like a sob.

"Here, let me clean you off," Ceff said.

Ceff's eyes glowed faintly as he used his water magic to pull moisture from the air. I held myself rigid as water flowed over me, washing away the worst of the blood and gore. But nothing could ever wash me clean. My lungs tightened and it hurt to breathe.

I forced a deep breath and closed my eyes. I was shutting out the reality of my battle ragged clothing, but the feelings that held my chest in a vice stemmed from more than a ruined jacket.

I'd killed spider fae and duergar today without a second thought. Sure, they were vicious killers themselves, but they were living, breathing creatures. When had taking lives become so easy?

"Better?" he asked.

I nodded and looked away. It was a relief not having to worry about touching my own clothes without risking a vision, but that wasn't the reason I was on the verge of tears. I

wanted to explain that to Ceff, unload some of the guilt that
was bubbling to the surface, but I couldn't trouble him with
that now. Because if I started, I didn't think I could stop—and
this wasn't the time or place to fall apart.

"Yeah, I'm good," I said, lying through my teeth.

"Good," he said, eyeing me warily. "Now who was
shooting at you back there, before we traveled to Emain
Ablach?"

Oh, right, the faerie assassins. Another thing that I'd
put off talking to Ceff about.

"The Moordenaar," Torn said, answering for me.

Ceff blanched.

"Then the courts have discovered your secret," he said.
"They have marked you as a traitor."

"Yeah, sorry, I was going to tell you...I just ran out of
time," I said.

My faced burned. That sounded lame, even to me. I
could have told Ceff about the Moordenaar while we traipsed
through the forest hacking away at spider webs, but I hadn't.

I let my messy hair fall into my face, shielding me from
Ceff's strained smile. I should have told him about the
Mooredaar sooner.

Ceff cleared his throat and I forced myself to meet his
watery gaze.

"They will not stop until you are dead," he said.

He was right. The Mooredaar are trained assassins,
zealots who believe wholeheartedly in wiping out those who
threaten the secrets of the faerie courts. They will come for
me, and eventually, they'd kill me. That truth sucked, turned
the blood in my veins to ice, but shaking in my boots wouldn't
help us. I tightened my hands into fists and gave Ceff a curt
nod.

"Well, they can get in line with the rest of the creeps
who want something from me," I said. "I doubt the glaistig
would appreciate them destroying her tool before she has a
chance to use up her two bargains."

Feeling sorry for myself, me? Okay, maybe just a little.
It had been a rough two days, and the battle was far from over.
At least I hadn't gone fetal like the gibbering voice in my brain
kept suggesting.

"You could seek sanctuary with The Green Lady," he
said. "Many of the carnival fae cannot create a glamour, but

the glaistig has special dispensation from Mab and Oberon to rule over her kingdom as she sees fit. Humans think that the oddities of the carnival are just part of an elaborate parlor trick and since they do not believe the carnival fae are real, fae who cannot control their powers are allowed to live there. You would no longer be considered a threat to the faerie courts if you removed yourself from the human world."

He held his body rigid, his face an impassive mask, but I could sense how difficult this was for him. If I sought sanctuary with the glaistig, I would become her lapdog. I would survive, but my ties to friends and family would be severed. The relationship that Ceff and I had only just begun would be over the moment I knelt and swore fealty to The Green Lady.

We both knew it, but he said the words just the same. He didn't want to lose me, but he also didn't want to see me die. And he obviously didn't trust his ability to keep me safe against the Moordenaar.

"No," I said, shaking my head. "I'm not a follower. I'd rather die first."

"Well, princess," Torn said. "You might just get your wish."

Ouch. Leave it to Torn to go for the jugular.

"Yeah, well, it might be preferable to what the glaistig has in store for me," I said. "I might be able to weasel my way out of our first bargain, but I still owe her one more favor of her choosing. Whether I swear fealty to her or not, I'm still bound to the woman—as much as I hate to admit it. And I doubt she'll be as easy to fool the next time."

"Too bad Ailinn didn't give you two apples," Torn said. "You could fool the glaistig by bringing your witch friend back and release yourself from your second bargain with the glaistig."

"Wait, what?" I asked. "How could an apple get me out of my bargain?"

Ceff and Torn didn't know about the second apple I'd grabbed on our way out of Emain Ablach, the half rotten twin safely tucked away in my jacket with its silver sibling. Until I fully understood what Torn was getting at, I wasn't sharing that little secret.

Torn rolled his eyes.

"Because, princess, dying gives you a clean slate," he said. "It's drastic, sure, but it's also possible if, you know, you had a way to come back to life."

Like if I had a magic apple.

I gently bit my lip, a plan already forming in my mind. I'd kill myself and use the apple to bring me back. I had, in fact, grabbed that second apple, but it was rotten and may not work. But that was okay, because if dying absolved me of my bargains, then I didn't have to kill Kaye. She didn't have to die—only one of us did.

But why hadn't anyone thought of this sooner? Did Ceff know about that little loophole? I looked over to see Ceff wince. Oh yeah, he knew. Who else knew about this?

"Does Kaye know that there's a way for me to break the bargain without her having to die?" I asked.

"Maybe," Torn said. "But then again, maybe not. It's not something we go around advertising to the supernatural world. And most fae can't bring themselves to fight the rules of a bargain. But I'm thinking with your mixed blood and pain in the ass stubbornness, you might be crazy enough to give it a shot."

If this worked, I'd be out from under that second bargain I owed The Green Lady. And if it didn't, well I wouldn't be around to find out what kind of nastiness the glaistig and the Moordenaar had planned for me.

"Kaye wouldn't have to die," I said.

"Ivy, please," Ceff said.

"No, you know I have to do this," I said. "You said it yourself, I'm a hero."

Today I'd gone on a hero's journey to Emain Ablach, faced a sea deity with a legendary sword, plucked a magic apple from the grave of Ailinn, and lived to tell about it. I was a hero—and heroes don't let their friends die in their place.

CHAPTER 44

Too bad Kaye had other ideas.

"We will both die and ride the apples back to life," she said. "It is obvious that's why Ailinn's spirit gave you two apples."

I wasn't so convinced.

"She may have told me to take the apples, plural, but I was the one who grabbed the second one off the ground—it's not like she handed it to me on a golden platter," I said. "And it's half rotten, so it probably won't even work."

We'd left Torn to deploy his network of *cat sidhe* spies to keep an eye out for the Moordenaar and proceeded to take a circuitous route to The Emporium, hoping to keep any potential assassins off our trail. But it was a brief reprieve. If I'd known how difficult Kaye was going to be, I might have tried doing this without her help. If nothing else, I should have listened to Torn's parting advice—don't piss off the witch.

The moment Ceff and I arrived Kaye grilled me for details on our trip to Emain Ablach. She demanded that I tell her everything that Ailinn said, word for freaking word—over and over again. She also wrung the truth from me about the second apple. Ever since then, she'd berated me about how this was going to go down—and I didn't like her plan, not one bit.

"Oberon's eyes, Kaye, I don't even know why we're having this conversation!" I yelled.

I breathed hard, trying to get my temper under control. Here I was, trying to do the right thing, and Kaye was bucking me every step of the way. It was enough to drive a girl insane.

My death would give me a clean slate, cancelling out both of my bargains with The Green Lady. Once that happened, I would be under no obligation to kill Kaye. Sure, not having sealed Kaye's actual death would make entering the carnival grounds nearly impossible, but that was a chance I had to take.

I'd use the fire imps as a distraction, and if I got caught on carnival grounds without permission, I'd face the consequences.

"Stop being so stubborn, girl," Kaye said. "You know you need my help, so let me do my part."

"But why?" I said. "I get you helping me and protecting the city from the fire imps at the same time, but you don't even like Jinx. Why help me gain access to the incubus?"

"Revenge, dear," she said. "That goat woman demanded my death. You could say we have a debt to settle."

Kaye's dark eyes glinted, lips pulling up into a grin, and I stifled a shiver. Torn was right. Don't piss off the witch. I sure as hell hoped I didn't end up on Kaye's bad side. But that didn't keep me from taking the rotten apple for myself.

If Kaye was crazy enough to follow through with this plan, I'd at least give her the best possible chance at survival. She just didn't know it yet.

"Fine," I said. "It's your funeral—literally—so how do you want to do this?"

"I have just the potion," she said. "Though I never thought I'd be drinking it myself."

Poison, we were talking about poison. My gut twisted and I tamped down the fear that rose in my throat.

"Will it be painful?" I asked.

"No, dear," she said. "You won't feel a thing."

"Arachne, come give me a hand," she said, pointing to her purple-haired apprentice. "Fetch a bottle of wine."

I watched Kaye and Arachne brew a death potion and mix it with wine. Kaye was smiling and chatting as if she were teaching the kid how to bake cookies. Meanwhile, Jinx slept in the spell circle covered in the blanket that Forneus had covered her with just hours before. The entire scene was so surreal that it was hard to believe that any of this was really happening.

Ceff came to stand beside me, his silent presence giving me strength. We stood like that for awhile, just enjoying being close to one another.

"I love you," he said.

I blinked away tears and gave Ceff a wan smile.

"I know," I said. "I love you too."

I wanted to reach out to touch Ceff, to have him fold me in his arms and pull me close, but I didn't have time to experience the visions of his tragic past. So I leaned against the counter, hands fisted at my sides. I'd wanted to get away with Ceff, spend a few days somewhere peaceful, just the two of us. Now, there was a chance that may never happen.

The rap of metal against metal brought me out of my brooding thoughts with a start. Kaye was beating a large spoon against the cauldron she'd carried from the stove and set on the counter between us. Mab's bloody bones, this was really going to happen.

I was going to die, and eat a magic apple to come back to life—if I was lucky. My mouth went dry. Yeah, probably not the best idea I'd ever had.

"Ready, dear?" Kaye asked.

I avoided looking at Ceff, instead keeping my eyes on Jinx's prone form, and nodded.

"Yeah, I'm ready," I said.

"Are you sure about this?" Ceff asked. "We could find another way to free Jinx from the incubus and keep you safe."

"I'm sure," I said, sliding away from the counter to stand up straight and meet his gaze. "This is my best chance at freedom and Jinx's best chance at survival...and Kaye wants revenge. If we had more time, we might have found another way. But time isn't a luxury we have. We need to do this now."

"I just wish it was not such a risky plan," he said.

"You know me," I said with a shrug and a wry grin. "I never do anything halfway. This will be risky, no matter the plan."

"I have faith in the apples," Kaye said, her tone brooking no argument. "Now let's stop dilly dallying. Give me the blighted apple."

I pulled out the perfect, silver apple and set in on the counter between us.

"Don't be silly, child," she said, narrowing her eyes and pointing a tattooed index finger at me. "That apple is for you."

I heaved a sigh and ran a gloved hand through my hair.

"The other apple is more risky, you know that," I said.

Kaye pounded a fist on the counter, liquid from the spoon in her hand spilling onto the stone surface. Arachne blanched and stepped away from the counter, her eyes ping-ponging between us.

"I'm an old woman," Kaye said, baring her teeth and giving an impatient snort. "I'll take my chances."

"No," I said, shaking my head. "If we're going to do this, we do things my way."

Kaye glared at me, but I stared right back into her sharp, kohl-rimmed eyes. She sighed and slumped against the counter.

"Fine, have it your way, girl," she said.

She plucked the apple from the counter, put it in her mouth, and took a bite. Judging from her grimace, it wasn't the tastiest of apples—the bitter fruit of faerie schemes rarely are. I pulled the bag from my pocket that held the second apple, ready to follow her lead, but Kaye shook her head.

"Not yet, dear," she said. "Wait and watch."

Kaye finished eating the apple, core and all, and nodded to Arachne.

"Add a spoonful of the potion to three fingers of wine," she said, instructing the young witch.

Arachne poured wine into two large goblets and spooned liquid from the steaming cauldron into each. I swallowed hard. At least the potion didn't smell bad. The scent of cinnamon, clove, and berries were thick in the air as Kaye lifted a goblet to her lips. She coughed, hand flying to her mouth and she lowered herself onto a nearby chair.

Kaye's hand came away stained with blood, not wine, but she didn't grimace in pain. She said that taking the potion wouldn't hurt and I trusted her not to lie, not about this. She smiled and sat back in the chair, hand dropping to her side.

I stood transfixed. There was no rise and fall of her chest, no light in her drooping eyes. Kaye was dead.

"What do we do?" Arachne asked in a whisper.

"We wait," I said.

As we watched, the tattoos on Kaye's skin began to retreat. Dark, black, intertwining lines faded first from her hands, then her neck and arms. Torn had said that dying would give me a chance to be free of the faerie bargains I'd sworn to, but I hadn't given much thought to what the experience might do to a witch as old as Kaye. Apparently, I wasn't the only one who was getting a clean slate.

Kaye had been cursed with those tattoos as part of the cost of using powerful magic. It was the price she had paid, one that would eventually catch up with her. Her magic had already weakened, but I suspected that she would die or burn out the last of her magic entirely if there was no longer bare skin available to allow the tattoos to spread. She'd come close to that during our battle with the *each uisge*, damn close.

I'd like nothing more than to see the clock turn back on Kaye's tattoos, but one truth echoed inside my head—having her magic at full strength wouldn't do Kaye any good if she remained dead.

I held my breath, the sound of Arachne's teeth grinding against her hair the only sound in the room. Come on, Kaye. Wake up. My eyes felt gritty and dry, but I didn't dare blink as I watched Kaye for any signs of life. Oh god, what if the apples were some kind of faerie trick? What if they didn't work at all? My stomach twisted.

What have I done?

Kaye gasped, a reverse death rattle from deep in her throat, and I covered my mouth with a trembling hand. Ceff stepped forward and bent to place his fingers against her throat. He nodded and smiled.

"She will live," he said.

The "but" hung heavy in the air. Kaye was back from the dead, but I didn't kid myself that everything was fine. Dying wasn't easy on the body and Kaye was hundreds of years old. There was still a chance that she had suffered irreparable brain damage. She may never regain consciousness.

Only time would tell.

I bit my lip and leaned forward, gloved hands shaking as I place them wide on the stone countertop.

"Kaye?" I asked. "You alright?"

"Give...me...a...second," she said between wheezing gasps for breath. "Always...so...impatient."

Her eyelids fluttered open, the dark eyes filled with their usual shrewd intelligence and, a hint of mischief.

Arachne rushed over to her side, waving a hand in front of Kaye's face.

"How many fingers am I holding up?" Arachne asked, leaning forward.

"Three," Kaye groused. "And if you keep waving that fool hand of yours in my face, that's how many big, ugly warts I'll put on that perky little nose of yours."

Arachne's hands flew to her face and she shook her head, backing away.

"You wouldn't," she said, voice muffled behind her hands.

"Don't test me, child," she said. "By the Goddess, I've just died and come back to life. It has been one hell of a day."

I let out a shaky laugh. Kaye was alive, thank Mab, and just as sharp as ever.

"Go on," she said, making a shooing motion with her hands—hands that no longer carried the tattoos of spent magic. "I can't breathe with you all hovering like a band of moroi."

"As you wish," Ceff said.

He stepped aside to give the woman space, but I couldn't help but step closer, eyes wide and shining. I was no moroi—phantoms who draw life from the living—but I was drawn to Kaye just the same. I couldn't stop staring at her skin.

"Kaye," I said, pointing. "Your tattoos, they're gone."

She held up her arm, pulling the lace sleeves of her dress away from the unblemished skin.

"Well I'll be," she said. "That is…unexpected."

I'm pretty sure that there wasn't much that surprised the witch, so I backed off and gave her a moment to let the implications sink in. If her bare skin meant what I thought it did, then her magic was back to full strength, or would be as soon as she recovered. Judging by the slow grin tugging at her lips, she'd just realized that as well.

The glaistig better watch her back.

"Feeling better?" Ceff asked.

I smiled, doing an internal inventory, and nodded.

"Now that you mention it, yeah, I do," I said. "I feel great. Never better."

It was the truth. No more bone crushing fatigue. No wobbly knees or shaky muscles pushed to the brink of exhaustion. The weight of one unfulfilled bargain—the compulsion to kill Kaye—was gone. I rubbed my gloved hands together thinking about just how much I was going to enjoy seeing the look on The Green Lady's face when I showed up later tonight with an angry witch bent on revenge.

"Arachne, fetch me the cot we keep in the back," Kaye said, frowning at me. "That potion packs more of a wallop than I expected. Best to be prepared, we don't want Ivy getting a concussion from hitting her fool head."

Without the yoke of the glaistig's bargain around my neck, I felt like I could take on anything. Too bad the first thing I had to face was death. I'd rather go knock some fire imp heads together than drink Kaye's potion. Such is life.

Arachne carried in a folding cot and set it up beside the counter where I stood. I'd been on that cot more times than I'd like to admit, usually with Kaye stitching me back together. Taking on cases involving the fae hadn't been good for my health.

"Go on, lie down, dear," Kaye said. "Might as well get this over with. We still have a lot to do tonight."

I sighed. Our plan had worked. Kaye had eaten her apple and drank a goblet of poison, died and been resurrected. Now it was my turn.

"You ready?" Arachne asked, shaking hands reaching for the second goblet.

Watching Kaye die had left me with some serious thoughts. It put things into perspective. And the fact that the witch had survived was no guarantee that the second apple would work on me. There was nothing in Kaye's books to reassure me. I was about to drink a poisonous brew, but I was no fool. There were no guarantees as far as I was concerned.

I may not make it back.

"There's a phone call I need to make first," I said, pulling out my phone. "Think you can keep The Emporium from eating me, or making me walk around in circles for hours?"

Kaye lifted her unblemished arm and waggled her fingers.

"Oh I can do a lot more than that, dear," she said. "So much more."

CHAPTER 45

I stepped out onto the sidewalk and took in a lungful of spring air. Mud and car exhaust never smelled so sweet. I just hoped I'd still be here to enjoy the coming summer.

But I didn't know, not for sure. That was why I needed to call my mom. I'd gone years resenting her for her distance. I believed it meant that she didn't love me, couldn't love the freak child that I'd become when my powers began to manifest. But that hadn't been the full truth.

My mom hadn't been afraid of me, she'd been afraid *for* me—and the geis that my dad put on her made it impossible for us to talk about my fae blood. We'd lost years to a misunderstanding and a well-intentioned, but misguided spell.

After figuring that out, I'd come to see my mom in a different light. We were beginning to have a better relationship with each other, but I was still guarded. There was so much left unsaid, and I didn't have the excuse of a magical geis. Before going through with my crazy scheme to unburden myself of faerie bargains, I needed to set things straight with my mom. I had to let her know that I love her.

Too bad the Moordenaar had other plans. Pesky assassins.

Thwap, thwap, thwap. Three arrows sunk deep into my flesh, each embedding their tips into vital organs—stomach, liver, heart. I noted the deadly strikes with a strange detachment, as if the injuries were happening to someone else.

My phone slid from my hand, shattering on the sidewalk. Shattering like the fragments of my soul. Where do half-breed souls go when they die? I'd never thought to ask, and now it was too late.

"Finish her," a voice like the whisper of a scorpion said from the growing shadows that blurred my vision.

At some point, I'd fallen. I could see approaching black and silver boots, but I no longer cared. I'd finally get some sleep. I let my eyes drift closed. It's funny how comfortable cobblestones are when you're dying.

A low, rumbling growl startled me awake, though I couldn't move. I lay there helpless, unable to reach my weapons. Just like in every nightmare I'd ever had, the monsters I saw every day were finally going to catch me—and there was nothing I could do about it.

"The gargoyle?" another voice asked.

"We have pierced her vital organs," said a third voice. "That and the poison will do the rest."

"Then leave the guardian, he has not been marked for death," the first man said. "The traitor will die before the day is out. Our work here is complete."

A monster loomed over me, casting what was left of my vision into shadow, and roared. Eyelids growing heavy, I sighed and let them drift closed again, no energy left for the monster. But it grabbed my jacket and shook me until I opened my eyes.

A grotesque face hovered close to mine. It was familiar, but it took my brain a minute to give it a name.

"H-h-humphrey?" I asked.

At least, I tried to say his name. It came out more like a wet, stuttering croak as I choked on my own blood.

"Do not speak," he said, words tumbling like rocks in a landslide. "I will take you to Mistress Kaye."

My head fell back as the gargoyle lifted me into his arms, spread his wings, and flew—actually flew—through The Emporium. I heard a gasp and then all hell broke loose. I couldn't help but laugh. It was too funny.

I let down my guard for one second and sidhe assassins come along and turn me into a half human pin cushion. Funny bastards.

"Ivy, eat," Kaye said.

I choked as someone shoved food into my mouth. It tasted like apples and mold and blood. I gagged, but someone held my jaw shut. I struggled against the vice-like grip. I couldn't swallow, couldn't scream for help...couldn't breathe.

CHAPTER 46

The visions went on forever. At least, I thought they were visions. Maybe this was the afterlife and I was doomed to an eternity of repeatedly playing out the painful moments of a young couple's tragic life. And it was a tragedy—that was for certain.

Faeries may have an obsession with The Bard, but Shakespeare got his inspiration from somewhere. I was guessing that Romeo and Juliet had Manannán mac Lir and Ailinn to thank for the bittersweet ending to their romance.

Manannán had three wives—Fand, Aife, and Iuchra—but when he met Ailinn it was love at first sight. The two were inseparable until the Milesians invaded the north. Manannán rode north on his sea chariot to help the Tuatha Dé Danann repel the invading army.

Fand, jealous of Ailinn and angry at her husband for ending her own affair with her lover Cúchulainn, saw her opportunity for revenge. She sent messengers to the border villages of the north, spreading the rumor that Ailinn was dead.

On his return journey south, Manannán was told falsely that Ailinn had died during his absence. He used Fragarach the Answerer to force the truth from the man, but since the man believed the rumor, he continued to claim that Ailinn was dead. In his grief, Manannán turned his sword on himself.

When news reached Ailinn that her lover had taken his own life, she too takes her life to be joined with him for eternity. But in a cruel twist of Fate, Manannán is not dead. His sword Fragarach did not hit any vital organs, and its blade was so sharp that his wounds knit in a day. In frustration, he rode home, learning along that way that he'd been tricked by Fand, but he was too late to save Ailinn.

When he arrived on the hillside where they'd promised to meet when the war was over, a tree bearing silver apples grew from Ailinn's fresh grave. The sea deity's tears flooded the land, creating Emain Ablach and turning the hill into an island.

I rode the visions that the apple gave me, my own tears falling to join those of Ailinn and Manannán mac Lir. Their tragic story was a lesson that I would take to heart, if I survived.

CHAPTER 47

"Feeling better?" Kaye asked.

I blinked against harsh light, memories falling into place. Sidhe assassins, Humphrey the gargoyle, Kaye's voice, the taste of apple...

"It worked?" I croaked.

I turned over onto my side and wretched, dry heaves wracking my body. I'd been brought back to life, pulled from the endless visions of Ailinn and Manannán mac Lir's tragic romance, but, for the moment, I wished I were dead.

"The pain and nausea will subside," she said. "You will live."

The faerie courts had sent their assassins and they'd finally caught up with me. They'd shot me full of poisoned arrows and left me for dead. If I hadn't grabbed that second apple...well, that was something to think about later. The universe sure worked in mysterious ways.

"Ceff?" I asked.

"I am here," he said.

I looked up into his face, taking in the dark rings that circled his red-rimmed eyes. He looked like he'd been crying. Normally, I'd look away or make some kind of joke, shrugging off our messy feelings. But memories of Ailinn and Manannán mac Lir flooded my mind and I reached out to hold his hand with my gloved one. I was done with being careful, with pushing people away.

"I missed you," I said, letting all those messy emotions into my voice.

"I never left," he said.

"Yeah, but I did," I said. "I'm sorry about that."

"It was not your fault," he said, dark green eyes going black. "It was the Moordenaar."

"Yeah, but I was going to do this to you anyway," I said. "The Moordenaar just beat me to it."

"I forgive you," he said. "I will always forgive you, Ivy, but I will never forgive the faerie courts. The Moordenaar tried to take you from me. That is not something I can ever forget."

The lights flickered and a booming sound like a gong rang throughout the building.

"What the hell is that?" I asked, trying to sit up.

"Something's tripped the wards," Arachne said, rushing over to Kaye's side.

Kaye was at her scrying bowl. She looked up, a slow smile sliding onto her face.

"It looks like we have visitors," she said.

Great, just great.

"Is it the Moordenaar?" I asked, pulling myself to my feet. "Fire imps?"

My knives hit my palms and I shook my head, clearing away the mental cobwebs. I needed to be alert if this came down to a fight.

"Even better," Kaye said, a glint in her eye. "Two demons and a *cat sidhe.*"

I sighed, slipped my knives into their sheaths, and rubbed a hand over my face.

"Whatever you have planned, don't kill them," I said. "They're with me."

"I was only going to have a bit of fun," she said.

"There isn't much time to prepare our attack on The Green Lady," I said. "We can use their help."

"I suppose you're right," she said, frowning.

"So can they come in?" I asked.

"Yes," she said, tapping her fingers beside the scrying bowl. "War certainly makes for strange bedfellows."

"You have no idea," I said, marching toward the door.

CHAPTER 48

"**P**rincess, you're alive!" Torn exclaimed, eyes wide.

"It appears that news of your imminent demise is highly exaggerated," Forneus said, tugging at his gloves. "More's the pity."

"What are you both doing here?" I asked.

At my voice, Sparky peeked out from behind Forneus' legs and ran at me, nearly knocking me off my feet. The little guy may not be linebacker material, but my knees were still wobbly from my recent brush with death.

"Iveeeeeeeeeee!" he squealed, grinning from ear to ear.

Sparky did a twirling dance, his floppy ears bouncing while he spun, my pant leg clutched in his tiny hand. Dang, but the runt was cute.

"Come on in you guys," I said, waving them all inside. "Better get in off the street."

Torn seemed to relax into the shadows, but Forneus hesitated on the sidewalk and continued to fidget with his gloves.

"Is the witch here?" he asked.

I knew he wasn't referring to Arachne. Kaye and Forneus hadn't got off on the right foot, and he'd be a fool not to wonder what she had planned, but the two were going to have to go the night without killing each other. If not, I'd do the honors for them.

We were all going to have to work together. The fire imps had to be contained, the glaistig needed to be taken down a notch, and we had to break the hold that her incubus had on Jinx. If nothing else worked, I figured that last point would get the demon on board.

"Yeah, Kaye is inside with Arachne and Ceff," I said. "Play nice."

"Jinx?" he asked.

"She's still sleeping," I said with a shake of my head. "Now come in before someone else gets filled with poisoned arrows. We're fresh out of magic apples."

Forneus raised an eyebrow, but stepped inside, the door slamming shut behind him. Apparently, Torn hadn't filled the demon in on our successful trip to Emain Ablach. Or who knows, maybe he did but they still thought I was dead. Magic apples aren't the most predictable of safety nets.

With all of our guests inside, I held my breath and scanned the room for signs of hostility. The Emporium creaked and groaned, but it didn't lash out against the demons and *cat sidhe*. That, strangely enough, made the shop a safer place than the street. I didn't need to risk being shot by anymore poisoned arrows, and Humphrey had looked ready to tear our guests limb from limb.

Judging by the way Forneus eyed Torn, the demon was having the same ideas about the *cat sidhe* lord. I shook my head and winced. These two were giving me a headache. It was going to be a long night.

"Yes, how is our Jinx?" Torn asked.

He smiled and winked. Damn the cat, he was toying with the demon. I'd wondered why Torn had shown up, and I didn't think it was solely out of concern for my wellbeing. We were allies, not besties. But Torn had been flirting up a storm with Jinx lately and the two had been spending a lot of time together ever since that night at Club Nexus. If I knew the meddlesome *cat sidhe*, he was here to mess with Forneus and screw up the demon's chances with my best friend.

I grit my teeth and tried to change the subject.

"So, learn anything new?" I asked Forneus.

Forneus was supposed to be doing recon. If we were lucky, he'd have learned something that could help our assault on the carnival.

"For some reason, they relaxed security half an hour ago," he said. "I came here to report back, but when this one relayed the information he had gathered from his spies, concerning your shooting, I assumed that the change in security meant that you were dead. But here you are, in the flesh."

The glaistig had relaxed security? It had to be in response to the completion of our bargain. She would have felt it and assumed that Kaye was dead. Little did she know that the witch had come back to life, and was stronger than ever.

I just hoped that the glaistig couldn't sense that there was no longer a second bargain between us. So long as she didn't figure that out, she'd keep me around, a tool to be used when needed. As far as she was concerned, I'd followed her orders and taken out the most powerful witch in Harborsmouth. She'd think I was a useful tool, indeed.

"Yes, princess, you look good for a dead chick," Torn said, suggestively licking his lips.

"I got better," I said with a shrug.

"I gather by your resurrection that you successfully completed the trials of Emain Ablach?" Forneus asked.

"Yeah, not my idea of a tropical getaway," I said with a grimace. "But I got the apple we went there for...and I managed to grab a second one on my way out. Good thing too, since Kaye was determined to use one of the apples. The second apple was half rotten, but it still held enough of Ailinn's magic."

"Hence your resurrection," he said.

I nodded.

"Ah, princess, *tsk tsk*," Torn said, wagging his finger. "You've been keeping secrets."

"Like you haven't?" I asked, raising an eyebrow.

"Touché," he said with a wide grin.

We strode into Kaye's spell kitchen and into a makeshift spell circle that pulled us up short. Damn, I should have noticed the chalk marks on the floor. Kaye had us trapped with her magic, unable to move a muscle. Forneus, Torn, Sparky, and I all hung in place like flies on fly paper.

"I have let you all into my domain because we have a battle to plan," Kaye said, eyes glittering. She pointed her wand at us and a trickle of sweat ran down my back. "But first, some ground rules."

Oh yeah, it was going to be a long night.

CHAPTER 49

I held my breath against the stench of the alley, but I wasn't complaining. Anything was better than being trapped inside The Emporium with my ragtag group of friends and allies. Forneus and Torn had managed to behave while we planned our attack on The Green Lady, but it was a close thing.

I rested my elbows against an overturned crate, steadying the binoculars I held in gloved hands. Lights winked out and the last few human stragglers were finally exiting the carnival turnstiles.

"Looks like they're closing things down," I said, my voice low and nasally.

I pinched my nose and tried to breathe through my mouth to avoid the stench, but it wasn't working. This alley had a clear line of sight perfect for observing the carnival gates, but it smelled like stale piss, French fries, and rotting fish. I wrinkled my nose, wishing we'd chosen a different spot for doing recon.

"About bloody time," Forneus muttered.

I nodded in agreement. At least we wouldn't be here much longer. With the humans clearing out of dodge, we were up next.

The plan was for me to carry the spelled demon vessel through the gates and onto carnival grounds. I figured the glaistig would be eager to hear all about how I took down Kaye for her. That should get me in through the front door and, hopefully, gain an immediate audience with The Green Lady. For maximum mayhem, I needed to give the glaistig an up close and personal introduction to the demon vessel.

A grin tugged at my lips. I'd never played at being a Trojan horse, but there was a first time for everything.

"Ceff, your people are in place?" I asked.

I stole a sideways glance at where Ceff crouched to my left, beside an oil slick puddle. Somehow he was using his water magic to stay in contact with the head of his royal guard.

"My guards are in place," he said, nodding. "They will remain in the harbor, on the perimeter of The Green Lady's domain, ready to use their magic if needed."

"Good," I said, giving him a curt nod.

The kelpies were the key to keeping any fires that the fire imps started contained. None of us wanted unnecessary casualties. Well, most of us didn't. Kaye looked like she was out for blood.

I handed my binoculars to Torn and turned to Kaye.

"Okay, let's charge this thing up," I said.

Kaye touched the demon vessel with her wand, strange words tumbling from her lips.

"That's it?" I asked.

"Yes, it is done," she said.

I gingerly slipped the artifact inside a zippered jacket pocket, one of the few remaining pockets without holes or tears, and checked my weapons one last time. I had my full complement of blades, holy water, and iron weapons. I was ready as I'd ever be.

"They closing up shop yet?" I asked, turning to Torn.

His cat spies hadn't reached me in time to warn me of the Moordenaar's attack earlier, and he seemed eager to prove their worth. *Cat sidhe* now lurked in nearly every shadow along the harbor. If anyone knew if the carnival had flipped their closed sign, it was Torn.

"They've powered down and the humans are gone," he said. "Only two satyrs at the front gate sharing a cigarette."

"Sloppy," I said.

Torn shrugged.

"The Green Lady thinks Kaye is dead and that you're her lapdog," he said. "With the rest of the city scrambling to deal with fire imps, she's probably feeling pretty confident right about now."

"Good, we want her careless," I said.

I ran a hand through my hair and pasted on a smile.

"Those satyrs still smoking?" I asked.

Torn nodded.

"Then that's my cue," I said.

My gut tightened as I stepped out of the alley and strode across the street toward the carnival turnstiles. I was about to go deep into enemy territory and unleash a swarm of pyromaniacal demons.

Talk about jumping out of the frying pan and into the fire.

CHAPTER 50

"**H**ey boys," I said, suggestively licking my lips. "What does a girl have to do to see The Green Lady these days?"

The satyrs perked up, ready for duty—and I'm not talking about their security detail. The hairy, goat men stared at me, their cigarettes long forgotten.

"So, is that a flute in your pocket, or are you just happy to see me?" I asked.

I flipped my hair and gave them a girlish giggle. Geesh, I'd rather clash blades than flirt, but these were satyrs. Their weakness was that their brains were located between their legs. If I wanted to get inside the carnival grounds without a fuss, this was the best strategy.

Of course, if the glaistig had left orders not to let me in, they might just kill me on sight and screw my lifeless corpse. Satyrs weren't known for their discerning tastes.

One of the men clomped toward me and I clenched my fists, resisting the urge to palm my knives. If I had a weapon in hand, I'd use it. I knew exactly what my first target would be, and although his leer made my stomach twist, it wouldn't be the satyr's fur covered face.

He unhooked the chain that was strung across the entrance and waved me through.

"Thank you, sugar," I said. His buddy came up beside him and they both were definitely happy to see me. I pushed out my bottom lip and shook my head. "Sorry boys, business before pleasure. I have to see The Green Lady, but I promise to make it quick."

I winked and the satyrs nodded. One led me down a sawdust-strewn path, which left only one guard at the gate. So far, so good.

The carnival was quiet, with most of the fae turning in for the night or kicking back with a drink or three. The amusement rides were shut down, the skeletons of the roller coaster and Ferris wheel dark voids against the starry sky. The grinning funhouse clown's teeth and eyes seemed to glow

in the dim light and I shivered. I never understood the appeal
of clowns. They were right up there with vamps and spider fae
for breeding nightmares.

We passed the funhouse and ducked beneath the flap of
a large tent. Fae reclined on pillows in various stages of
undress, long pipes in their hands. It was no secret what these
faeries were up to. The air was thick with the sickly sweet
smell of opium. My nostrils flared and I flushed hot as I took
in the disheartening scene.

Apparently, the glaistig had found another way to keep
her workers compliant—as if swearing eternal servitude wasn't
enough. I clenched my jaw, teeth grinding so hard it was a
miracle they didn't break. These fae trusted The Green Lady
to take care of them and instead she used them as free labor in
her carnival and then pimped out drugs to them in their off
hours. She claimed to love her people, but she was as bad as
Puck dealing Ice to the patrons of Club Nexus.

I wanted to wring the faerie queen's neck, but instead, I
kept a smile pasted on my face and my blades up my sleeves. I
needed to gain the glaistig's trust and find her pet incubus. I'd
leave her fate in Kaye's capable hands.

I followed the satyr to a dark corner, all the while
keeping an eye out for threats. He beckoned for me to pass
behind a sheer curtain and I resisted the urge to tuck tail and
run. If the satyr was taking me here to drug and rape me, he
had another thing coming—namely, a date with my friends
Sharp and Pointy.

CHAPTER 51

I ducked as the satyr held the curtain back and I caught sight of a familiar face. The glaistig was still fully shrouded in an emerald green cloak, but semi-naked men sprawled like puppies on the cushions she lounged on. A girl covered in red fur, wearing a gold bikini that would make Jabba the Hut proud, fanned The Green Lady with an honest to goodness palm frond.

I was here to behave, but I couldn't resist cocking an eyebrow at the foliage as climate control. Hell, with the satyr at my back, this room didn't need any more wood.

"Is that shrubbery?" I asked. "And look at me empty handed, no herring in sight."

Sometimes there was just no controlling my mouth.

"I see that you are as insolent as ever," the gaistig said.

"Well, I figure I deserve a little gloating…now that I've fulfilled our bargain," I said.

"Yes, I felt the witch's death," she said, smiling and licking her lips. She sipped wine from a golden goblet, not unlike the one which Kaye had drunk the death potion that had at least temporarily killed her. "But if you are here for a reward, you are sadly mistaken. You have fulfilled the terms of our bargain, nothing more."

I nodded, keeping my eyes averted. Let her think I was sheep, she'd feel my claws soon enough.

The satyr bent down and whispered something into the glaistig's ear. Her eyes widened and a slow smile crept across her face.

"Yes, splendid idea," she said. "I will have use for you tomorrow, so spend the night enjoying my hospitality." By hospitality, I'm pretty sure she meant the groping hands of the satyr. "Return to me at dawn."

An invitation to stay was exactly what I wanted, but I couldn't afford to sound too eager.

"Oh, no, I couldn't…" I stammered, my eyes on the pillow-strewn floor.

"I insist," she said, eyes narrowing.

"Um, okay, if that's what you want," I said meekly.

The glaistig nodded.

"My satyr has taken a particular shine to you," she said. "Go and make merry, but do not think of leaving. I have something special planned for that second bargain you owe me."

I kept my eyes averted, hiding the fiery rage that simmered within. She thought she could send me off to fuck her satyr's brains out and then order me to implement another one of her foul orders. The woman was a faerie queen alright. She was an evil, self-serving, manipulative bitch.

A twisted part of me wanted to know what her second request would be—Which one of my friends would she want me to kill this time?—but I didn't want to press my luck. Best to look beaten and avoid further scrutiny.

I palmed one of my knives and followed the satyr out the door.

CHAPTER 52

I let the satyr lead me far from the glaistig's tent before putting on the fake waterworks. Nothing like a red face and snot to ruin the mood, and keep an amorous satyr at arm's length, right?

"The Green Lady is sending me away in the morning," I said, lip trembling. "I need to see my friend Delilah before I go."

The satyr shook his head and reached for my jacket. I slapped his hand away with the flat blade of one of my knives. My lip curled and I bared my teeth—so much for snot and tears.

"No," I said. "I need to see Delilah."

The satyr shoved me, hard, and my head hit the side of a food truck. My ears rang with the force of the blow, but I shook it off. My knees wobbled, heart racing at the thought of this guy touching me—and it wasn't just the threat of visions that made my gut twist.

He stepped forward, trying to press his body against mine and I rammed a knee between his legs. He let out a high-pitched bleating cry, but I didn't stop there. On the downward motion, I kicked out to the side, using my momentum to ram my boot into his knee. As he buckled forward, I shoved his shoulders, pushing him away from me and onto the ground.

I grabbed a metal box of napkins that was on the fold-out counter of the food truck, and cracked him over the head. The bleating stopped.

"No means no, buddy," I said. "You should have listened when I said it the first time."

I left the satyr curled in a ball, hugging his family jewels even in sleep. He'd live, but he might think twice before forcing himself on the next woman who told him no.

I brushed my gloved hands together, smoothed out my hair, and slipped into the shadows. One satyr down—one succubus and one incubus to go.

CHAPTER 53

I found Delilah just as the alarm rang out. The smell of smoke mingled with the breeze off the harbor and I knew that Kaye's spell had worked. I patted the demon vessel in my pocket and grinned. The fire imps had come.

I scanned the area for threats, but the only person in sight was the succubus who was tugging down the skirt of her skimpy dress. I may not have caught the succubus in flagrante, but she looked sated. Hopefully, her recent feed would make her slow and not strong as hell.

I palmed a throwing knife in one hand and grabbed a holy water grenade off my belt with the other. I kept the weapons behind my back and slipped out of the shadows, looking more like I was out for a stroll than ready for a fight.

But looks can be deceiving.

"Hello, Delilah," I said. "Fancy meeting you here."

Here was a dark patch of grass covered ground beside the fortune teller's tent. But the area didn't remain dark for long. The rage at what the succubus had done to Jinx rolled through me like wildfire, warming my body, and setting my skin and eyes aflame.

Delilah hissed and jumped back into a crouch. But when she saw that it was just little old me, albeit a glowing me, she relaxed.

"Oh," she said, pulling herself upright and straightening her dress. "It'sss you. What are you doing here?"

I stepped forward, closing the distance between us. In one fluid motion, I held the balloon filled with holy water aloft and brought my knife to her neck. I swallowed hard, but kept my hand steady. It was risky being this close to the succubus, but I'd taken some precautions.

After leaving Kaye's I'd made a pit stop back at the loft where I suited up in two layers of silk long underwear. The neck of the turtleneck was pulled up high and my thumbs were securely through the holes in the top's sleeves. With my gloves, jeans, tall boots, and leather jacket worn over the long

underwear, there was barely an inch of exposed skin. I'd also
added a skullcap from my pocket, which I'd pulled down over
my ears moments before. If I kept her from touching my face,
I'd be safe from unwanted visions.

"I know about your role in hurting Jinx," I said. "You
rufied my best friend. I can't just let that go."

"I wasss jussst following ordersss," she said, eyes wide.

I shook my head.

"Not good enough," I said. "Jinx is my vassal, which
gives me the right to take your head."

Delilah licked her lips, face shifting from fear to
seduction.

"Perhapsss we can come to an underssstanding," she
said.

She heaved her more than ample bosom, rolled her
tongue along pouty lips, flashing a tiny fang. I shuddered and
Delilah smiled, but my reaction wasn't desire. The succubus
may be sex incarnate, but a) she wasn't my type, b) sex with a
succubus is a death sentence, and c) she'd drugged my friend
and handed her off to a horny incubus.

Nope, I'd rather eat glass than touch Delilah with
anything other than my blades.

"Keep that up, Delilah, and I take your head," I said.
"You can't seduce me and if you call for help, no one will
come—your coworkers have their hands full battling a horde of
fire imps. But if you help me find the incubus who's feeding on
Jinx, I'll let you live. We'll call it even."

She pretended to think about my offer, but it was all
show. It was within my rights to take her life, but instead, I
was giving her a chance at redemption. It was a deal and she
knew it.

"I will take you to Adam, on one conditsssion," she said.

"And what would that be?" I asked, eyes narrowing.

"You take me with you when you leave," she said.

Take the succubus with me? Now that was unexpected.

"Why would you want to go with me?" I asked.

"Onccce The Green Lady knowsss I've helped you, I am
as good asss dead," she said.

I thought about it. If I'd become the glaistig's lapdog,
would I be looking for a way out? I didn't have to dig too deep
to know my answer.

"Come on, show me where I can find this Adam, and I promise to take you with me," I said. "But I can't promise your safety."

"Deal," she said. I backed away, feeling the bargain settle between us. "Thisss way. Adam isss working."

What did an incubus do for work? I was tempted to ask Delilah, but shook off the idea. Some things were best left unknown.

CHAPTER 54

Delilah was as good as her word. She showed me the way to Adam's place of employment. I frowned, cursing myself for not asking what the incubus did for work.

"That's the glaistig's tent," I said.

"Yesss," she said with a nod.

We were ducked behind a sign for the strongman. Delilah crouched behind an oversized cartoon thigh, eyes flicking up and down the path. Harried carnival fae ran in every direction carrying buckets of water, weapons, or both.

"So, is Adam the glaistig's...concubine?" I asked.

"Concubinusss," she said. I raised an eyebrow. "Concubine is female, Adam is male."

Ah, okay. Now that we had the terminology straight, I tried to wrap my brain around what was going on inside the forest green tent. Bile rose in my throat at the idea of The Green Lady using her subjects for sex, even if the man was an incubus.

I spit to the side and surveyed our options. The fire imps were keeping the carnival fae busy. In the chaos, it would be easy to slip inside The Green Lady's tent. I just didn't want to think too hard about what I'd face when I got there.

"Okay, you stay here," I said. "I'll try to gain access to Adam. If I'm lucky, the two are done knocking boots and I'll catch him on a smoke break while the glaistig sleeps."

Delilah gave me a dubious stare, but nodded.

I palmed my knives, not worrying about brandishing weapons out in the open since most of the carnival fae were currently armed, and ran toward the tent. I slipped around to one side and carefully pulled back the fabric flap.

I gasped. I'd expected to see the glaistig sweaty and naked with her concubinus. Or if my luck held, they'd be fast asleep. What I didn't anticipate was The Green Lady in a faceoff with a pack of fire imps.

"Mind if I join the party?" I asked, drawing the glaistig's wide-eyed gaze.

"Come, half-breed, douse these flames," she ordered, pointing to her bed.

The sheets were smoldering and it had nothing to do with the scantily clad incubus tied to the headboard.

"Why haven't you untied him yet?" I asked, body tensing.

"Him?" she asked. "He is just a slave. Now put out those flames and help me lift these strongboxes. The items these contain are priceless."

I pulled out the demon vessel and rubbed it three times like Kaye had instructed. She said that it would accelerate the spell and attract the fire imps like pixies to salt. With a tittering laugh, six more imps bounced into the room to join the four already facing the glaistig. Flame sprung from their fingertips as they eyed her long, green robes and a table covered in maps and scrolls.

I remembered the vision I had while riding a fire imp's blood. *Fire, fire, fire*! All these demons cared about was finding things that were flammable...and making them burn.

"Consider this a gift from Kaye," I said, holding up the demon vessel.

I was about to toss the vessel at The Green Lady when she blanched and pointed behind me. I spun around to see Kaye stride in, the bells on her skirts jingling merrily.

"You!" the glaistig cried.

"You look surprised to see me," Kaye said, eyes glinting in the growing flames. "I wonder why that is."

"You are supposed to be dead!" she yelled. She twisted her head my way. "You were bound by our bargain to kill the witch."

I smiled and shrugged.

"You said I had to kill her," I said. "You didn't say anything about her staying dead."

My grin wavered as a cough racked my body. While we were having our chat, the fire imps were getting busy doing what they did best—burning the place to the ground.

The fire imps had reached the table beside the glaistig and were setting fire to books, maps, and scrolls. Judging by the bulging eyes and the veins popping out along her temples, The Green Lady wasn't taking it well. She was madder than a bald bugbear in winter.

That would have pleased me more if I could breathe.

"Um, Kaye, a little help here?" I asked, blinking against the smoke.

Kaye lifted her arm and with a flick of her wrist, the tent flew away into the night. The smoke dissipated and I drew in a ragged breath. I started toward the bed where the incubus was strung up, but a familiar chirping voice made me stop.

"Iveeeeeeeeeeee!" Sparky cried.

The little guy threw himself at me, Forneus close on his tail.

"What the...?" I asked.

"Sorry," Forneus said. "He insisted we come, and I was not swift enough to stop him. Sparky is surprisingly agile for one so young."

"Um, okaaay," I said. I looked down into Sparky's serious face. "What's so important that it couldn't wait?"

He pointed to the demon vessel in my hand and shook his head, then pointed to the fire imps, then himself and nodded.

"He can send the fire imps home," Forneus said. "He can remove the threat without trapping them inside that cursed vessel."

I looked down at the little demon clinging to my leg. Sparky could do that? Color me impressed.

"Okay then, change of plan," I said. "When we're ready, Sparky can give his method a shot. But first, I have something I have to take care of."

Forneus nodded and Sparky let go of my leg. I spared one glance toward the glaistig, but Kaye was keeping the faerie queen busy.

I ran to the huge bed where the incubus was tied. He was alive, but his wrists were bloodied where he'd struggled to pull himself free. The bottom of the bed was in flames and the pillows on which he crouched were beginning to smolder.

If I left him here to burn, he would die and Jinx would live. Death would break the incubus' hold on my friend. I grit my teeth and palmed one of my blades.

"Pleassse," he begged, tears streaming down his face. "Don't kill me."

I had every reason to want him dead. I gripped my knife and stepped forward.

CHAPTER 55

I raised my hand and used the knife to slash at the rope that bound his wrists. The incubus sagged in relief.

"Why?" he asked. "Why sssave me?"

That was a good question, one I'd think about later.

"No one deserves to die as someone's slave," I said. "You're more than a piece of property."

Heck, the glaistig had been more concerned about her precious treasure chests than this man's life.

"But I hurt your friend," he said.

Something inside me shifted and I met his gaze.

"Yeah, you did, but you were under orders, right?" I said. "You couldn't resist."

He was a slave, chained to a powerful faerie queen. The Green Lady was the one responsible for Jinx's failing health, not Adam.

"Yesss," he said, nodding.

"That's what I thought," I said. "Look, you can still make this right. Release your hold on Jinx and I'll do what I can to get you out of here."

He covered his mouth with a bloodied, soot-covered hand, eyes wide and shining, and nodded. The hope in his eyes was painful to see. How long had it been since someone thought this guy was worth redeeming?

"Yesss," he said. He placed his hands together at the level of his heart and nodded once again. "It isss done."

"Good," I said. "Now come with me."

Adam staggered, legs unsteady, as I showed him where Delilah waited.

"Go with Delilah," I said. "I'll meet you two as soon as we take care of the fire imps."

He nodded and limped away. I turned back to see Forneus standing rigid, nostrils flaring.

"You let that scoundrel go," Forneus said, biting off the words.

Flame flickered in his eyes and I had the distinct feeling that I was standing on a powder keg ready to go up in smoke—and it didn't have anything to do with the fire imps that converged on us.

"Yes, I did," I said. "He was just as much a victim here."

"But Jinx..." he said.

"She'll be fine," I said. "He released his hold on her."

He scowled and lifted a sleek cell phone from his pocket.

"Forgive me if I do not take the incubus' word for it," he said.

He punched in a number, the other person picking up on the first ring.

"Little witch, this is Forneus," he said. "I require an update on Jinx's status."

Forneus rapped his fingers on his cane, eyes dancing.

"Splendid!" he said. "Yes, I will let her know."

He hung up, a smile on his lips. Tears welled up, but I blinked them away. Jinx was doing better, thank Mab, but I wasn't done here.

"Your efforts to persuade the incubus, though misguided, were successful, and just in time," he said, waving a hand at the surrounding devastation. "As you can see, things are getting out of hand."

I surveyed the wreckage of the carnival and sighed. Fires were not raging completely unchecked, Ceff and his kelpie guards were making sure of that, but even doused flames left behind scorched property and greasy smoke.

There were fire imps on nearly every surface, scampering from tent to tent, ride to ride. Smoke hung thick in the air, but the imps showed no sign of slowing down. Flame shot from their fingers as they danced around the carnival, eager to watch it burn.

"Make them stop!" the glaistig screamed.

Yeah, it was time to put a stop to this. But that didn't mean I couldn't make a few things right at the same time.

I stomped over to the glaistig and folded my arms across my chest.

"If I do, then I want your word that you let your incubus and succubus go free," I said.

"But this is your fault!" she yelled. "How dare you demand a boon from me?"

"You started this when you ordered Adam and Delilah to attack my vassal," I said.

She looked from me to Kaye and back again.

"Perhaps we can bargain for the lives of the succubus and incubus..." she said, licking her lips.

"I want more than just their lives," I said. "Removing the fire imps from your territory will fulfill any remaining bargains that they owe you. Deal?"

Forneus cocked an eyebrow at me, but I ignored the demon. Thankfully, he didn't interrupt. He went back to babysitting Sparky and watching my back, his cane sword drawn and ready.

"Yes, fine, you have a deal," she said, grinding out the words. "Now get these fiends out of my domain before they burn everything!"

Kaye flicked me a questioning gaze, but I shook my head. We weren't using the demon vessel I still held. Not yet. I crouched down and gave Sparky a nod.

"It's all you, buddy," I said. "Send them home."

Sparky nodded, long ears flapping, and lifted his spindly fingers. As if conducting a symphony I couldn't hear, the little demon gestured and tugged at the air, unraveling reality. A small portal opened, just large enough for a fire imp to pass through. I covered my nose and mouth with my arm, trying to block the stench of decay, sulfur, and brimstone from the other side.

Sparky had opened a portal to Hell.

I swallowed hard and watched as fire imps came racing forward, drawn to the fiery land. Sparky waved his hands and chattered at the imps in a strange tongue. The imps bounced from foot to foot and proceeded one by one through the portal. When the last imp crossed through, Sparky waved a hand and the gate slammed shut, making my ears pop.

Sparky brushed his hands together and turned to me with a smile.

"Good job, Sparky," I said with a grin. I handed him a sparkly pencil and a pack of chewing gum. It was all I had, but the little guy seemed to like it.

I walked over to Kaye and handed her the demon vessel.

"Guess we don't need this anymore," I said.

She nodded and took the vessel, slipping it away in one of her skirt pockets.

"We will talk later about your new friend," Kaye said, eyeing Sparky warily.

"Yeah, I thought you might say that," I said with a sigh.

"But now you should take your friends, and the succubus and incubus, and leave," she said.

Yeah, I wanted to get out of here, go see how Jinx was doing, and take a week long shower. I walked past the glaistig who was staring at the remains of her carnival.

"Thank Mab, this day is over," she muttered.

I didn't have much sympathy. The woman had brought all of this on herself.

"You're forgetting one thing," Kaye said, lifting her wand and moving toward the glaistig. "You have not yet settled the debt between us. This battle is far from over."

I'm no coward, but I had no desire to get between Kaye and The Green Lady. I waved to Adam and Delilah, collected my friends, and ran.

CHAPTER 56

Ceff waited for me at the waterfront, his body dry, but a pool of water at his feet. He'd pulled himself from the harbor as soon as we cleared the carnival turnstiles.

My friends and I weren't the only ones to turn tail and run. Most of the carnival fae had evacuated to the strip of land just inside the gates. They could not leave The Green Lady's territory, but that didn't mean they wanted to stick around while a powerful witch and a faerie queen duked it out.

"Thank you," Delilah said. "You helped usss essscape."

I shrugged. "Just don't make a habit of us meeting like this," I said. "Stay out of trouble."

"You too," she said with a wink.

She grabbed Adam's hand and they slipped away into the night. I glanced back to the carnival, seeing the pained look I half expected would be there. There he was, holding his bow with white-knuckled hands, staring after Delilah.

The archer had a crush on Delilah, but this turn of events might be for the best. If the two of them ever got intimate, she would feed on him, draining his life energy until he was dead. You had to be as powerful as a faerie queen if you wanted to knock boots with a succubus, or incubus, and survive.

"You are really letting them go?" Forneus asked.

"Yeah," I said, stifling a yawn. "It'll probably come back to bite me in the ass, but I couldn't leave them with the glaistig."

"No," he said. "I suppose you could not."

Nope, I just wasn't made that way.

"Let me get Ceff and we'll go see Jinx," I said. "Any idea where Torn is?"

I hadn't seen Torn amidst the chaos, but I was sure he was around here somewhere. Forneus scowled, but nodded.

"The *cat sidhe* is brokering secrets," he said. "He said to thank you for a non-boring day."

"That sounds like Torn," I said. "Okay, I'll be right back."

I limped over to where Ceff stood waiting. Now that the adrenaline was wearing off, every ache and pain was a new agony. I moved stiffly, but I couldn't help the silly smile on my lips.

Ceff was gorgeous, standing there in low slung jeans and a button down shirt that pulled tight across his chest and broad shoulders. I moved in close, breathing him in, letting his sturdy presence sooth my battered soul.

"Hey," I said. "Thanks for keeping the fires under control. There were a lot more imps than..."

Ceff pulled me into a fierce kiss, his arms wrapping around me, pulling me close. As our lips met, I was hit by the visions that his skin held. But I'd grown used to riding these particular visions. I experienced the many tragedies of his life, and a few particularly good moments that we'd shared.

I knew just from our touch that Ceff hadn't suffered anything severe during our altercation with the glaistig. If he had, I would have experienced it firsthand through the visions. The fact that he left himself open like that, allowing me glimpses of the man he was and what he had endured, took my breath away. Trust didn't come easy for either of us, but somehow we'd managed to find each other and lay our hearts open. That never ceased to amaze me.

When the visions passed, our lips were no longer touching, but Ceff had slipped his hand inside my shirt to rest on the skin at the small of my back. My pulse quickened as my body became hyper aware of his touch.

We'd learned that if we wanted to keep touching, then it was best to maintain constant skin on skin contact or risk another round of visions. This was Ceff's way of telling me he wasn't letting go. That was good because I wasn't done with him either.

"What was that for?" I asked.

His hand on my back worked in slow circles and warmth flooded my body.

"I lost you today," he said.

"I got better," I said.

"It is not funny, Ivy," he said. "You died. I keep telling myself that you are here, you are whole, but my mind does not quite believe it. I need to feel you, to know that you are really alive."

I licked my lips and smiled. I wanted to go visit Jinx, to see with my own eyes that she was okay. But Ceff needed reassurances too, to know that I was safe and whole, just in a much more tactile kind of way. If I listened to my heart, I had to admit that I needed that too.

Visiting my friend was important, but that didn't mean I couldn't take a detour along the way.

"Change of plan, Forneus," I said. "Ceff and I have to run an errand. We'll meet you and Sparky at The Emporium."

"An errand, right," he said, rolling his eyes. "Fine, but I am not sticking around if Kaye returns. That witch is scarier than a starving pack of hellhounds."

I turned back to take in the battle still raging within the carnival grounds. Multicolored light and smoke streaked the air. Kaye was scary alright. She struck fear into me before when she was at half strength. Now that her powers had returned, she was downright terrifying.

I shivered and Ceff pulled me close. His fingers trailed along the inside of my waistband and I shivered again, but this time the response had nothing to do with fear.

"You. Me. Loft. Now," I said.

It had finally happened. Ceff had turned me into a monosyllabic sex fiend. If Jinx were here, she'd throw me a party. But I didn't need a party—all I needed was Ceff.

I grabbed his shirt and started dragging him down the street toward my apartment, Forneus chuckling behind us.

CHAPTER 57

Ceff's hand sent shivers up my spine as we entered the loft and kicked shut the door. Shedding my jacket and weapons while continuing to touch each other, skin on skin, was like a game of naked Twister. Fun, but challenging.

I removed each of my blades, a dozen stakes, and a utility belt full of charms and Ceff pulled a trident and a small blade from sheaths on his leg and back and tossed them onto the growing pile of weapons. He lifted my burner phone from his pocket and set it on the counter.

"My phone," I groaned. "Jinx is going to kill me."

"Why would she kill you?" he asked.

"That phone's not waterproof," I said. "I should have thought of that before you went swimming in the harbor."

"The phone is dry," he said. "I formed a pocket of air around the device, keeping the water at bay."

"Your water magic can do that?" I asked.

"You would be amazed at what my water magic can do," he said, eyes shifting to pale green and beginning to glow.

"Then amaze me," I said.

"I thought that you would never ask," he said.

His mouth slanted over mine and I moaned. The fatigue that had held me down all day vanished with the flick of his tongue. Our kisses deepened and Ceff pulled me further into the loft apartment.

"Shower or kitchen?" he asked, lips moving from my mouth to my neck.

"Shower," I said.

Now I was the one doing the pulling. I dragged him into the bathroom, shedding clothing as we went. I fumbled at the button on Ceff's pants and growled.

"Here," he said, his lips grinning as he kissed my neck. "Allow me."

His hands slid between our bodies as he deftly undid his pants. His hand brushed against my body and I moaned. Desire rose up through me and my skin burned.

I tugged at his jeans, growling again as they caught on his hips and toned buttocks. Ceff's body was a thing of perfection, absolute beauty, and it was all mine.

He stepped out of the jeans and I pulled him closer. He turned on the shower and my skin began to tingle. His skillful hands returned to my body, and additional tendrils of water began to slide across my skin, coaxing it into a frenzy of desire.

"You are really here," he said, voice ragged. "You returned to me."

My magic rose up to meet his, water and fire filling the room with steam. Tears mixed with water and sweat, but I smiled as I laced my fingers in his hair.

"I will always return to you," I said. "You can't get rid of me that easy."

I raised myself up on tiptoe as I guided his head down toward mine.

"I never want this to end," he said, his breath whispering across my face.

"Then don't let go," I said.

I pressed fiery lips against his and water and heat filled the room. For this precious moment, the rest of the world slipped away. We didn't let go of each other, not for hours.

CHAPTER 58

I pulled a tank top on over my head and winced at the pain in my chest, side, and abdomen. My skin had knit together over my wounds, but the areas where I'd been shot with poisoned arrows were still tender—a constant reminder of the danger I'd faced, and would soon face again.

I wasn't going to kid myself. The faerie courts may think I'm dead, but that wouldn't last. As soon as the Moordenaar realize that I am alive, they'll be back to finish the job.

The only way I'd ever be safe from the faerie assassins was to learn how to control my wisp powers. Then I'd have to go before the faerie courts and prove that I wasn't a menace— well, no more so than any other law abiding fae.

I just wished that learning how to control my powers was as easy as signing up for a class, but there was no correspondence course for what I needed to learn. The one person who might be able to help me control my powers was my father, and he was still missing. With no other strong leads, I'd have to wait until the summer solstice and use my key to enter the door into the wisp court. Until then, I'd have to keep a low profile.

That was going to be a challenge.

I shrugged into a black hoodie, zipped it, and pulled the hood up over my head. I cast a forlorn look at my leather jacket and shook my head. There was nothing salvageable left. We'd have to throw a funeral for it when Jinx got home. Instead of my favorite leather, I grabbed a denim jacket and tossed it on over the hoodie. I slid on a pair of dark sunglasses and checked my reflection.

I looked like a gangbanger, but at least my eyes and skin were covered. I couldn't risk anyone on the streets recognizing me, or seeing me glow.

"Should I cut my hair?" I asked.

"Oberon's eyes, no," Ceff said, eyes wide. "Why would you do that?"

"You know, to hide my identity," I said with a shrug.

"You cannot even see your hair with that hood up," he said. "And I have never seen you in that jacket."

"True, I do look...different," I said.

Of course, that could have been due to the goofy grin I couldn't seem to lose no matter how many times I scrubbed at my face. I'd heard of earth shattering sex—maybe we'd shaken something loose inside my brain.

My phone beeped and I sighed, texting Forneus a quick reply. Texting while wearing gloves sucked. My "be right there" had more misspellings that an ogre's ransom note—and I should know, I'd had to decipher one while working a kidnapping case last month.

"Okay, time to go," I said, heading for the door.

"That is the seventh call from Forneus," Ceff said.

"He's just worried about Jinx," I said. I took the stairs two at a time. Was there a spring in my step? Hell yes, even with my injuries I felt better than I had in days. "After that little scene earlier, Arachne doesn't want to wake Jinx up until we get there. She's worried she'll have a pissed off Jinx and an injured demon on her hands."

"Ah, that makes sense," he said.

I frowned, slowing my pace.

"Actually, I'm more worried about her trying to wring my neck, not Forneus'," I said.

"Why would she be angry with you?" he asked.

I swallowed hard, but answered truthfully.

"You know that night I told you about, when we killed Puck and put a stop to the drug dealing and prostitution at Club Nexus?" I asked.

He nodded and I looked away.

"Well, Forneus saved Jinx's life and from the way their lips were locked, I'd say she was very, very appreciative," I said.

"Those two finally kissed, and the world did not end?" he joked.

"Nope, but then things went sideways and Forneus saved her life again...but this time Jinx hit her head," I said. I bit my lip, face flushing.

"What happened?" he asked.

I was walking fast again and we were nearly at The Emporium, so I stopped and met Ceff's curious gaze.

"I screwed up," I said. "To save Jinx, Forneus had to take on his fully demonic form and...and I freaked. He was everything I feared. He was a monster, evil incarnate. So, Torn and I hauled Jinx's ass out of there and when she woke up and couldn't remember that kiss..."

"You pretended it never happened," he said.

I sighed, throat feeling tight.

"Yeah, I never told her," I said.

"You were trying to protect her," he said.

"But I knew better," I said. "Deep down, I knew that Forneus genuinely cared about Jinx, but I'd spent my entire life afraid of the monsters that no one else could see. So I pretended that I was doing the right thing, protecting her from a monster, but who am I to judge? I'm not human. I never was. And now I've gone and lied to my best friend, because I'm too afraid to see the good in people."

"She will forgive you," he said. "Give her time."

"I don't know if I deserve forgiveness," I said.

And that was the crux of it. How could Jinx forgive me if I couldn't forgive myself?

"We all deserve second chances," he said. "And you do see the good in people. You saw the man I wanted to be when I was broken and beaten and at my worst."

"That was easy," I said. "You are a good man."

"You took in Marvin and gave him a family when he looked and smelled like a bloodied garbage heap," he said. "You gave him a chance when most people would have looked the other way."

"He was just a kid," I said.

"You, Ivy Granger, do see the best in people," he said. "If it took you time to believe in Forneus, then maybe there is a reason for that. Maybe he has not always been worthy of Jinx."

I thought about what Ceff had said. Forneus had been an irritating, arrogant, manipulative, self-serving prick when we first met. It was only more recently that I'd begun to suspect I'd made a mistake in keeping Jinx from him. Maybe Ceff was right.

"Even so," I said. "I don't think Jinx will see it that way."

"There is only one way to find out," he said.

I took a deep breath and strode up the hill, closing the distance to The Emporium. It was time to face the music.

CHAPTER 59

Jinx was surprisingly quiet. Instead of raging at me or lashing out at Forneus, she just wrapped her arms around herself and mumbled her thanks when Arachne woke her up.

Before leaving the loft, I'd packed her a change of clothes, figuring the rockabilly fashion maven would feel more comfortable in a strappy dress than the turtleneck she'd worn to cover the marks the incubus had left on her skin. But even a cherry red dress and platform pumps weren't enough to break her from her funk.

"No thanks," she said, slowly shaking her head.

I gave her a probing gaze and she hunched into herself. That was so unlike Jinx that I flinched. Jinx was spunky and confident and vibrant and alive.

"Hey, um, Ivy, can you help me with this?" Arachne asked, waving me over to the other side of the kitchen.

"Sure," I said, keeping one eye on Jinx. When I reached the corner, I looked more closely at Arachne who was twitching like a kid on a sugar high. "What's up?"

If she'd unleashed another horde of fire imps, she was going to have to find someone else to clean up the mess. I was officially dead, and on vacation.

"Um, it's just, you know, I think Jinx just needs some time," she said, tugging at her hair.

"What do you mean?" I asked, heart starting to race. "She's getting her energy back and healing from the incubus attack right?"

"Yeah, she's fine, physically," she said. "It's just, I had this friend from school who got taken advantage of at a party...and Jinx reminds me of her."

"Jinx reminds you of your friend?" I asked.

I wasn't following what Arachne was saying, but that was partly because I was only half listening. Forneus was over trying to talk to Jinx, but she just sat there looking at the floor. There was something seriously wrong with my friend. There were plenty of pointy objects in the kitchen and Jinx hadn't grabbed a single one.

"By the Goddess, Ivy, look at me," Arachne said.

I pulled my eyes from Jinx and cocked an eyebrow at the kid.

"Sorry," I said. "I'm listening."

"It's not that Jinx and my friend look or dress the same or anything," she said. "What they have in common is that they were both raped...and all I'm saying is that you need to give her time. She's not going to heal from this overnight."

"Jinx wasn't raped," I said, shaking my head.

Arachne rolled her eyes.

"It doesn't matter if it was a full on rape or not," she said. "And just so you know, Jinx is too fuzzy on the details to know exactly what happened—that's obvious. But even if that incubus didn't force sex on her, what he did was still a form of rape. It's normal for Jinx to feel violated."

Mab's bones. Anyone who didn't think a teenager could be wise or profound had never met one. Arachne was right about Jinx. My best friend had suffered a trauma and I was going to be there for her in any way that she needed me until she was better again.

"Thanks, Arachne," I said. "I'm an idiot."

"No you're not," she said, blushing. "Just don't ask her to change her clothes and stuff with people standing around."

I nodded and walked back over to Jinx and Forneus. Sparky was hamming it up, dancing like a drunk clurichaun, while Forneus tapped out a beat with his sword cane. Jinx even had a small smile on her face.

Ceff was gathering our things and cocked an eyebrow. His unspoken question was obvious. *Everything alright?*

I nodded. It would be.

"Okay, everybody ready to hit the road?" I asked. "I don't know about the rest of you, but I'm starving. I'm thinking pizza delivery."

"Pizzaaaaaaaaaaaa!" Sparky squealed, clapping his hands.

"I do not wish to intrude on your homecoming, but I will walk you home," Forneus said, holding out a hand to Jinx.

My friend ignored his offer and pulled herself to her feet.

"I'm not in the mood for pizza, but I'd rather not be here when Kaye gets back," Jinx said.

"That makes two of us," I said. "Come on. Later Arachne!"

"Bye, take it easy," she said, giving me a knowing look.

Yeah, this thing with Jinx was going to take time. Good thing I was in hiding. We'd have plenty of time to hang out at the loft between now and the solstice.

When we stepped out onto the sidewalk I tossed Humphrey a smile and a wave. I hesitated a moment then moved to walk beside Ceff, giving Forneus room to slide into step with Jinx. I was here for Jinx, but I was done being overprotective. Look at where that got us.

"May I be so bold as to inquire if you would have dinner with me this evening?" he asked, falling into step beside Jinx. "Or perhaps a drink to celebrate your continued existence on this mortal plane?"

"No," she said.

Forneus flashed Jinx a pained look, but nodded his head. God, even I felt sorry for him. He'd saved her life, again, the truth of what had happened in the basement of Club Nexus had come out, and he still didn't get the girl.

"Very well, if that is your wish," he said.

"I've been asleep for days and I still have another dude's lip marks on my skin," she said. Forneus' eyes widened. Jinx wasn't saying no, just not now. "I'm sure I look like crap. Call me tomorrow."

That was all the encouragement the demon needed. Titania save us all.

"You are a sight, indeed, a radiant vision," he said.

"With this bed head?" she asked.

"Angels cry from the heavens with envy over your raven-hued locks," he said.

I wanted to roll my eyes, maybe even throw up a little, but Jinx had perked up, already looking better. If it took a demon to bring my friend back from the brink of death, and keep her safe, then I would keep my trap shut...for now. The guy had earned that much.

Plus, I'd learned my lesson. As much as I felt compelled to protect my friends, I had to respect Jinx's wishes. If she wanted to date a demon, I wasn't going to stand in the way. He just better not hurt her, or all bets were off.

I lingered behind, letting the two lovebirds saunter up ahead. Forneus was insisting on escorting Jinx home and though she protested, I could tell her heart wasn't in it. The two walked side by side, their fingers almost touching.

Yeah, I knew where Jinx's heart was—it was being carried by the well-dressed demon at her side. She may have forgotten the kiss that she and Forneus had shared back in Club Nexus' basement, but she had always felt passionately about the guy. It had started as a love-hate attraction, but through his actions, the demon had found a way to tip the scales in his favor.

I still didn't completely understand her attraction to the guy, but who was I to judge? I was taking home a demon of my own. Sparky bounced along at my side, singing about pretty eyes and dancing flames with childlike glee. If you'd asked me yesterday if I'd befriend a demon, agree to kill the most powerful witch in the city, or try to pull a fast one on The Green Lady, I'd have said you were crazier than a *boo hag* who'd lost her favorite skin.

I smiled and shook my head. I guess you never can tell what the future will hold—just another reason to have an open mind and sharpened blades. In Harborsmouth anything can happen.

EPILOGUE

Ceff barely stirred as I rolled out from under his arm. I stared at the ceiling and let out a lengthy sigh. I couldn't sleep.

I slid out of bed, shrugged into my robe, and tiptoed out to the kitchen. I pushed aside a pile of empty pizza boxes and found the coffee maker. I could help Jinx clean this place up tomorrow. Maybe she'd want to do one of her obsessive-compulsive spring cleanings. Normally, that would make me cringe, but if scrubbing floors would bring us closer together and help my friend heal then I'd do it in a heartbeat.

In fact, a house cleaning was a good idea. We needed to clear out the rest of our anti-demon charms. I'd disengaged the door wards and shoved the more deadly charms into our junk drawer, but that wouldn't keep curious hands safe—and Sparky sure was curious. I bent over to peek at his tiny form sleeping in a dog bed beside the couch.

I smiled at his squeaky snores. Jinx always wanted a dog, hence the dog bed that usually was the perch for a stuffed bulldog one of her ex-boyfriends had given her. Now the plush toy was gone and Sparky was snuggled under a blanket, his floppy ears hanging over the sides of the bed. I had a feeling the little guy was here to stay.

Sparky wasn't the only demon that might be spending more time here at the loft. Forneus had been good to his word and didn't intrude on our homecoming, but I knew he'd be visiting soon enough. Whether I approved of it or not, there was no denying the attraction between him and Jinx.

Yeah, getting rid of our anti-demon charms was definitely on my to-do list.

I put on a pot of coffee and turned to the remains of my leather jacket. A trip to a clurichaun tailor for a new one was also on my list. The sight of my poor jacket brought tears to my eyes. We'd been through a lot together, that jacket and I.

I sighed and grabbed the jacket, setting it on the counter. I might as well empty out the pockets before tossing it out and sending it to the big jacket heaven in the sky.

As quietly as I could, I dumped charms and weapons onto the counter. Turning the jacket inside out, I noticed a crinkle of paper where something had slid down inside the lining. I reached into the inner pocket, my gloved fingers retrieving something small and square. I pulled it out and held it up to the light.

It was Jenna's note, the one that Jonathan had slipped to me at the Hunters' Guild headquarters. So much had happened since my trip to Master Janus' office, I'd forgotten all about it.

I unfolded the envelope, only to find a blank piece of paper inside. What the heck? I held the note up to the light, turning it over in my hands. Had Jenna written a message in invisible ink?

The coffee maker beeped and I got up to pour a cup. Maybe I'd be able to figure things out with a clearer head. I set the full cup on the counter and it sloshed onto the paper.

"Damn," I muttered, grabbing a towel.

I wiped up the coffee spill, but paused. There were coffee stains on the paper, giving me an idea. If someone wanted to send me a message that only I could read, how would they do it?

Coffee isn't the only thing that leaves stains behind. Strong emotions leave their marks on items as well.

I took a deep breath and tugged off my glove.

"I hope I'm right about this," I said.

I reached out and placed my bare hand on the paper. The room tilted and I gasped at the pain, but it was coming from my other hand. The hand was calloused from the constant use of a sword and blood dripped from a gash in my palm. I looked away from the blood and up into a familiar set of eyes.

Jenna's face stared back at me from a bathroom mirror.

"Hey, Ivy," she said. "I hope this works. Otherwise, I just slashed open my hand for nothing."

Jenna's wry grin made my heart race, or maybe that was her heart racing. Inside a vision, it's often hard to tell the difference.

I felt metal scrape on bone and knew the nausea was all Jenna's. She knew how my visions worked and she was using pain to leave a strong enough imprint on the paper, a psychic message that only I could read.

Clever girl.

"They're sending me away tomorrow," she said. "I don't have much time, but there's something you need to know."

Sweat beaded on her lip, and a sad smile tugged at her lips.

"There's a war coming, Ivy," she said. "And the fae and the undead will be at the center of it. The Guild is already gearing up for the coming war...I think my being sent away has something to do with that, but they hold their secrets close. I shouldn't even be telling you any of this."

She looked down at her bloodied hand, then up again.

"But you need to prepare," she said. "I don't know when the war will begin, but I may know where. I overheard Master Janus arguing when I came to his office earlier. I never saw the other person, but a man's voice was demanding aggressive training for all young Hunters. He claimed that the first battle of the coming war would take place in Harborsmouth."

My stomach twisted.

"Take care of my city, Ivy," she said. "Good hunting."

I blinked and the mirror was gone. I padded back to the bedroom and slipped into bed, pulling Ceff close. He stirred, a smile forming on his lips.

"Hello," he said.

I let my hand glide down his chest as I slid my body closer to his.

"Hey," I said.

Tomorrow may bring the world down on our heads. War was coming. All the more reason to show those I cared about just how much I loved them. And I knew right where I'd like to start.

Coming in 2014

The first novel in the Hunters' Guild series
set in the world of Ivy Granger

Hunting in Bruges
By E.J. Stevens

Read on for a sneak preview.

HUNTING IN BRUGES

I've been seeing ghosts for as long as I can remember. Most ghosts are simply annoying; just clueless dead people who don't realize that they've died. The weakest of these manifest as flimsy apparitions, without the ability for speech or higher thought. They're like a recording of someone's life projected not onto a screen, but onto the place where they died. Most people can walk through one of these ghosts without so much as a goosebump.

Poltergeists are more powerful, but just as single-minded. These pesky spirits are like angry toddlers. They stomp around, shaking their proverbial chains, moaning and wailing about how something (the accident, their murder, or the murder they committed) was someone else's fault, and how everyone must pay for their misfortune. Poltergeists are a nuisance; they're noisy and can throw around objects for short periods of time, but it's only the strong ones that are dangerous.

Thankfully, there aren't many ghosts out there strong enough to do more than knock a pen off your desk or cause a cold spot. From what I've discovered while training with the Hunters' Guild, ghosts get their power from two things—how long they've been haunting and strength of purpose. If someone as obsessed with killing as Jack the Ripper manifests beside you on a London street, I recommend you run. If someone as old and unhinged as Vlad the Impaler appears beside you in Targoviste Romania, you better hope you have a Hunter at your side, or a guardian angel.

The dead get a bad rap, and for good reason, but some ghosts can be helpful. There was a woman with a kind face who used to appear when I was in foster care. Linda wasn't just a loop of psychic recording stuck on repeat; this ghost had free will and independent thought—and thankfully, she wasn't a sociopath consumed with bloodshed. Linda manifested in faded jeans and dark turtleneck and smelled like home, which was the other thing that was unusual about her. Most ghosts are tied to one spot, the place where they lived or died. But Linda's familiar face followed me from one foster home to another. And it was a good thing that she did. Linda the ghost saved my life more than once.

Foster care was an excellent training ground for self defense, which is probably why the Hunters' Guild uses it as a place for recruitment. Being cast adrift in the child welfare system gave me plenty of opportunities to hone my survival instincts. By the time the Hunters came along, I was a force to be reckoned with, or so I thought.

The Hunters' Guild provides exceptional training and I soon learned that my attempts at both offense and defense were child's play when compared to our senior members. I didn't berate myself over that fact; I was only thirteen when the Hunters swooped in and welcomed me into their fold. But learning my limitations did make me painfully aware of one thing. If it hadn't been for Linda the ghost, I probably wouldn't have survived my childhood.

The worst case of *honing my survival skills* had been at my last foster home, just before the Hunters' Guild intervened. I don't remember the house mother. She wasn't around much. She was just a small figure in a cheap, polyester fast food uniform with a stooped posture and downcast eyes. But I remember her husband Frank.

Frank was a bully who wore white, ketchup and mustard stained, wife-beater t-shirts. He had perpetual French fry breath and a nasty grin. It took me a few weeks to realize that Frank's grin was more of a leer. I'd caught his gaze in the bathroom mirror when I was changing and his eyes said it all; Frank was a perv.

Linda slammed the door in his face, but that didn't stop Frank. Frank would brush up against me in the kitchen and Linda would set the faucet spraying across the tiles…and slide a knife into my hand. My time in that house ended when Frank ended up in the hospital.

I'd been creeping back to the bedroom I shared with three other kids, when I saw Frank waiting for me in the shadows. I pulled the steak knife I kept hidden in the pocket of my robe, but I never got a chance to use it. Now that I know a thing or two about fighting with a blade, I'm aware that Frank probably would have won that fight.

I tried to run toward the stairs, but Frank met me at the top landing. Frank reached for me while his bulk effectively blocked my escape. That was when Linda the ghost pushed him down the stairs. I remember him tumbling in slow motion, his eyes going wide and the leering grin sliding from his face.

Linda the ghost had once again saved me, but it seemed that this visit was her last. I don't know if she used up her quota of psychic power, or if she just felt like her job here was finally done. It wasn't until years later that I realized she was my mother.

I guess I should have realized sooner that I was related to the ghost who followed me around. We both have hair the same shade of shocking red. But where mine is straight and cropped into a short bob, Linda's was wavy and curled down around her shoulders. We also share a dimple in our left cheek and a propensity for protecting the weak and innocent from evil.

Linda the ghost disappeared, a wailing ambulance drove Frank to the hospital, police arrived at my foster house, and the Hunters swooped in and cleaned up the aftermath. It was from my first Guild master that I learned of my parents' fate and put two and two together about my ghostly protector.

As a kid I often wondered why Linda the ghost always wore a dark turtleneck; now I knew. Young, rogue vamps had torn out her neck and proceeded to rip my father to pieces like meat confetti. My parents were on vacation in Belize, celebrating their wedding anniversary when it happened. I'd been staying with a friend of my mother's, otherwise I'd be dead too.

I don't remember my parents, I'd only been three when I was put into the foster care system, but I do find some peace in knowing that doing my duty as a Hunter gives me the power to police and destroy rogue vamps like the ones who killed my mother and father. When I become exhausted by my work, I think of Linda's sad face and push myself to train harder. And when I find creeps who are abusive to women and children, I think of Frank.

That's how I ended up here, standing in a Brussels airport, trying to decipher the Dutch and French signs with eyes that were gritty from the twelve hour flight. It all started when my friend Ivy called to inform me that a fellow Hunter had hit our mutual friend Jinx. Ivy didn't know how that information would push all my buttons, she didn't know about Frank or my time in the foster system, but we both agreed that striking a girl was unacceptable. She was letting me, and the Hunters' Guild, deal with it, for now.

I went to master Janus, the head of the Harborsmouth Hunters' Guild, and reported Hans' transgressions. It didn't help his case that he had a reputation as a berserker in battle. The fact that he'd hit a human, the very people we were sworn to defend against the monsters, was the nail in the coffin of Hans' career.

I was assured that Hans would be shipped off to the equivalent of a desk job in Siberia. I should have left it at that, and let my superiors take care of the problem. But Jinx was my friend. Ivy's rockabilly business partner may have had bad luck and even worse taste in men, but that didn't mean she deserved to spend her life fending off the attacks of the Franks in the world.

Hans continued his Guild duties while the higher ups shuffled papers and prepared to send him away. Hans should have skipped our training sessions, but then again, he didn't know who had ratted him out—and the guy had a lot of rage to vent. I stormed onto the practice mat and saluted Hans with my sword. It wasn't long before the man started to bleed.

We were supposed to be using practice swords, but I'd *accidentally* grabbed the sharp blade I used on hunting runs. I didn't leave any lasting injuries, but the shallow cuts made a mess of his precious tattoos. I just hoped the scars were a constant reminder of what happens when you attack the innocent.

One week later, I received a plane ticket and orders to meet with one of our contacts in Belgium. I wasn't sure if this assignment was intended as a punishment or a promotion, but I was eager to prove myself to the Guild leadership. Master Janus' parting words whispered in my head, distracting me from the voice on the overhead intercom echoing throughout the cavernous airport.

"Do your duty, Jenna," he said. Master Janus placed a large, sword-calloused hand on my shoulder and looked me in the eye. I swallowed hard, but I managed to keep my hands from shaking. "Make us proud."

"I will, sir," I said.

"Good hunting."

Ivy Granger World
Don't miss these great books set in the world of Ivy Granger.

Ivy Ganger, Psychic Detective Series

Shadow Sight
Welcome to Harborsmouth, where monsters walk the streets unseen by humans...except those with second sight, like Ivy Granger.

Blood and Mistletoe: An Ivy Granger Novella
Holidays are worse than a full moon for making people crazy. In Harborsmouth, where many of the residents are undead vampires or monstrous fae, the combination may prove deadly.

Ghost Light
Holidays are worse than a full moon for making people crazy. In Harborsmouth, where many of the residents are undead vampires or monstrous fae, the combination may prove deadly.

Club Nexus: An Ivy Granger Novella
A demon, an Unseelie faerie, and a vampire walk into a bar...

Burning Bright
Burning down the house...

Birthright
Being a faerie princess isn't all it's cracked up to be.

Hound's Bite
Ivy Granger thought she left the worst of Mab's creations behind when she escaped Faerie. She thought wrong.

Hunters' Guild Series

Hunting in Bruges
The only thing worse than being a Hunter in the fae-ridden city of Harborsmouth, is hunting vampires in Bruges.

Coming Soon

Blood Rite

Ivy Granger psychic detective takes on a simple grave robbing case, but in Harborsmouth nothing is ever simple when dealing with the dead.

Warning: This book features grave robbing, an abandoned amusement park, necromancy, and zombie clowns.

Tales from Harborsmouth

Short stories set in the city of Harborsmouth.

Dressed in White

Something old, something new, something borrowed, something blue...

On the eve of Jinx and Ivy's double wedding, a sinister figure is terrorizing Harborsmouth.

When reports of a homicidal jilted bride threaten their wedding plans, Ivy and Forneus set out to put a stop to the string of heinous acts. What they discover might just send the faerie and demon straight to Hell, and set Ivy on a path to rectify more than one evil deed.

Will Ivy tie the knot with her kelpie king, or will she be saying "I do" to the king of Hell? Her father's curse is on the line, and lives hang in the balance. No pressure.

Praise for the World of Ivy Granger

"Stevens draws you in instantly with well-developed and likeable characters."
-Ted Fauster, author of the World of Faerel series

"Move over Harry Dresden fans, Ivy Granger is here."
-Kelly Abell, author of the Haunted Destiny series

"I haven't met an Ivy Granger story I didn't like. ...I love a good Urban Fantasy and the Ivy Granger series is not just good it's great."
-James A. Moore, Bram Stoker Award nominated author of the Seven Forges series

"If you're a fan of Kim Harrison or Patricia Briggs kind of Urban Fantasy then you will love the Ivy Granger series."
-The Keeper Shelf

"E.J. Stevens did a great job creating a unique Urban Fantasy world."
-Parajunkee

"There is romance, action, mystery, plenty of things that go bump in the night, all told with humor and style."
-Paranormal Romance Guild

"Stevens has done a fantastic job with bringing her world to us."
-Urban Fantasy Investigations

"Want a clever, fun and unique Urban Fantasy? This is the series to check out."
-The Jeep Diva

"The Ivy Granger Series is fantastic!"
-Book Bite Reviews

E.J. Stevens is the author of the HUNTERS' GUILD urban fantasy series, the SPIRIT GUIDE young adult series, and the award-winning IVY GRANGER urban fantasy series. She is known for filling pages with quirky characters, bloodsucking vampires, psychotic faeries, and snarky, kick-butt heroines.

BTS Red Carpet Award winner for Best Novel, SYAE Award finalist for Best Paranormal, Best Horror, and Best Novella, winner of the PRG Reviewer's Choice Award for Best Paranormal Fantasy Novel, Best Young Adult Paranormal Series, Best Urban Fantasy Novel, and finalist for Best Young Adult Paranormal Novel and Best Urban Fantasy Series.

When E.J. isn't at her writing desk, she enjoys dancing along seaside cliffs, singing in graveyards, and sleeping in faerie circles. E.J. currently resides in a magical forest on the coast of Maine where she finds daily inspiration for her writing.

CONNECT WITH E.J. STEVENS

Twitter: @EJStevensAuthor
Website: www.EJStevensAuthor.com
Blog: www.FromtheShadows.info

CPSIA information can be obtained
at www.ICGtesting.com
Printed in the USA
LVHW081324071019
633420LV00012B/420/P

9 780984 247554